DEADLY REASONS

(THE BEGINNING)

TONY HANTKE

©2021 Tony Hantke
All rights reserved

CONTENTS

Chapter 1	5
Chapter 2	13
Chapter 3	19
Chapter 4	31
Chapter 5	41
Chapter 6	51
Chapter 7	59
Chapter 8	67
Chapter 9	77
Chapter 10	89
Chapter 11	99
Chapter 12	105
Chapter 13	115
Chapter 14	121
Chapter 15	131
Chapter 16	139
Chapter 17	153
Chapter 18	163
Chapter 19	173
Chapter 20	183
Chapter 21	191
Chapter 22	203
Chapter 23	213
Chapter 24	233
Chapter 25	239
Chapter 26	247
Chapter 27	261
Chapter 28	269
Chapter 29	277
Acknowledgments	291

ONE

About halfway to the wrong town, I realized the Greyhound bus was traveling north and not east. The ticket bought in Louisville showed my error. At the Columbus, Indiana, bus stop, not Columbus, Ohio, I unfurled my body from a short but needed nap. Stepping off the bus and stretching, I saw the station. It was a small covered awning just large enough to protect a small group of passengers. The immediate area was emerald green and plush. The bus stop smelled of diesel, but a breeze in my face swept the odor away quickly.

An old-time motel was visible a short distance away and a crappy room was, of course, available. It was a fairly brisk, cool afternoon with a setting sun splashing colorful rays throughout the area and over the motor lodge parking lot.

I reran my steps in Louisville to determine my bus ticket mistake. I had taken the cash used for the ticket from an addict near the Louisville Slugger baseball field. In a hurry to leave Louisville, I had only glanced at the departing bus schedule. I read Columbus ... well, there you go.

I saw a truck stop across the road, and a diner's kitchen smells reminded me of how hungry I had become. Walking towards the aroma, I read a roadside advertisement for a local cinema showing the movie *The Sixth Sense* later on that evening. Now, that was a cool movie. I still get goosebumps when that little kid says to his mother, "I see dead people." I read a discarded newspaper that sported a little spilled coffee and jam. I found my way through the front doors of the Red Caboose Diner, and my life forever changed.

I was lucky, or unlucky, depending on your view. I met him at the kitchen counter. Terry Langfeld was probably forty-five to fifty, with short black hair just long enough to comb. He parted it on the right side and carried himself with confidence. His fingernails were clean and well-cut. A desk job? A loose-fitting, long-sleeved T-shirt printed with Queen's "The Game" album cover hung over his dark blue jeans. A day off? He was known by the diner staff and was welcomed with a warm good morning as he strolled in and sat at the counter to my right. He placed a rolled-up newspaper on the counter with his left hand. No wedding ring nor wristwatch either. He was probably six one and of medium build.

They decorated the Red Caboose like an old 50s and 60s type diner replete with red vinyl seat covers and red checked tabletops. An old-time soda fountain was the central attraction. The wall behind the counter was all glass, reflecting the fountain and creating that illusion of a larger area. The interior was well lit, almost too bright. An exterior wall on the street side was all windows with red checked drapes looped over "RC" drape wall hooks. It seated fifty-six customers at eight tables and four booths, seating four customers each with another eight at the counter. The linoleum floor doubled as a dance floor with black and white checkers surrounded by a solid red border. An old-time jukebox provided the dance music, and Chubby Checker was singing "The Twist", along with the cook and one of the waitresses. It showed some wear but was charming and disarming all at the same time. Two women were working, plus only one cook that I could see and hear. The diner smelled of frying sausage and bacon, even though it was later in the day. There was, or had been, bread baked recently, causing my nose to track its scent like a dog.

I was sitting several stools away from him. Eventually, Langfeld asked me, "Do you live around here?"

"No, I said as I continued to look at the local newspaper. I'm just passing through."

"Where to?" he asked.

I wasn't sure if he was simply making conversation or was one of those guys that just had to talk. "What do you care where I'm headed?"

"Hey, take it easy, kid. Just making small talk."

We both stayed quiet. He ordered a cheeseburger and onion rings. For me, the chicken sandwich and fries with mustard.

He looked at me with a wry smile. I assumed it had to do with my fries and mustard combination. Ever since the movie *Sling Blade*, I have eaten fries with mustard.

I broke the thick silence which I had caused.

"I'm going up around Toledo to visit an aunt," *I lied*. "That is if she still lives there."

"That's a haul, son. That's gotta be 250 miles or more. How are you getting there? I didn't see a car outside."

The waitress, a cutie, maybe thirty, brought us our orders and asked if we needed refills. Coffee for me and a diet 7up for Langfeld. I agreed to the coffee refill, turned to Langfeld, and said, "It's 281 miles to the city limits from here."

Langfeld looked at me curiously. "That's a pretty exact figure. I guess you've made that trip before."

I stared at him and said, "I told you I've been there before."

Langfeld said, "No, you said you were going to visit an aunt there if she still lives there. You hadn't mentioned you were returning."

I didn't respond. Again, I wasn't sure if he was feeling me out or that he was a precise sort of guy. "Yeah, well, that's where I'm thinking of going," I feebly replied.

The chicken sandwich was good. I hadn't eaten too well

recently. I asked Ashley, the waitress, for a piece of apple pie. She smiled that flirtatious way that elicits better tips (and it did). Langfeld turned to me, introduced himself, and asked me my name. "It's Woody."

He probed. "Short for …?"

I hesitated but told him, "Woodford."

He looked at me out of the corner of his eye. He said, "Hmm, no car and a little jittery. You running from something or someone?"

"Someone."

"You have family around closer than Toledo?"

"No, I don't have any family,"

"Really? You mean none living or none close?"

"I never knew my mother. My dad normally was in prison. No siblings either. You always interview people you've just met?"

"No, I'm sorry. Again, just making conversation," he answered.

His telephone rang, and after a brief exchange, he excused himself. He walked outside to continue the conversation. The waitress refilled my coffee with a smile and a swish of her butt.

"When are you leaving for Toledo?" Langfeld asked as he returned, but didn't sit.

"Not sure, why?"

Throwing a ten and a few ones on the counter, he said, "I eat here almost every day. Maybe I'll see you again before you leave to see your aunt."

The next morning began with a beautiful sunrise and a cup of coffee from the hotel lobby. Even though the motel was terribly cheap and somewhat filthy, the coffee in the lobby was superb. I asked the gray-haired guy behind the counter if there was somewhere I could go for a walk. He looked me up and down, recognizing I wasn't one of his usual type of guests. He suggested the "People's Trail."

It wasn't far from the motor lodge. I rented a bicycle at the small but quaint entrance gate and rode the trail for the better part of two hours. During the ride, I saw a few robins and cardinals. I was told the robin was the state bird, even though I knew that to be wrong because the cardinal was. I had read that once in a book that contained all the states' birds. The People's Trail was an easy ride. That part of the U.S. is smooth as glass. As the ride went, thoughts of my conversation with Langfeld hung over me. I was not sure what to make of it.

It was a little warmer than the day before. Clear light-blue skies showed even warmer hours ahead. I took my time in the park and tried to enjoy the freedom and alone time. I still hadn't decided if I was going to the Red Caboose for lunch or to Greenville, Ohio, and Aunt Jennifer. I hadn't wanted Langfeld to know where I might actually be headed, only because I didn't know his interest. It felt as if Langfeld had given me a not-so-subtle invite to stay. I was curious why. I played yesterday's interaction over and over and went early and discuss Langfeld with the cute waitress.

Ashley was working and was quite busy when I arrived. Another waitress was scurrying around with her, so I had little time to start or carry on a conversation. I nodded at her when I sat at the counter and she mouthed hi to me before bringing me a cup of coffee without my asking. She couldn't stop to chat, but I thought I saw in her eyes that she wanted to. The diner, again, smelled of breakfast fare during the early lunch period. The same cook was now singing "The Loco-Motion."

A couple walked in that Ashley knew well; she met them at a booth, smiled, and continued a conversation they obviously had had recently. The other waitress, her name tag identified as Martha, came over to me, but I told her Ashley had already taken my order, pointing to the coffee. Every time I thought I might have a chance to speak to her, she couldn't stop because of business.

Langfeld arrived before I ever talked to her. He sat next to me and smiled like the proverbial Cheshire cat.

"Good morning, Woody. How was your evening? Mine was great."

I nodded with a jut of my chin.

"Have you ordered yet?"

"Nah, I just got here."

Today, he was decked out with a tie and sports jacket. A far cry from yesterday's attire. Definitely a desk job. Ashley eventually came over and asked for our orders. We ordered, and Langfeld excused himself and went off to the shitter. As Ashley walked by, I asked her where Langfeld worked. She said he was a bigshot at Baxter's Engine Plant, not too far from the diner. She cocked her head, half squinting an eye in a way that asked, why I was asking?

I answered her unasked question, "I'm just wary of strangers."

"I'm a stranger, and you're talking to me," she toyed.

"Well, I make exceptions for pretty girls."

I saw Langfeld had stopped on his way back to the counter and took a telephone call. He returned before Ashley and I could continue our chat. Martha, the other waitress, carried our plates of food to us, winking at Ashley.

"Ok, let's eat," Langfeld exclaimed. It wasn't hard to notice that the phone call had been good news. "I'll buy," he added.

He turned to me and said, "Are you still on your way to your aunt's home in Toledo?"

"You sure seem to be concerned about my travel plans," I countered. "Why?" I asked.

He leaned over to me and softly said, "I have a job I can offer you."

I wasn't sure what to make of this. Was he coming on to me? Was he setting me up? Was he being honest? Ashley said he was a big shot at a local engine plant. I didn't know what that meant, but I wasn't really in any position to argue. "Doing what?"

He motioned me to a table away from other customers and the waitresses. "I work at the Baxter's Engine Plant as the Chief Financial Officer, but I came up through the Transportation Division, which is where we could use you. We transport much of our engines and parts to McAllen, Texas, by rail, but there are some things we do by truck because it's more cost-efficient. Until last week, we had two drivers handling each truck load. They're on a twenty-one-day revolving route. However, last week one driver was arrested on immigration charges and deported. So, we need a driver."

"So, all you want me to do is take turns driving with your other guy?"

"Yep, basically just a helping hand. Oh, you wouldn't happen to have your CDL, would you?"

"What's a CDL?" I asked.

"Well, that answers that question. It's a commercial driver's license needed for all over the road truck transports and other delivery vehicles such as UPS, etcetera."

"Yeah, well, I don't even have a regular driver's license."

"What?"

"I mean; I've driven since I was 14 but never took a test for it."

He thought a bit and said, "We can get you through a class here at Baxter's. I'll have to make some calls for your Indiana driver's license. If you're in, I'll get you started in HR tomorrow to get your employment package and all that shit in the pipeline."

I didn't have to think long about if I was in or not. "Yeah, count me in. I doubt driving a big rig is too awful hard," I bragged without the slightest idea what the hell I was in for.

TWO

The morning of the third day in my crappy motel room was much like the prior two except that a future as a paid truck driver approached. It had been a long-time since I rubbed legally gained money together. I needed a place to live. I went to the Caboose and began with the local paper ads of apartments for rent. Ashley brought me a hot cup of coffee. "Hi, Woody. Ooh, how was your date with Mr. Bigshot?" she smirked.

"Great. He offered me a job, so now I'm looking for a place to stay."

"Ooh, hey, congratulations," she said, while she poured a cup of coffee for a guy at the end of the counter.

The cook wasn't singing today, and I missed his voice. In fact, the jukebox wasn't playing at all. The diner still smelled wonderful. I circled a few rentals in the paper and asked Ashley for two eggs over-medium with sausage and whole-wheat toast. She glanced at my circles and went on back to the kitchen line.

Keeping with the overall atmosphere, the diner had an old-fashioned telephone booth, so since I didn't have a cell phone, the rotary phone was a nice touch. I called regarding a prospective rental apartment on the other side of town. The apartment owner explained she had just rented the apartment, but she had another apartment opening at the end of the week if I wanted to look at it. While she spoke and identified the amenities of the apartment, I wondered how I was going to get around. I had never owned a car. I thanked the lady and said I had other places I wanted to see too, but I would call her.

Ashley brought me my order. "Well, how's it going?"

I told her about my conversation. She was peering over the napkin holder and the diner sign on the counter to see my scribbled circles and x-outs. "Do you know of any place for rent?" I asked.

A smile appeared. "Ooh, I have a garage with an apartment. I could rent to you. My parents own the house, but they've moved permanently to Florida. I live there with my eleven-year-old daughter." *She had me at "I could rent to you."*

I said, "Sure, if you're okay with it, but I have some baggage."

"Luggage or baggage?" she asked.

Shaking my head, "Baggage like in trouble with the law. It's all juvenile crap, but still. You should think this over, Ashley. I don't want to impose, and hell, we only just met."

"Listen, the bottom line is that the extra money wouldn't hurt, plus having a man around the place might be good. I'm a single mom, and, well, it would just be safer."

"Well, I certainly need a place, and if you're okay with it, I'm willing to give it a run. Thanks. I'm probably going to be gone more than I am going to be around, anyway."

"Do you want to know how much the rent is?" "Not really. I'm sure it'll be fair."

Terry Langfeld picked me up, and we went by his home long enough for him to grab something he had forgotten. He lived in an average house outside of town with maybe five acres of fairly flat grassland. The two-story house was all brick, with white siding on the dormers. There was a two-car attached garage and another two-car detached garage assumingly for lawn equipment sufficient to maintain five acres of grounds.

Terry nonchalantly intimated he wasn't married any longer. His daughter and son were out on their own. He changed vehicles at his place, an Audi for a Ford 250. The drive to the plant took ten minutes, and it was a picture-postcard view for most of the drive with rolling hills and a few winding turns alongside a darkish creek. The ever-present breeze was refreshing.

Langfeld told me his assistant, Michelle Freeman, would meet me at Baxter's. Freeman was finishing a telephone conversation. "Yes, sir. Of course." She hung up and said to me, "I'm sorry, sir. Let me show you around the plant."

She was quite attractive, maybe five foot five inches, with wonderfully long, straight black hair. Hispanic? Italian background? She clearly worked out at a gym or was involved with some other type of regular exercise program. She had an air about her, much like a manager would have. For some unknown reason, I felt she had been picked as his assistant to take over and run the plant when he retired.

The plant was huge. I learned from Michelle that the building was over six hundred thousand square feet, with plans for expansion that would make it close to a million. We rode in an EZGO golf cart, winding between yellow painted lines. She had access to all areas of the plant. The floors were surprisingly clean, although the smell of oil and diesel hung in the air, which was humid, not quite a tepid temperature, but muggy nonetheless. The large floor fans were loud but helped move stagnant air out the large bay doors. We wore ear protection with an internal radio set so we could talk to each other. They muffled steel and iron machines striking on sheets and blocks of materials. The sounds were almost deafening and after a short while had a musical pattern ... boom ... boom ... screech ... bang ... boom ... boom ... screech ... bang.

As we traveled throughout the plant listening and smelling lubricants, Michelle described the various diesel engines built along with the engine parts needed for the after-market. The tour was impressive. The walls of the plant had to be sixty feet high. I had never been in such an enormous structure. There were rails with hanging engines or parts of engines gliding through a maze of tubes and tracks. Impressive. The design engineers were required to visualize where all those rails needed to be placed in order to be drawn on paper, all solely for Baxter's. Everything had to be custom made. The costs surely reached out of this world.

As we neared the offices and the end of my tour, Michelle pointed out railroad tracks leading out into the "yard" and then on out to a not-yet-visible train.

I asked, "How many trucks roll out of here a day?"

"Well sir, we run about six a week, which sounds low, but actually it's pretty substantial because mostly everything is done by railcar." She said that we assigned each truck a pair of drivers, and each truck had specific routes.

I asked, "How long have you worked here?"

"Just over seven years. It's a great company. Good benefits, and the paychecks are comparable to those of other large corporations. They're loyal, and we get Christmas bonuses in November, so we have time to buy presents." A female employee stepped onto the bay floor and caught Michelle's attention with a wave of her hand. Michelle strode to the employee and after a quick conversation, I heard Michelle say, "No, ma'am. No need to fix it until the parts department has signed off. Call me later, if you haven't been contacted."

Langfeld met us in one of the bays. Michelle told him I had been shown the needed areas and given a quick rundown of the plant before she walked away. Langfeld followed her with his eyes, then turned to me and, seeing I had noticed, said she had been his right hand for a while; he relied on her more than most. "Don't hesitate to ask her for anything if I'm not around. She probably knows as much about this plant as I do." I thought to myself, *"there's the reason."*

Langfeld pushed me through HR quickly, and for the first time in a long time, they asked me to fill out personal information forms. I knew my social security number, but I didn't know any of my family's medical history. I didn't have any family members for emergency contacts. The middle-aged woman pointed to the blank lines under family history. I shrugged with open hands.

I gave her a brief thumbnail sketch of my family. "I was born Paul Anthony Woodford in Kentucky and raised somewhere in southern Indiana or Illinois, depending on if my dad was in prison. When he was imprisoned, I stayed with my Uncle Pete and Aunt Jennifer. I was nicknamed 'Woody' when I was little and don't know anyone that ever referred to me by Paul. My mother left when I was around two. I was never shown pictures of her, and none of my family ever discussed her." The nice little old lady was stunned, gave me that 'I feel sorry for you ... look,' and wasn't sure how to respond, but no further family questions were asked.

Langfeld had the pull that Michelle spoke of. James, who introduced himself as an Indiana State Police Trooper, contacted me. He would be my driving instructor. Now, I've got baggage, and my recent interaction with the addict in Louisville made my heart jump as James spoke, but there was no inkling of problems, so breathing resumed.

He picked me up in a late model Audi A4, not the biggest of vehicles, especially since James was as tall as me. Thankfully, the test would be on a Peterbilt. It helped that I had driven several cars before. Using an ignition key, rather than a screwdriver and needle-nosed pliers, was new, though. By noon, he felt I was ready for the truck lessons.

"What do you mean there are ten gears?" I yelled over the pinging of the big diesel engine.

He laughed and said, "Only one is used at a time, big guy. You'll get used to it."

He worked with me on a stretch of road near I-65, so every once in a while, we would enter and exit the freeway, getting acquainted with downshifting and gaining speed too. By early evening, I had become somewhat adequate in my abilities and asked about the test. He looked at me like I had three eyes. "Boy! You already passed; you can thank Mr. Langfeld."

I had to pinch myself. No one, and I mean no one outside of family, had ever helped me as Langfeld had. I owed him big time, and that eventually would become a major problem.

THREE

Ashley drove us to her house. She was quiet, anxious, and a little nervous, too. I could sense she might be concerned now about this drifter living on her property. Still, she handed me the keys to the garage apartment. I grabbed all my belongings, which were in a small duffel bag.

Still sensing she was worried, I said, "Ashley, if me renting here is going to be an issue for you or your daughter, just say so."

"No, that's not it. I ... I received a letter today from the state. Brittany's father lost his job and can't pay the back child support he owes me," she said softly but with eyes welling up.

I didn't know what to say, so I said nothing. I just stared down at my size thirteens. It was obvious she needed extra money and probably would have agreed to rent to anyone, so I was glad to be that anyone because I would not harm her or her daughter.

The babysitter, Mrs. Daniels, an enchanting black lady with small braids, greeted Ashley in the front yard with Brittany. Brittany was a clone of her momma, beautiful with a sparkling smile and a twinkle in her eyes. Mrs. Daniels introduced herself and said she had heard about me; I should call her Mrs. D. I glanced at Ashley, who was staring at her feet, which were not thirteens. I continued looking at Ashley but answered Mrs. D. "Well, let me tell you about the good things too," I joked.

The trace of electricity in the air was disrupted, thankfully, by Brittany. "Are you going to live with us?"

I stammered an ah well. Ashley jumped in and said that I was Mr. Woody and I was going to live above the garage.

Brittany seemed to approve. "Where are you going to eat?" she asked.

Hadn't thought of that and not knowing what the apartment comprised, I mumbled, "Young lady, I'm too big as it is. I probably could go a whole month without eating."

Brittany and Mrs. D smiled; Ashley said, "Honey, Woody can eat with us anytime he's in town, but his work is going to take him out of town a lot, okay?"

"All right," she replied. A frog croaking down in a small swale of a ditch at the road broke her concentration.

Mrs. D said goodbye and drove off. Ashley and I sat down in separate rocking chairs on the covered front porch.

Ashley looked at Brittany, walking toward the croaking of the frog. I assumed she felt the need to explain Brittany and her ex-husband, but she didn't have to. She said, "Her Daddy and I hooked up in high school. I got pregnant my last year in school and dropped out. My so-called friends were brutal towards me. They stopped asking me to go with them to the mall or the movies. In a short four months, I found myself alone with nobody."

I interjected, "Kids at that age are cruel or over-the-top compassionate. I'm sorry your friends were in the cruel category."

"We were so young. Marriage just would not work out, but we both thought we should marry. He at least was working, so there was that. My folks were … hurt, maybe more disappointed. I guess that would be the best way to describe it. They had built the garage apartment, so that's where we lived. At first, everything seemed manageable, but soon after Brittany was born, our ages and immaturity were obvious. We'd argue, and I'd cry and run over to the house and my mom. It was awful for us both. Besides that, we were both experimenting with who-knows-what drugs."

"I understand a little of what you went through. My mother left me when I was two, and my father was in and out of jail much of the time. I stayed mostly with my Uncle Pete and Aunt Jennifer. Uncle Pete was a burly man with huge biceps. I'm not sure how much schooling he had, but he never dissuaded me from going to school. He had been a pipe fitter for several machine shops in the general area. I recall my Aunt Jennifer as a petite brown-haired woman with hazel eyes. She was everything I would have hoped my actual mother might have been. She was as petite as Uncle Pete was large, but she ruled the roost."

"It sounds like you were pretty close to them. Do you see them much?"

"No, not much, even though they filled the role of my 'parents.' Drugs crept into my life too; I left under less than good conditions. Don't get me wrong; if I showed up today, they would be welcoming."

"I understand the drug issue. You know, I didn't take drugs while I was pregnant; I was naïve, but not stupid. My parents sensed it, as I'm sure your Aunt Jennifer did, too. Brittany's father also left us when she was two, looking for work in Indianapolis. He found work but never returned. We divorced a year later. My folks helped some, but the relationship became strained. I think that's really why they started spending more time in Florida. Rather than give me money to help, which they figured would go to drugs, they instead titled the house in Brittany's name. It was the best thing they could have done. It made me more self-sufficient. But with all the normal costs of raising Brittany and paying Mrs. D for her time, I always seem to live paycheck to paycheck."

"Your folks did you a great service, Ashley. Putting the house in Brittany's name assured them she had an inheritance and you couldn't refinance it to buy those drugs. They obviously love you. I've never really known if my mother ever loved me. I doubt it.

My dad probably doesn't possess that emotion, or at least knows how to express it. Aunt Jennifer was a bookkeeper for a local tax accountant. She used to bring some basic bookkeeping work home and let me help her do some simple tasks. The basics seemed easy for me, but before long my immaturity showed and I drifted."

"Well, Mr. Langfeld seems to think you're an okay guy to get you a job so quickly. I sure hope it works out for you," Ashley noted.

"You at least have Brittany to show for your work. I've got nothing of value to show for myself. Is there another guy now?"

"Nope, not yet, at least." Her smile told me if I didn't screw things up, I might be that guy.

"How has Brittany handled the absence of her father?"

"She's done remarkably well, I think. Sometimes, she'll ask about him; if she's having issues with friends. I think mostly she's kept those feelings hidden."

"My dad kept nothing hidden. He was raised in an awful family of poorly educated folks. He'd say they were all cretins and then spit a wad of chewing tobacco to nowhere in particular. Dad wasn't around much, and more times than not, I wished he had stayed away. He beat me a lot, and not with an open hand, but a wide leather belt. I was probably ten when he began using his fists."

"Oh my God! That's awful. You were only ten? How did you protect yourself?"

"Well, at first I couldn't fight back. He would hit me harder or longer if I cried, so I learned early not to cry. At some point, I began not to care. He drank and used drugs; he got violent at the drop of a hat."

"Damn, I thought I had it bad," she said. We kept talking. I told her of my time in the Evansville Juvenile Detention Center and others in the Midwest and the South.

I said, "Looking back now, I think it may have been beneficial.

I certainly learned life experiences early on, including survival techniques."

It was weird to tell a "stranger" about my days of selling drugs to survive. But her eyes revealed her thoughts of both of us exposing some of our deepest secrets at such an early stage. Sensing that, I remarked, "I apologize for throwing my life story at you. There has been only one other person I've shared this with, but I haven't seen Tawon since I left Dallas."

"You shouldn't apologize. I should apologize to you; laying all of my crap at you wasn't much of a welcome-to-the-neighborhood sort of speech."

"You know, that Langfeld got me a job sure is a good reason to quit the other shit in my life. About time for some good luck."

"I'm glad you're being honest with me," she answered. "That means a lot."

I felt a little more comfortable telling her about some of my life because she had had to raise Brittany on her own and I figured she knew how life throws a curve.

We continued sitting on the front porch, enjoying the sunset. The front of the house faced the west and the setting sun washed a wonderful array of reds, yellows, and a little orange across the sky. It was a Hallmark moment featuring some songbirds whistling and a cricket or two chirping to each other. The evening breeze was … clean and relaxing. Brittany came bounding back to the house wanting a dessert, but I think she really just wanted to be part of the conversation. I didn't want to overstay my first night, so I excused myself for the evening and walked over to my new home.

In the morning, I went for a walk around the subdivision. Last night's sunset was a glimpse into the morning's start. Ashley's parents certainly selected a friendly area to buy or to build. The lots seemed quite large to me. Most of the homes were two-story vinyl-sided classic suburban abodes, as was Ashley's, but she had a wrap-around porch running the entire width of the front and north side. The garage was detached and set to the north side of the house. The front of the garage faced the street and a little forward of the porch. The driveway was gravel except for the last thirty feet, which was paved for two cars to park. The yard appeared to be about an acre, and there was plenty of space between neighbors. The garage was an extra-wide two-car bay with the stairs to my new home on the outside closest to the house. My home had a gabled roof with an inverted "V" ceiling. It would cause me an issue only when plugging in electrical cords; I've been called a block because of my square build.

I walked around the front until Ashley came out onto the porch and invited me in for a cup of coffee before taking me to the Baxter plant. The coffee could have been sludge; I was focused on Ashley. She drove me over to Baxter's and then rode with a friend to the diner. She said to use her car until I could get one of my own. One of my own? That's a weird thought.

I found my way to the Transportation Division office. I assumed the office might look like the typical office in a large warehouse or manufacturing plant. It was all glass on the side facing the main floor. The backside had a two-foot by two-foot window for some natural light. The furniture was straight out of a military-looking movie set. Fatigue green desk and cabinet, with a matching swivel chair. Not what I thought I'd see for such a large company.

I was met by Stan Eddy, the office manager of domestic services. He introduced me to Miguel Cortino. Stan and Miguel took me out to the truck bay and told me almost word-for-word what Langfeld had said. Stan said the truck would already have been loaded before our trip as he swept his arm across the length of the bay, pointing out the various loading docks. We walked back to Stan's office. Miguel spoke to me in Spanish, and when I just stared at him, he spoke in English. "Just checking, mi amigo," He said, smiling. Stan added we unload in North America at other Baxter locations. Our load would then be transferred to other trucks in which most of the loads went to auto and truck plants in Mexico.

Miguel said, "Baxter's pay for all of our travel expenses, so there's no need to bring a lot of cash."

I said, "I had no cash anyway."

He grinned and said he had a corporate credit card and would be given some cash out of their petty cash account.

"Whatever, Miguel. I'm just along for the ride—no pun intended."

He laughed and said, "You're going to be doing a lot of driving. It's over 1,400 miles and we can't speed, so we only average about fifty miles per hour. We don't normally arrive there until late Friday night and don't offload until Saturday morning. Stan wants us to stay overnight one night on the way there, one night in McAllen, and one night on the return trip."

Stan interjected, "It's a safety issue, Woody. The feds are very strict about hours behind the wheel, so we just don't push it. We don't need to push it."

Miguel said, "I normally stop in Texarkana at a new casino there. They have a large parking lot and good rates, especially if you gamble. Do you gamble?"

"Nah, I've never really had the cash to lose. When do we leave?"

"This Thursday morning around seven."

"Ok, do I meet you here in the bay or where?"

"Si, my amigo. Our truck is number 4345."

"Okay, 4345, got it, thanks," and I turned to continue reading the orientation packet.

Miguel said laughingly, "Don't forget a change of clothes," as he walked out.

Thursday was in two days. Langfeld said after I finished the orientation business that there was no need to be at the plant until Thursday and said to get my personal things set up.

"You know, Terry," I said. "I've never asked how I'm paid or how much I'm paid. Don't get me wrong. I'm grateful to just have a job. How does the 21-days on work for pay?"

Langfeld explained, "You'll get paid a salary for forty hours a week, but only have to show up to the plant on the days you travel out. You're going to be working for about 120 hours on each round-trip, and each trip is about 3-weeks apart, so it works out to forty-hour weeks."

"Okay, I follow." I said.

He said, "By the way, you've got a paycheck - a signing bonus because of our urgent need to hire, so congratulations. Also, Baxter's includes expected travel costs for meals in your checks, but the lodging is paid directly through a business credit card. Miguel or Stan will explain it all to you."

I didn't know what to say or how to say it. I just sort of gawked until he said, "Don't worry about it. You're filling an immense need for us."

The check was for $1,580 and I still didn't know how much I was being paid, but at that point ... who cares. A quick calculation in my head said that was at least eighty grand a year, and after taxes! Holy shit!

I drove Ashley's car to the Caboose and asked her where she banked. With her answer, I went to open up my very first bank account. Again, I was confronted with forms that made me recall my crappy life up to then, but I walked out a new man. A job, a home, and a bank account!

Back at the Caboose, I gleefully asked Ashley out to celebrate my new life. She smiled, grabbing her cell phone. "Absolutely. I'll just call Mrs. D and see if she can stay longer." I heard Mrs. D's voice, "Of course, sweetie, I'll stay, but don't you need to freshen up a bit?"

In response to Mrs. D's question, Ashley, blushing a little, turned away from me and spoke softly to Mrs. D. I turned away before she could see me smiling, but I have to admit, I was now more than eager for our "date." Date loses its clout when the woman drives, but I didn't care and I doubt Ashley did either.

"Ooh, let's go see a movie after we get a quick bite," she suggested.

"That works for me. Which movie?" We ended up watching *Analyze This* and laughed our asses off. Sitting there with her was relaxing, and I think I made her feel comfortable too. We held hands at the cinema and kissed on the way to the car. She let me drive back to the house. Mrs. D was awake and excited to see I was in the house, not at the garage apartment.

After Mrs. D left, we continued our date in her bedroom. We both hesitated, quivering and nervous like two teenagers. We fumbled a little with our conversation, trying not to make the other think this was our normal behavior. Neither of us wanted to mess up this opportunity. We giggled a lot because we were both intent on proceeding slowly, although I could tell we both were starved for intimacy. We finally succumbed to nature and made love to each other, not sex.

Afterward, I told her, "I'm going to go back to the apartment. You don't need to explain this to Brittany," I said. "I don't want her hurt. Ok?"

She said she understood, but I knew she wanted me to stay. So did I. That felt good.

I had nothing much to do the next day, so I walked to the YMCA. It was about two miles away, but it felt good to be out moving around. I joined so I could use the weight room and the exercise equipment. I've used the YMCA facilities frequently, mainly for showers, but now I just thought it would be a good way to stay in shape. They offered a boxing class twice a week; the first class would happen while I was on the road, but I was assured each class was individually geared. I've always been a solidly built guy and had been in fights on the street, but I had fought trained boxers and learned quickly size doesn't scare everyone. I appreciated the boxer's craft, especially street fighters with boxing knowledge.

I never backed away from a fight, but I always respected the other guy because I knew what it took to be hit with a fist, a rock, or worse. Most of the fights I was in ended quickly. Either I won or I got beat. Not too many of the latter. I enjoyed fighting, and I understood that if someone was badly injured, or worse, the legal ramifications were less for fighting than having used a weapon.

I had spent a lot of my earlier years lifting weights and throwing bare-knuckle punches at a punching bag. I had been a fairly large sixteen-year-old kid. I wasn't picked on too often, and when I was, I fought dirty. There is no reason to be polite or to follow any rules when your ass is on the line. Dad hadn't ever been polite, and I don't recall him losing any fights.

I was going to have a lot of time on my hands, as a passenger or at my home over the garage, waiting for the next haul. I didn't have any books or magazines to read. I remembered a book Aunt Jennie had that I had just read when everything ended there. It was an accounting book—not really a sexy read, but I did like to read, especially subjects I knew little about. Here, I had some interest because of Aunt Jennie; I went to the local library and checked out Accounting Principles and Banking and Finance 101; both had audio versions, too. I figured I would not be a truck driver forever and Langfeld was now in the Finance Division. Since he was on the finance side of an extensive business, I could ask him questions about finance and stay connected in the hopes he might move me to his division. I wanted something to do during the long drive, anyway; Miguel and I wouldn't have too much in common, so at some point, I would have to pass the time. There isn't anything sexy about the basics of accounting and finance, but I knew that everything we do or want to do in our lives is based on green-backs.

Ashley had to attend a parent-teacher conference Wednesday night, so I was on my own. Well, not entirely on my own. Brittany and I sat in her living room. I read while she watched a TV show.

Every once in a while, she and I would exchange brief comments. It felt … right … like what I assumed a normal family might be. When Ashley returned, I told her goodnight. I needed some sleep because my first day started early in the morning. She understood, but clearly, we both would have liked to continue last night's affair.

Thankfully, my apartment had a television and wired for cable. It also had a radio/CD player. I always had time on my hands when I was younger. Although I was intelligent, I didn't pay super attention in school. I spent more than my fair share of school time in detention halls. I listened to lots of music: rock, country, and even some big band sounds. I put on a John Prine CD, *Lost Dogs and Mixed Blessings*. I loved that album. He is such a talented songwriter and lyricist, one who hadn't yet received his due from the public.

Brittany came up to my apartment and asked if I would help with a math question before going to bed. I sat down on my Amish-made dining room chair and between us; we figured out the answer. I knew the answer right off the bat, but acted otherwise, so she had to slog her way to the answer. Ashley must have told her I was going to be around for a while. Brittany was not afraid. I was an okay guy that treated her and her mom well … I was safe. She was such a wonderful kid. Tall, blonde, blue eyes and a wispy physique. Smart as a whip and determined. Brittany asked a few questions about me, to which I responded truthfully, but with some lack of details. When we finished her math problem, she left with a, "See you tomorrow, Woody, and thanks for helping me."

Before going to bed, I sat outside the garage on a fold-out lawn chair I found next to the garage refrigerator, viewing another beautiful evening. This could be a wonderful life.

Langfeld picked me up Thursday morning. "Is everything going okay for you, Woody?" he asked.

"Yeah, you've been great, and everyone I meet seems to fall all over themselves to help. How are things with you?" I returned his inquiry.

"Just one day at a time," Terry answered.

"Hey Terry, what do we bring back from Texas, anyway?"

He paused a little, searching for the correct words to use in his answer. He finally said, "Miguel will have that information."

Truck 4345 wasn't hard to find. I rolled my luggage of clothes, books, CDs, and a utility bag to the rig. Miguel showed with a big smile, "Hey, amigo! Are you ready for a drive?"

"Let's do it, Miguel."

FOUR

Not long thereafter, Miguel and I pulled out of the Baxter plant onto I-65 south. I took in the day and the weather. It was clear, a little crisp, but not harboring many clouds. I checked weather reports along the route. It looked like we would have smooth sailing. At least any rain forecasts weren't for severe storms. About half an hour out, I saw an exit for Seymour, Indiana—the home of John Cougar Mellencamp. I started singing "Jack and Diane," and Miguel sang along with me, but in Spanish. We laughed because neither of us could carry a tune in a bucket, but it broke the ice. We were going to spend a lot of time together.

Miguel told me he was born and raised in Indiana around Indianapolis. His father had immigrated here legally, Miguel said with an emphasis on "legal." He married Miguel's mother, who was also a naturalized citizen. Miguel said they were very proud to have started their lives here legally. The crime in Mexico is devastating and touches every part of life there. They both have family and friends in Mexico, so they're aware of the issues. They understood the reasons many come to America illegally, but Miguel's parents felt they should have applied for citizenship as they had done. Miguel's wife, Stacy, and daughter, Elizabeth, were as proud as Miguel to be Americans.

"We'll be dropping off this load on Saturday morning, and then we'll be told where to pick up our return load," Miguel said without my asking.

"So, what stuff does Baxter's buy that we bring back?"

Miguel hesitated, like Langfeld had, and said, "I don't know, my friend. It changes each trip, and it's on a need-to-know basis. I just go where I'm told."

"What do you do in between the runs to Texas?"

He grinned and sheepishly said, "I work at the Mexican Restaurant in Columbus."

"Good, I know where I can get a good Mexican meal."

For the next hundred miles, I read my book, and by Louisville, we needed to switch. Miguel had worked last night and needed a nap. So, at Shepherdsville, Kentucky, we switched. I was a little nervous, no, a lot nervous, but soon got my confidence. I stuck the audiobook in and Miguel rolled up into the sleeper. As we approached Bowling Green, Kentucky, we needed diesel, so I woke Miguel and asked if he wanted to eat while we fueled up. He told me there was a truck stop at the next exit. It was the typical highway truck stop, complete with diesel odors and revving engines and transmissions, a large bay for truck washes, and the fried grease smells of the diner. While at the truck stop, two guys were talking about their recent visit to the Corvette Museum in Bowling Green. I made a note to take that in on one of our trips. When Miguel took over, he asked me how I came about getting the job. I told him about the Red Caboose meeting with Langfeld.

"You didn't start your life last week in Columbus, my friend. Where's your family?"

We would spend many hours together so he might as well know my crappy life story. The speech given included brushes with the law, no family to speak of, my explanation for the books with me, my current residence, and Ashley. To Miguel's credit, he never questioned my past or asked about my goals. He nodded and said it made sense. Sense? That was a strange observation.

We picked up I-40 in Nashville and continued on our long southwesterly journey. In Little Rock, we merged onto I-30 towards Dallas. I can say now that the drive was enjoyable, but after a while, it all seemed to look the same to me. Concrete and idiot drivers.

We arrived in Texarkana around eight that night. Miguel filled in the logbook and showed me the requirements, where initials were needed to record our individual portions of the trip, and what types of remarks needed to be recorded. We ate at the casino, and Miguel went to his room for a nap before venturing out later. I went to the gaming tables and played some Roulette. I hadn't played often because of a low cash flow, but when possible, playing just a few numbers seemed the best strategy. I won twice, but in the end, I donated one hundred dollars to the local Indian Tribe. That's why they call it gambling and not winning. I was tired by then and crashed into my bed. It was remarkably quiet for a large gathering of drunk gamblers. I fell asleep thinking of Ashley and imagining seeing her in a few days.

Miguel woke me up the next day by calling the room at seven-fifteen. He said we needed to eat breakfast and get on the road. After a fantastic meal and a full tank, we were driving on I-30 for Dallas by eight-thirty. We picked up I-35E and stopped in Waco and had ordered lunch, and refueled. Although each truck stop was different in some ways, they all smelled the same, and I recognized the nuances of each. I drove to San Antonio, where we switched. We ate at a roadside Mexican eatery that Miguel was familiar with. The food, he said, was authentic. It differed from the fare of most Mexican restaurants I had eaten at before. Miguel knew some people there and spoke to them in Spanish. They looked at me a lot, but I assumed it was because I was his new partner. Miguel returned to our table and, pointing over his shoulder, said, "Those guys want to know if you're a fed," he said, smiling.

"Why would they think that?"

"They're pretty sure that my previous partner was arrested because someone had turned him in and they're nervous."

"I imagine there are a lot of immigration arrests down here; doubtful the feds need tips."

"Well, if you're down here and you're a gringo, you're on top of their list."

"We're just driving a truck with engines and parts," I said.

Miguel looked down and away from my eyes and said nothing. He just looked at the other table with his hands splayed out, but they kept looking.

Miguel drove the rest of the way. He picked up I-37 outside San Antonio and then onto the Baxter facility in McAllen, which was several miles north of the city. We arrived a little later than normal, Miguel said. It didn't matter because he reminded me, we couldn't offload until the morning. He provided paperwork at the entrance. They let us in and we were escorted by a pickup truck to the far side of the building. It was a big plant, but not nearly as big as Baxter's. Miguel told me to grab my overnight stuff, and we got in the pickup. The driver and Miguel knew each other. Miguel introduced me to Antonio, who spoke to me in half Spanish, half English accent I had heard before. Miguel and Antonio spoke in Spanish as we drove out of the plant and to a hotel fairly close by. We were tired. I was exhausted, and Miguel said we needed to be back at the plant in the morning around eight. I hit the bed, and the next thing I knew, the phone was ringing, and I groggily said something that sounded like hello.

Miguel said, "Let's go, mi amigo, it's seven o'clock; we need to eat and get on the road."

I met him in the lobby, still groggy, but the coffee brewing smelled like heaven.

He said, "I got a call this morning telling us we're going to a new location. I was told to get moving because it would be a longer run. So, we have to get a move on."

Dazed, I asked why or if new plans were the norm, but he

handed me a cup of coffee in the lobby while waiting for our ride. All seemed okay. Another driver showed up with the same truck that picked us up and we were on our way to breakfast, and then to the facility. Strangely enough, we did not eat at a Mexican restaurant but at a McDonald's. Miguel said Mickey D's had better coffee, anyway. When we arrived at the entrance gate, Miguel had to do some explaining about who I was. Apparently, last night, the security man ran my name through the Baxter employment files and came up with nada. He made a note for the morning crew. A couple of phone calls, and I was okay. When we arrived at our truck, Miguel told me to sit tight while he went to pick up our instructions. I said okay, but I felt something wasn't right about this. It seemed strange, the security, the secrecy. But I was new, so silent I stayed.

Miguel was in a conversation with someone who handed him a telephone. Miguel spoke, or more precisely, listened. After a few moments, he hung up and came back to the truck and said nothing. I could tell he was miffed or perturbed. He just fired up our truck and pulled out without a word. "Well, what are we getting and from where?"

He was silent. Nothing. Just crickets. I let it be for a few minutes and asked again.

"Miguel, what the hell is so secret about hauling engine parts! This is absurd. Everyone is acting like we're transporting a nuclear bomb and not letting me know what's going on sucks. I really don't want to drive fourteen hundred miles in silence. If you don't tell me, so help me, I'll punch your lights out right now!"

He looked at me, upset, defeated, and nodded. He pulled over at the next rest stop behind a row of red maples and just before the rest area building. There were only a few vehicles parked and none close to us.

"Get out, my friend. I'll show you what we're hauling."

"What do you mean? We haven't picked up anything."

He opened up the trailer. I saw crates of fruit and vegetables.

They were not fresh. It stunk to holy hell as one could only imagine. "What the hell is this, Miguel, I asked, holding my arm over my nose? Why are we hauling rotten food? This makes no sense. Where's the regular stuff to haul back?"

"Mi amigo, we always haul back rotten food, but there's been a change in the location. We're not going directly back home. We're going to Atlanta first, and we need to make that seventeen-hour trip in fifteen! So, please just get in, and I'll try to explain."

I grabbed his shoulders and angrily asked, "Rotten food? What the hell? That's ridiculous. Who hauls rotten food almost fourteen hundred miles?" I smelled something fishy, and it wasn't the rotting food in our trailer. "Miguel, nobody hauling rotting food goes through the security and secrecy we've been through, so what's really in the back of this truck?"

A little shiver, a nod, and ultimate surrender. "Tell me," I insisted.

He just looked so small and defeated. "My friend," he reluctantly confided. "I'm so sorry, but we're hauling drugs ... crank."

I froze. Jesus, meth? What the hell? I took a deep breath and then immediately became paranoid. Who else there at the rest stop heard us talking? Who had seen us open the back end and saw me cursing at Miguel? I finally exhaled. "Is this your first time?"

"No, but I hoped it wouldn't start up again. I thought it would stop after the other driver was arrested and deported. I guess the shit wasn't found."

My head was whirling like a top at the county fair. Jesus! I was hearing bursts of recent conversations with Langfeld. The unusual luck I had, being offered a job so easily, the interview about my family; the fact no one was expecting me to visit. Miguel's comment, *that makes sense*. It was now clear to me.

"I get why Langfeld hired me. I'm basically a vagrant with no family ties. Easily an expendable pawn. If we get caught, he could claim I did this on my own. But why you?"

"My daughter, Elizabeth, was diagnosed with brain cancer a few months ago."

"Oh Christ, Miguel, I'm sorry," I said, truly concerned.

"It's at least treatable with a new cocktail of drugs, slight use of chemo, and other things I don't understand. It's going to be expensive to see it through all the way. Langfeld was told about this and came to me with an offer. He would pay me extra for the regular hauls as long as I would haul this crap, too. I was scared, but I could provide my little girl a chance, you know? I agreed, hoping it wouldn't last very long. My partner last week wasn't arrested for immigration. He got popped while he was unloading another truck with the crank we were supposed to be hauling. It was never connected to our Baxter's truck, and as far as I know, he never talked."

I thought about what he had told me. It was a no-brainer that Miguel agreed to the offer. Who wouldn't do anything to save their kid? Hell, I would do it for Brittany, and I've only known her for a couple of weeks.

"Miguel, you said you only made runs every three weeks?"

"We do, but because of last week, Langfeld had to replace the missing load as soon as he could. We can't do this with just one driver, and when you happened to be available, well, it just fell into place."

I thought for a while. My life was pretty shitty before this week; I now had a way to improve it financially just by keeping my mouth shut and doing the job offered. I had much less to lose than Miguel, and I sure as hell would not hurt his chances of helping his kid, nor Langfeld.

"Ok, Miguel, listen to me. I'm not opening my mouth. You need the job to care for your daughter. I would never screw you over something like this. I don't know how long I can continue this crap, but I've got reasons to keep this gig going too. So, when Langfeld asks you about the haul, you just tell him I didn't care about what we hauled or where it went. Ok?"

"Si, amigo, I don't want to hurt nobody." We began driving

north to Houston, where I figured would be a good place to stop for fuel and a quick bite of food. "Hey Miguel, have you dropped off in Atlanta before?"

"No, I've gone many places before, but not Atlanta."

"Did you haul rotting food each time?"

"Yes. Strange, I know, but explainable."

"How? Wouldn't it be hard to explain that a Baxter Engine Plant truck was hauling rotting food?"

Miguel explained, "Langfeld developed a contract to haul fruits and vegetables as a sub-contractor for a distributor named Schmidt's Distributors & Parson's Fruits and Vegetables. Langfeld said if we were stopped and searched to show them the documents for Schmidt's, the company in Texas, we were contracted to haul for. Nothing really links Baxter except the use of the truck. He wasn't worried about that connection. In fact, I think that Schmidt's actually sells rotten or rotting food to hog farms and other users across the country. I don't know how Schmidt's is protected if we were stopped. Our paperwork stated we picked up the cargo there."

I pondered that for a long time. Langfeld, Miguel, and I were trafficking illegal drugs across state lines for Schmidt's. The ultimate buyers were unknown, but Baxter's would have been number one on the list. However, since the haul wasn't going to Baxter's, the receiver, of which I yet didn't know, could also be the ultimate buyer. We were not involved in any money exchange, at least to my knowledge. Therefore, was Baxter's a broker? Was Schmidt's a broker too? I knew Miguel wasn't aware of all the player's roles. He wasn't a drug dealer and didn't have the stomach for that world, a world I knew a lot about.

I hadn't seen the quantity of the meth in our trailer. It could be any amount. I assumed the rotting food must hide or confuse a K9 drug dog from alerting. It's the only explanation why Langfeld and others weren't too worried about being stopped. Jesus, as soon as I thought I had put that life behind me, I found out that I was exposed even more.

We picked up I-10 in Houston and drove east through Baton Rouge, then on to Mobile. We stopped again for fuel, both for the truck and us. Before we rolled out of Mobile, it began to rain, and I mean, it was a cloudburst if I ever saw one. It was daylight, but the rain was so hard that the lights of approaching vehicles glared so badly that I put on my sunglasses. We eventually had to pull over under an overpass. Miguel said he had seen it rain harder before, but this was the worse I had seen. It rained for about forty-five minutes, so we were concerned about making the deadline given to us.

I asked Miguel how Schmidt gathered all the rotting food waste. He said that it was his understanding they included their own unsold foods with area restaurants and grocery stores. The rain finally scaled back enough for us to head up I-65 north to Atlanta. Somehow, we made it by the seventeen-hour deadline given to us. In fact, had it not been for having to wait on the rain of the century or the fact we had to drive near the airport, we might have made it in sixteen hours.

Schmidt's had a medium-sized warehouse just east of the airport off Conley Road in what would be described as an industrial area. There were many warehouses of all types of industries. So many flat-top roofs with sheet metal siding that I could see the benefit of loading and/or unloading the drugs in the industrial park. When we arrived at the location, we were again escorted to an area of their building that appeared to be more or less abandoned. This time I thought I saw a side-arm on the passenger.

Miguel backed us in and just sat in the cab. I looked at him. He felt my eyes and he said, "We don't get out of the cab, so we can't see what is unloaded nor who is unloading us."

"Now that makes sense, Miguel. Plausible denial and in this case actual denial of facts." After about an hour, someone banged on the side of our trailer, and off we went. I saw no one except the gate guard, and I couldn't have picked him out of a line-up of two.

We made it home with no issues. I had continued reading or listening to my boring Banking and Finance 101 material. When I didn't have the headphones on, we both listened to various musical artists. There was no need to talk about what we were doing. We also knew that it was to our benefit financially to just keep the secret to ourselves.

Miguel dropped me off at my apartment, and as much as I wanted to see Ashley, I was gassed. I left her a note on her door explaining that and telling her I would stop by the Caboose in the morning. Even though I was exhausted, both physically and mentally, I couldn't sleep. I lay there and ran the facts that I knew over and over. How much had we delivered? How many at Schmidt's were involved? How many at Baxter's? Schmidt's was the primary key to this trafficking organization. Was Schmidt's the only distributor? Was meth the only drug? With all of those questions and my involvement, I still knew this might be the only way I could survive financially and have some resemblance of a stable home life. Right then and there, I had made my decision; this was going to be my life from here on out. Come hell or high water, I was in it for the long haul … no pun intended.

FIVE

Months went by before I learned Langfeld was aware I knew what we were hauling. I overheard him on his office phone saying Miguel and Woody were straight-up guys and we wouldn't talk. He answered another question by stating, "Javier, I pay them enough to guarantee loyalty. Don't worry. You just do what you do, and I'll do what I do."

During the next months, Miguel and I hauled to St. Louis, Oklahoma City, Nashville, and Milwaukee. We never were pulled over and we never saw an employee of Schmidt's other than a gate guard. The freight was always loaded and ready for us at their warehouse each Saturday morning that we ran. We had no mechanical breakdowns, which was more of a concern than the police stopping us for some traffic violation. My check was directly deposited every Monday. Ashley and I were getting closer and closer, but I didn't let on how much I was being paid, which, of course, was absurd.

Brittany and I continued our relationship, sort of older brother connection at first. I was only about ten years older. It actually was beneficial for me. I was helping her with homework, which meant I was seeing an awful lot of academic material for the first time. I could help Mrs. D, especially when she had her own errands to run.

Several more months passed and school was out. Although Brittany went to a sort of summer camp, it wasn't all day nor all week. Ashley was working long hours at the Caboose. Although I could have afforded to pay for everything, I couldn't let her know I was a drug trafficker.

Langfeld hadn't yet approached me about our arrangement, and I didn't want to seek him out. Stan was actually Miguel's boss for our runs. Stan had to have known too, but he never let on that he did, and Miguel never told me that Stan knew. I struggled to believe he wasn't in on it, but he surely didn't act like he was part of the group.

The runs hadn't deviated from the 3-week schedule. By the school year in September, I had hauled with Miguel on eight trips. We went to Atlanta and Kansas City twice, and the other sites just once. I noticed that the stops in Milwaukee, St. Louis, and Nashville were at unmarked warehouses.

Miguel's Elizabeth was being seen by doctors at the Mayo Clinic in Rochester, Minnesota. I drove with Miguel and her once because it was going to be a turn-and-burn trip. The actual drive was pleasant because of no traffic accidents or major road construction delays. However, the air was thick with concerns and anxiety. I don't recall which number trip this was for them, but it didn't matter which trip it was; they were all equally suspenseful. I attempted to start a few conversations, but they were each met with solemn replies, so I stayed mum. Miguel explained why the Mayo Clinic in Rochester, Minnesota, and not Cleveland, Ohio, which was at least five-hours closer, had been chosen. He said that Elizabeth's type of tumor was treated specially by the Rochester medical team. Miguel chose to avoid Chicago by traveling west to meet I-39 north through Rockford, Illinois, up through Madison,

Wisconsin, and eventually to Rochester. Traveling through Illinois is an extremely flat trip, especially on I-39, and except for the huge windmill farms, I saw nothing out of the ordinary, just acres of wheat, corn, soybeans, and alfalfa.

Even though Baxter's medical insurance was top notch, the amount of out-of-pocket costs had to be high. Langfeld made sure Miguel was compensated appropriately.

I had now read, actually listened to, three books on finance and accounting. I had wondered how Langfeld was hiding what had to be an outlier in Baxter's expense accounts for employee-related transportation. Miguel had let it slip one day that he was getting almost $2,500 a week after taxes. I was getting $1,580, so for two drivers, Baxter's was paying more than $212,000 a year! No way you could hide that for long from the Executive Board unless Langfeld somehow hid the expenses. One part of me was curious, but the other part wondered why I even cared. I was quickly beginning to enjoy the job. I put my head in the sand and convinced myself that since having never seen the loads; I was innocent. I wasn't the person selling drugs to those on the streets and, therefore, not responsible for the overdoses.

I had eventually moved into the main house with Ashley and Brittany. The move was seamless, mainly because over many months; we had moved clothes, odds and ends, and other items occasionally. Brittany and I had developed a pretty good bond by then. She sometimes would ask me questions I felt a daughter might ask a father and not the mother. Ashley and I had fallen in love and we began talking about marriage.

Ashley hadn't seen my anger and rough side until one night when we were out having a few drinks and some guy copped a feel. Ashley jerked back, and before she said or did anything, I drove my fist into the guy's stomach and kicked him. I was in his face, screaming to leave my girl alone. When he stayed bent over,

I hit him on the back of his head. He went down like a pile of bricks bleeding from several places. Ashley screamed, "Holy shit, Woody! Where did that come from? He was just being a jerk."

I said, "He was being a jerk to you, Ashley. No one does that to me or someone I care for without paying the price. That's the thing my dad, and the streets, taught me. My most important fighting talent, or gift, wasn't that I hit like a ton of bricks. It was that I didn't care if they hit me with a ton of bricks. Nothing seemed to hurt me, especially when I was pissed."

"Damn, Woody. You caught me off-guard, but thanks, I think."

I said, "My dad unknowingly, or maybe in some weird fatherly way, taught me not to feel the punch or the kick. I began becoming apathetic to the punch or kick. I also don't like to quit. So many times, I think I just scared the hell out of the other guy."

"Well, you scared the hell out of me. Do you really not care?"

"Yeah, I would keep coming at whoever, even after being dealt serious blows. Uncle Pete described my style as a modern-day Joe Frazier. Years later, I read up on Frazier and learned that a sports announcer once said Frazier would block his opponent's punches with his face until the other guy became tired and wore out. Then Frazier would knock the guy out. I guess that's a fair description of this side of me. I'm sorry for scaring you, but that guy deserved it."

"Remind me not to piss you off," she said, but at least with a smile.

Nothing much changed for us until after September 11. Obviously, a shitload of changes was required then. By then, Miguel and I had completed at least thirty or forty runs. Elizabeth was in remission, and Miguel had succumbed, long ago, to the fact she was healthy only because of our illegal hauls.

Not long after that fateful day in September, Ashley had seen my monthly bank statement. I had saved more than $90,000, so it didn't take a rocket scientist to realize I was making more money than a normal truck driver. Ashley waited on truck drivers day and night. She asked me by saying, "Baxter's must really be doing well these days." She held the statement in her petite hand.

I knew this day would arrive, but it didn't help. I explained to her how it all had begun for Miguel and me. It took most of the night to describe how all the puzzle pieces fell into place. She asked all the obvious questions. She seemed not to be torn about how our relationship evolved because it had never been about money. I told her I had recently added Brittany to my checking account. In case something happened to me, she could go to college without a financial burden on her. Ashley didn't know if she should cry or be mad that I hadn't told her. So, she punched my arm, gave me a bear hug, and cried on my shoulder, but she did ask, "When were you going to tell me?"

I told her the truth. "I don't know, honey. It isn't something ... you can plan for."

I had taken a few finance quizzes online offered by a few colleges in order to test the waters. I had done well enough that I contacted a college admissions office regarding how to get a degree while being a long-haul truck driver. The school was starting an online degree program in the business school. We spoke and shared faxes containing my quizzes and she felt I would be a great candidate, possibly even an advertisement, if I succeeded. We negotiated an agreement to earn an associate's degree in accounting and finance by being allowed credit for classes I had tested previously through other schools, to avoid redoing the same courses. Brittany and I discussed accounting occasionally. Not your usual father-daughter type of subject. She was smart and inquisitive. I had only become interested in the subject solely because of Aunt Jennie, so I had to study a bit more to understand the matter. Thankfully, the long hauls gave me the additional time, and Miguel was typically listening to music with headsets or on his telephone with his wife or Elizabeth. It helped a lot to ask and answer questions with Brittany. She enjoyed it too, and suggested she would major in accounting and finance when she went to college.

Seldom was I found at Baxter's because of the unique shift work. However, from time to time, I had to sign a form or take one of the mind-numbing mandatory human resource classes. One day, Langfeld learned I was at the plant and asked me to his office. I entered and he closed the door. He showed me to sit without a word. This was it, so I was ready for the rug to be pulled out from under me, but he surprised me. "I understand that you've been taking some finance courses," he said with a grin.

"Yes, doing okay too."

Pouring a cup of coffee for himself and me, he said, "I'm impressed, which is why I want to ask you to do something else for me. I have been moving all of … the money through various other companies. I've been asked, no, told, to take on another role in the business, but I need someone I can trust to handle laundering the money and everything it entails. I'll teach you the ins-and-outs as I know them, and hopefully, soon, you'll be able to do it without me."

I was shocked he felt I could do the job but grateful and said, "Sure Terry, but what more of the business could you possibly have time to do? You're already overworked." His look said not to push it. "Okay, but what am I going to do here at Baxter's."

"You'll be in the Accounting Department under me."

My dreams or hopes years ago were coming true. I would be off the road and my hands would not be touching the cargo. I would be learning another side of the business, albeit an illegal one. But it was exciting, and I was truly appreciative of Langfeld for the chance.

I began an accelerated program on 'How to launder drug proceeds' under the guise of a legitimate business. Langfeld explained, "Over the years, I have scoured the country for cinemas, car washes, and other cash-intensive businesses that were for sale or could be bought. As a result of my wishes, Baxter's has purchased twenty-seven businesses; fifteen car washes, seven cinemas, and five money service locations in larger cities. I have set up, or had set up, those new businesses in the names of homeless people as the officers and owners or names borrowed from death certificates. We have always filed and paid the taxes on the income from each, but we reduced taxable income by creating fake expenses and ghost loans so we could wire money out of the companies to businesses in Mexico, among other places, for the payment to our sources. We even began to create loans between the companies so we could siphon off money to pay us, including you, through Baxter's. It's begun to be all I can do to keep track of the books. So, you're the guy that's now going to learn this and keep this thing afloat."

"Who are we working for? I never asked you before, but if I'm going to be this involved, I need to know my bosses' names," I said, more exploring than accusatorially.

He pondered my question for a moment, "Yeah, I guess I owe you that."

"Schmidt's is owned by another corporation, Rotten Tomatoes. Rotten Tomatoes is owned by another company, maybe in Mexico. I'm not aware of all the owners or who is the top dog. What I can tell you is the dog I answer to is Javier Muchido. I don't know who he answers to, but that person's reputation is that he is ruthless."

"How did you find yourself involved in this, Terry? I know Miguel's and my story, but what's yours?"

"I met Javier when I was the Transportation Manager at our Texas location. I had recently been divorced, and I guess I was feeling sorry for myself. She took almost everything I had, Woody, including the kids. Over a lot of tequila one night at a local watering hole, I told him of my plight. He suggested he had an answer for me in which the family court would never know about and, therefore, my alimony and child support requirements wouldn't be increased. I wasn't concerned about the child support, but that goddamn alimony check was choking me every month that I had to write it, so I listened."

"The owner of Schmidt's now is Franklin Schmidt. He had done a short stint on a state drug offense. Javier has been in the business now for almost twenty years and had been arrested twice. The Mexican arrest went away after a series of large bribes to the officials. The arrest in the Texas cost him 27 months in state prison. That's where he met Franklin, the nephew of the head of the family that owned Schmidt's Distributors and Parson's Fruits and Vegetables. The Parson, in the business name, had long since sold out to Mr. Schmidt. Franklin was the only relative who wanted to continue the family business. His uncle gave him the second chance he needed, being a felon and all, so when Mr. Schmidt died, Franklin, who had been out of prison for several years by then, was left to run the operation."

Langfeld continued, "Javier eventually approached Franklin; they set up the rudimentary supply routes and retail side of the business. Over the years, they had been able to avoid law enforcement detection. Javier had prided himself on keeping control over the business. Franklin was fine with letting him control the security and enforcement side of their business. Franklin probably didn't have the stomach for violence, and Javier did. Anytime a message had to be sent, Javier knew how or who could carry out the appropriate message."

I learned from Langfeld that they were much smarter than most by not living large and bragging about their money. Javier and Franklin had been using contract drivers to do their hauling when Javier and Langfeld met. Over more tequila, they came up with the idea of using Baxter's trucks because several times a month Baxter's truck traveled to McAllen. They figured they could send one back with their merchandise.

According to Langfeld, he was able to convince one particular driver coming out of Illinois to take hauls outside of the regular route. The driver began to ask questions Langfeld couldn't answer, so he closed it down for a month. Javier went ballistic. Langfeld was told, with no room for error, that it was to be fixed now.

At the same time, the Transportation Manager at Baxter's was retiring, so he begged the Plant Manager for the lateral transfer. "I assumed I could find someone that I could rely on because the Columbus plant was our largest engine plant, and I knew we could justify an extra run a month. So, I felt it was two birds with one stone, I could get Javier off my back long enough to land the job and then set up more hauls. Soon thereafter, I found out about Miguel and his daughter's situation. I approached him with the famous line, 'I'll make you an offer you can't refuse.' It worked on him as it did on you. And, yes, I'm a prick, but I had to do it because I'm way too far into this to walk away."

"No apology needed, Terry. I'm a big boy and I had a choice. Anything else to know about Javier or Franklin?"

"Not now."

The next day, we resumed our discussion about our drug organization. I now found myself square in the middle of without knowing all the players. Langfeld said Javier had explained the basics of the organizational structure to him without revealing the drug name. I guess Javier thought that protected him and me. I was desperate and thought I'd be financially set and get out of it quickly, but once you're in for a penny, you're in for a pound. Yeah, that was a concern for us all. Langfeld acknowledged that the financial apparatus we were using had been copied from some other unknown organization he was a part of, or learned of, which is why this new group had been so well run.

"I guess I should apologize to you for putting you in this same situation, but Javier can be very … ah, well, convincing when he wants to be."

"No need to apologize. I'm in just like you, but I guess Javier doesn't know me yet."

"That's true for now. I'll bring him up to speed as soon as you can effectively take over for me."

SIX

Langfeld described Javier Muchido as a very busy businessman, which I thought was a redundant announcement. He was a bigshot of a middle-sized drug trafficking organization in which newspaper and magazine articles describe as DTOs and being responsible for flooding America with methamphetamine. The appetite Americans had for the drug was astounding, and with no noticeable let-up in sight. Law enforcement in America, or anywhere, couldn't handle the overwhelming number of dealers, especially since many politicians and their communities were beginning to abandon their support of law enforcement agencies. Many of the law enforcement officers in Mexico could easily be bribed. The bigger DTOs, or cartels, were vicious and dangerous. They weren't concerned about being arrested and imprisoned because they killed and murdered anyone who talked during the drug investigation; including family members. Fear is a powerful motivator and intimidator. Javier knew all that. Muchido had set up the major parts of the organization, but Baxter's fulfilled the distribution portion within America. Muchido didn't have the needed associations, but others in the DTO did, therefore, he needed Langfeld and vice versa.

Langfeld said, "I'll be able to show you the company names and individual aliases involved as we go over the books. No note-taking Woody. You just have to remember names, passwords, locations. I've tried to avoid documenting my actions, and I suggest strongly you do the same." I did, and I have ever since.

So, over the next four months, reading became my life. Thankfully, the weather and our front porch were comfortable for much of the time. The analysis of more transactions than I would have ever imagined had been overwhelming at first. When at Baxter's, I asked Langfeld questions. Many questions. I took trips to speak to our managers at almost all of our businesses. We guarded against using a company credit card too often for travel expenses, so a personal card of mine was used and paid for through several other businesses. Understanding foreign exchange rates and how they might affect us if we grew to that size was extremely difficult, and not well digested by me. I made many phone calls to confirm numbers and locations, and I bugged Langfeld to no end. The research never ceased nor seemed sufficient. I googled different financial issues, especially when it came to taxes. We both agreed that besides the DEA investigating us, it would be worse if the IRS were involved. The IRS wouldn't need to prove hand-to-hand drug transactions to prosecute for money laundering, which was frightening, not to mention the All-American tax audit. We made a concerted effort to ensure we were okay with the IRS.

Langfeld mentioned he had set up some businesses in homeless persons' names. He even went as far as filing tax returns for them, always ensuring that they had collected small refunds but applied the refunds towards the next year's taxes, avoiding any form of communication with the IRS.

When the weather was poor, I went to the garage apartment and read with guaranteed silence. All the original furniture was still in place, the sofa with the throw pillows Ashley bought me; the kitchen table; the CD player; and my reading chair. The refrigerator was stocked, and I knew how to prepare my favorite lunch - macaroni, cheese, and sausage. I had done so many times when I stayed all day reading. The telephone line was used for Internet connection, and nothing billed linked to Baxter's.

Risking showing the details of the organization, I used large sheets of paper taped on the living room walls of the apartment. Locations were pinned and connected by colored string lines to and from Baxter's and McAllen. Red string to show direct links to McAllen; yellow string to Indiana; green pins showed the various Schmidt warehouse locations. There wasn't a need to identify any of the pinned locations by name. The businesses we owned, actually investments of Baxter's, were pinned with large blue flags as noted in the Baxter accounting books.

The organization became clearer, and the structure of Langfeld's laundering of the drug proceeds illustrated his attention to detail. Langfeld had encouraged me to grasp and understand the entirety of our organization, but then specifically how to expand and grow it.

I began to visualize, or more specifically, wonder what the actual differences were of legal and illegal businesses. Answering my own question with the startling fact ... nothing. A successful business plan for either legal or illegal enterprise reflects the same goals ... profit. I asked myself how to take our successful business to another level. It was obvious we were increasing in size, although not having a firm handle on the sales portion of the organization was an obstacle.

Money laundering aspects seemed simple enough; the receipt of green dollars/cash for drugs and changed to something appearing to be legitimate. The act of making deposits and eventual withdrawals to clean the money on paper also seemed easy. It is the eventual use of those deposits/withdrawals that is the difficult portion of those in illegal businesses ... they just had to be big men on campus and braggarts.

The benefit of my new job was that, except for the few times I traveled to see our other businesses and managers, I was home every night. Ashely and I discussed my new position, and she was glad about my being home more, but she also stated the obvious. "You're now in the middle of this shit-show, and no longer going to be shielded. You won't be able to hide behind the defense that you're not seeing the product."

I had thought for some time that an alias might shield me from the organization if it crashed and burned. Ashley and I discussed how to create a fictitious name only she and I knew. We had to have an SSN and a DOB, so a driver's license and passport could be secured. We couldn't ask anyone in the group for help without telling them why. We resigned ourselves to the fact that unless we discovered a professional forger; we had to accomplish this on our own.

During some point in my life, I had read about a famous conman who had created new identities for himself by using the names of deceased children born around his birth date. The guy walked through cemeteries to find a grave marker for a male that had died very early in life and was close to his year of birth. Upon learning of a likely name, he went to the county courthouse and searched and acquired the proper documents to apply for a replacement birth certificate. The conman never did this in small populated counties. Those employees had more time to properly conduct their due diligence to prevent such a fraud.

The conman also had stayed in homeless shelters to avoid law enforcement from time to time and recognized some shelters kept files on their longer-term residents. He felt the homeless person was easier to finesse a new alias.

"You think that might work to get actual SSNs and DOBs?" I asked Ashley.

"I guess so, but you just can't go up and ask for them. How do you plan on doing it?"

"It's been a while, but I lived on the streets for some time. I may still be able to blend in long enough to finagle a way to find some records." We had to try.

We had to wait two weeks for me to grow out a scraggly, and I mean a scraggly, beard. I didn't wash for the last five days, which was disturbing to Brittany, but Ashley told her I had developed an allergic reaction to the new soap she had bought. Brittany was a little suspicious and pinched her nose and laughed at me. She was okay with the explanation and enjoyed teasing me.

We drove north on I-65 to Indianapolis, a simple and uneventful drive. The view out either side of the car was the same: flat farmlands. Ashley dropped me off in the downtown area near a Goodwill store. She made sure I didn't have my wallet or any form of identification with me and counted out thirty-one dollars for me to use. I found an oversized green corduroy pair of pants; a smaller but still larger sized pair of blue jeans than I normally wear, two fresh shirts - one, a cream color, the other an ugly plaid also too big for me but perfect for my needs. The purpose of the loose-fitting pants accomplished several needs. One, loose-fitting clothes are preferred by vagrants and the homeless because these can layer clothes, making it easier to keep warm or to stay cool. Two, weapons and other needs are better hidden in loose clothing. An old pair of low-riding, hiking boots filled out my attire.

We found one of the larger shelters was connected to a Catholic church, both physically and spiritually. It was a cathedral because I noticed a Bishop was assigned to the location. At the main entrance, two high-rising spires with a green patina rose at least three, if not four, stories. I guessed all or most of it was copper to exude such a hue. There were several entrances to the principal portion of the church, but one had persons hanging around and being served water, which made me assume it was a shelter.

Walking into the shelter with a slight limp, I sat down, not saying anything to anybody. Just waiting. I didn't want to speak if I could avoid it. I wouldn't have had the correct slang or mannerisms for the area. What I needed was a stretch to look into the records kept at the shelter's office. The office, or what I assumed was the office, was next to the entryway. Watching and waiting. I was good at waiting. Had done it many times as a surviving kid. I just hummed songs in my head.

For almost three hours, I observed how the residents walked and communicated with each other, and specifically with the shelter's staff. In case I was forced to speak, I had to have some idea what the local slang or speech pattern might be. I looked for cameras or where cameras should have been located and saw none. Only two people approached me. Both were workers. One female asked if she could help me. A few long seconds of my staring ahead and ignoring her caused her to walk away. I saw her tell a fellow employee to monitor me. He eventually approached me and asked my name. I stuttered a few unintelligible words as if I had Tourette's. He tried in vain to communicate with me and asked if I was hungry. I tried not to look at him, and just hid my head and he finally left me alone.

About thirty minutes later, the office and the main lobby emptied of staff and residents. I had seen a column of mostly men and workers walking away from the main lobby through a long hallway. Must be dinner time. I got up and limped to an open office. It was a typical-looking office, not unlike some at Baxter's. A large glass pane window with vertical pull blinds looked out at the main area. The office allowed for a person seated behind the desk to see the front entrance door.

The end of the long hallway began to evoke chatter and some clanging noises. Soon, the smells of cooked hot dogs and pork and beans caught my nose. For sure, it was the cafeteria.

Peering through the large office window, I saw the office contained a short wall of green government-type cabinets. Some were marked Reports, Vendors, Admin. But two of them were just labeled top to bottom A-M and N-Z. About the time I started to enter the office, a janitor started down the hallway towards me. I shuffled towards him, and the cafeteria, staring at my boots.

His eyes penetrated my attempt to ignore him. He stopped me by placing a firm hand on my shoulder. He asked, "You okay, son? You're late for chow. Better get a move on or it'll be all gone."

I stuttered an "okay" and he kept on walking past me and out through the main entry door.

When he turned the corner, I poked my head into the office, and it revealed it was empty. I was more than a little concerned now about being seen. Paranoia? Making sure no one was paying any attention, I slithered into the office, as slithering as someone my size can do with oversized clothes. I pulled a drawer of A-M cabinet and, Jesus Christ! It screeched like Edward Scissorhands dragging his hands across a blackboard. Holy crap! Then, without thinking, just reacting, I slammed the drawer shut with an equally loud Bang! Oh, this is going well. I scooted out into the hall and flopped down with my back to the wall opposite the office. I was sweating and breathing much too hard for a practical explanation if asked.

Yes, now paranoia set in. It was consuming me with a fear that everything, and everyone, was observing my every move. In a few minutes, I gathered enough intestinal fortitude and stood and walked back into the office.

This time, N-Z, I pulled and slowly. Much better. No sound. I sat down crossed-legged on the floor next to the desk with a handful of manila files. The entry door was visible to me.

I figured the best name for me to pick, if possible, was something similar to my name. First file, Francis B. Watson, age fifty-seven ...nope. Second, Kevin Winston, age sixty-two. Jesus, I hadn't considered that so many of the homeless might be old. There was only one other "W", a Lance Wheeler, age fifty-five ... crap! Before I could read the next file, I heard steps in the hall getting closer. I grabbed for the files I had taken, but I couldn't gather all of them. Those I could I threw into the drawer and the three left on the floor I swept under the desk.

I peeked out the door and down the hall. A worker was heading for this office. Ah, shit! Think! Think dammit! I saw the visitor's chair. Oh, what the hell, I sat and waited … and waited. The woman stepped into the office wearing jeans, a red blouse, and black hard-soled shoes. She walked directly to the desk, grabbed a pen and steno pad, turned and said hi, and walked out. I was so shocked I couldn't even respond with a hi.

I quickly looked at the file marked "William, Paul Anderson." No age had been written on the paper. I folded the three pieces of paper in the thin file and put them into my clothes. I threw the other two file folders into the N-Z drawer. The exit was uneventful except that the janitor saw me again and asked if I had made dinner. I nodded and kept walking.

I met up with Ashley at Willard Park, as we had agreed. She looked worried because it had taken a long time and I didn't have a way to tell her I was okay while at the shelter. I explained me not finding a probable file. Ashley asked what was it I found.

"Some guy, Paul Anderson William. I haven't looked yet at the documents."

She took the file and said, "He's a year younger than you. I thought you said his last name was William?"

"It is. See the folder label. William comma Paul Anderson."

"Honey, someone must have mis-marked it. His name is Paul William Anderson."

"Really? They also put it in the wrong cabinet drawer."

Anderson had given no family contacts or an emergency number. His medical history form showed a few issues, including high blood pressure and some sort of skin malady.

I hugged her, but she pushed me away.

"What's up? I couldn't call you to let you know everything was fine, and look, it worked out fine," I exclaimed.

"No, that's not it. You stink!"

Ha! I forgot I had been sweating all day, and had not showered for a few days. "Sorry." We laughed, and I ended up changing my clothes in a McDonald's bathroom before heading to a local steakhouse to celebrate. I said I should have taken a female file for her too. We agreed if it became necessary, we could try it again.

SEVEN

I needed to lessen my workload and stress on me when it came to managing all the financials for the companies. Just managing the bank accounts was a massive and tedious undertaking. Langfeld trusted very few of the outside managers to handle the banking duties. He said the managers were yet to be trusted, which required him either to have the financials mailed to post office boxes only he had access to or to handle them electronically online. Therefore, those managers didn't know how the businesses were doing, per our books. They recorded the deposits and expenses they paid on-site. The additional deposits were made remotely by Langfeld and others he hadn't yet revealed to me. The expenses via online. Although the managers weren't seeing the bottom-line figures of their location, the managers at several locations would have had to have been blind not to see that an infusion of cash kept the doors open and the lights on.

The numbers that were being generated and deposited over the breadth of the entire organization were astronomical. I couldn't help but wonder about the numbers in the truly large Mexican cartels. We had built up to an average of about $2 million cash deposits a month. I had yet to have seen how our product was paid for, so I was not yet clear how Langfeld determined the amount of cash to be added to the weekly deposits in the businesses.

In his office, one gray and dismal morning, I asked, "Hey Terry, I know how we're hiding the sales, but how have you handled the purchases?"

Langfeld was in a pretty good mood. He topped off my coffee, sat down at his desk, and propped his feet on it. "What Javier and I worked out with our sources is to pay them one-half of the total purchase price in cash. The price is a discounted price because of how we pay it all back. We create a loan equal to one and a half times the remaining amount plus interest in various companies owned by the supplier. That loan is then paid over a few years. For example, we bought $52,000 through La Haba Burrito the other day. We delivered $26,000 in cash to them. I set up a loan payable to that company for $39,000 to be paid over five years at three percent interest for something around $675 a month. I think it was. Anyway, they get a legitimate stream of revenue that actually pays them more than the original sale price! And, better yet, the IRS is kept happy. Since our suppliers also have several businesses set up to run the cash in, we're able to spread out our loan payables, so no one business should be red-flagged. Sometimes we've merged loans to make the accounting easier. We make approximately four to five times our original purchase price. Half of all that cash is eventually deposited into our legitimate companies as sales. Half the original purchase is done in cash, so we keep out half of each sale for upcoming buys. Also, we each get a draw of the profits from those companies as owners, so again, the IRS is happy."

Langfeld was proud of his and Javier's setup. He continued our conversation much like a pleased parent does when telling a friend of their kid's accomplishments. "Every month, we wire funds identified as loan payments between all the companies. It looks a bit like an airplane magazine destination chart, you know, the crossed lines in color and encompassing the last few pages of the magazine. The payments are minimal; they're not thousands of dollars each month to the same business."

I remarked, "That is a lot to do for one person."

But the best part, Langfeld still on his soapbox said, "is that me, Javier, and others higher up the food chain agreed that at some point when we all walked away to retire, the companies were still on the hook to pay out our salaries through draws from those companies for five years."

My pay, I was told, was calculated based on a percentage of the net profits for the organization. He said, "Javier and Franklin agreed to pay you two and three-quarters percent of the profit each week or month, your choice. He said Javier and Franklin took the bulk of the profit."

Langfeld said they paid him seven percent; our salaries went through regular companies, so the withholding of taxes was made. "We don't want the fucking bean counters on our heels."

I calculated in my mind that I would make over $17,000 a month! This would not be a normal forty to fifty hour a week job.

I sauntered out of his office, down the hall, and almost straight into Michelle. We both jumped. "Oh, I'm sorry, Michelle. I was lost in another world."

"Not a problem, sir. Have a good day," she said, smiling as she went into Langfeld's office, shutting the door.

After several months of an accelerated review of our financials; and a book on investments, I concluded that Baxter's and a few of the other companies should move into real estate. It would further layer the money, and it would be another way to create legitimate businesses. I wasn't sure when or how to suggest my idea. I invited Terry to dinner at a local steakhouse to broach the subject. A good steak and some drinks couldn't hurt.

I had told Terry that we needed to talk about business, and since Ashley was working a late shift, I thought a splendid dinner was in order. He had agreed. Mabel's Steakhouse was out of town a few miles and had always been known for great steaks and quality seafood.

We drove separately. He found me at the bar with a drink ready for his hand. We exchanged the usual pleasantries. I had been on the road recently, so we hadn't seen each other in a week or two. The bar wasn't, or couldn't, hide the kitchen smells of great food. Every once in a while, a whiff of garlic and heated bread caught my nose. A loud and obnoxious drunk was at one end of the bar and an extremely good-looking young red-haired lady was trying to evade his advances. The bartender waved to an unknown person who arrived just in time to prevent the boozer from forcing her to dance with him to a song playing in the bar. The savior was a pretty good-sized man who didn't have any trouble escorting the oaf to the door. His actions reminded me of days gone by when I interceded on behalf of someone, too.

At dinner, I explained to Terry my basic idea of investing in real estate. I admitted I was still searching for types and locations, but was convinced that real estate was the way to go for us. I described the need to continue to create legitimate avenues to place our money. He said he had considered it too, but hadn't had enough time to go to Javier or Franklin with a sound concept.

"Woody, take some time and draft a quality letter detailing your thoughts. Show exactly how we could implement it through the organization. Javier, for one, will want to see the specifics - to see the numbers. Franklin is an unknown to me, meaning I've never sat in a meeting with him regarding the finances. He always relied on Javier, me, or someone else for an accounting."

"Sure thing, Terry. Is there a timeframe for this, or is it just when I think I'm ready?"

Langfeld ordered another round of drinks and a dessert. "How much initial work and research have you done so far?"

"Well, I've always been interested in real estate but just in the last several months specifically have I considered how we might do it."

"Why don't you see if you can have a working draft done in three weeks. The last time I spoke with Javier, he had mentioned possibly stopping in on his way to … well, I can't remember where, but you get the gist. Three weeks' work for you?"

"I hope so," I countered with a little bounce in my voice.

Over the next several weeks, I lived on our porch and at my office over the garage. I pored over the real estate industry, reading various books on the different real estate: commercial, residential, land, HUD housing, time-shares. If it weren't for bourbon and the wonderful shelter of the porch, I might have given it all up. Ashley sometimes would curl up beside me on the loveseat with her head on my shoulder. Brittany joined sometimes in her favorite hanging chair on the porch. I realized three weeks was too short a time to make any type of quality presentation to Javier and Terry. Langfeld said extending the time wasn't a problem because Javier had to cancel a previous date, anyway. He asked if two more weeks would be good and invited us down to Houston for a dinner.

In Houston, during what had to be the hottest and most humid day in my life, we taxied from the George Bush Intercontinental Airport to the restaurant in a high-rise hotel Javier had selected. I was terribly uncomfortable because of the sweat and my nerves. Javier met us with open arms and showed us to a private room at the rear of the restaurant. It was dimly lit with sounds of strings and piano in the background. There were large indoor plants in equally large floor vases, embracing each of the private room's open entries. Our room had a view of the city and part of the Gulf. The white linen tablecloth was heavy and glinted a polished look and feel. A bottle of champagne was in a chilled container and, according to the waiter, was "a perfect selection by Mr. Muchido."

The dinner table was set for three. Apparently, Javier had requested it to be large enough for a work dinner/meeting. We ate and drank and talked about everything but work until Sopaipillas, Tres Leches Cake, Caramel Flan, and Mexican Wedding Cake were served. Javier then whispered to me, "Well, let's have it, Woody. Terry has told me the project he and I had asked you to do is ready for a review."

Over the next hour, nervous at first, I began laying out the basics of our real estate business. "Guys, I feel there might be too much scrutiny on us if we invested into large commercial real estate, you know, like large high-rise offices and established entities which would entail accountants doing deep dives in our books."

"Yeah, we don't need that shit," Javier noted, and a nod from Langfeld made it a unanimous vote.

I took a good swig of my bourbon with a splash of water and sighed relief. I gained more confidence each time I presented a part of the plan for large real estate companies, but nixed it for the same reasons as before.

In summary, I said we should strongly look into smaller properties, such as resort homes and apartments near vacation destinations. I explained that creating a few real estate companies would allow for the purchase of and management of the properties. I argued we had the capital resources to service the debts. Javier interrupted, "I don't like where this is going, Woody. I don't want my name on any loan documents to purchase anything."

"Okay, fair enough. My error in noting how we would make the investment. I propose we create real estate companies with loans from our own businesses. We can decide whether we want Baxter's involved on paper or not. But the other businesses could be the pipeline of money for the loans. The real estate companies would be in our names or in a corporate name using funds borrowed from the already established businesses we funnel the money into now." I let that soak in and was preparing for a fight, but Terry said, "Javier, this would resolve the issue that you said the others had questioned you about recently."

Javier, still looking at me, answered Langfeld with a smile, "Yes, I believe it would. How long before you can get this off the ground and running?"

I truly didn't know and didn't want to suggest I had a time in mind, so I said, "I don't have a good understanding of how long because I need to determine how many real estate companies we would want to create."

Javier suggested I set up the real estate companies in a few fictitious names in which he would provide me and fund them through the other company loans I had mentioned. Time wasn't really the concern, but security and safety from the government were, so he strongly advised me to do it right.

In the following weeks, as I implemented my plan, I called a football audible and hired a national real estate company to locate and purchase real estate properties based on specific guidelines. I established one corporation in Delaware, funded from investments from almost all of our other businesses. I included land and required no less than two acres within municipalities that already provided sewer and other utilities, at a cost only three percent higher than the last similar sale within two years. We would only pay higher costs if a sufficient amount of documentation was provided, demonstrating an extremely high speeding up real estate market.

The company I hired wanted us to consider existing brick and mortar properties. I let them know subtly that we didn't want others looking over our shoulders. I was assured that they would have their own CPA firm do the audit. I realized they had gone down this road before. I talked to Terry, who said for me to try it and see how it plays out. We would assess whether it was worthwhile; we could expand later. The company stated that they would require of the seller two years' worth of books and records along with copies of the corresponding tax returns. Those instructions were strictly to be adhered to. They would use their own CPA firm to conduct a market value assessment of the proposed property, and if it showed an increasing value, then we could be notified of a workable purchase. We had picked up several tracts of land and several existing businesses in which we allowed to operate, with no infusion of capital from our activities.

The roll-out of the entire project took several months, but seemed to go well. It turned out to be a calm before the storm.

EIGHT

Over recent years, I had felt and sensed the unraveling of the internal core in our organization. Javier was becoming paranoid, which wasn't at all like him. He had always been the rigid and stable one. But now he seemed out of sorts, looking over the proverbial shoulder. No reason he should that I knew of, but I guess that's the definition of paranoia. He was scaring us with the prospect of violence only because his reputation was that of a violent man, even though none of us had ever seen violent outbursts. He introduced us to dreams of worries and crazy shit all the time. Irrational crap. No one ever really knew what to say around him. Most were walking on eggshells, including me. It just wasn't like him to act the way he was.

But the business kept chugging along. Nothing out of the ordinary happened. No one had been arrested at any spot in the chain. Several drivers, including me and Miguel, had been pulled over by the police in recent years. Only once had Miguel and I been asked to open up the trailer by police, which we did without fear. The older officer peered in with his Maglite and recoiled when the smells overtook him. He paused again while looking at the shipping documents we had provided and gasped, "Are you out of your fucking minds! That's putrid. Go, get out of here." We watched him leave with Cheshire smiles on our faces. The smell avoided a call for a K9 dog.

My days were routine, the same thing virtually every day, going to the online bank accounts to check all the activities, and making sure all of our legal and fictitious company accounts had no unknown transactions. I checked emails for any news from the real estate company. I contacted the various managers either by email or by phone to discuss their business activities. My bank accounts continued to swell and caused me to pinch myself every day.

I hadn't been out to any of the managers for a while, so I had driven to Charlotte to check with one of our businesses and speak to the manager, who was wondering how they were still in business. I convinced the manager that the "mother ship" will put good money after bad money, hoping things would turn around. I explained the losses counteracted gains which were good for taxes. He bought the story.

I left the following day. The drive is beautiful through the Mountains in western Virginia and in southern West Virginia. There I was, driving through central Kentucky on my way back home, thinking about Javier, Franklin, and Terry.

It was a beautiful day late in the afternoon. The trees were still radiantly colored, and the winds were coming in from the north with a bit of a chill. Although I was traveling west, the sun hadn't yet fallen far enough to make it difficult to see. I was asking myself what types of trees I was seeing, maples, oaks, something I think they call the coffee tree. Gorgeous! The sun just started to dip low enough to envelop the trees within a cast of peach rays and the smallest hint of coral.

Traffic was fairly heavy on I-64 towards Louisville and just past Frankfort. I was scanning the countryside around me and wondering how in the hell the woman in the car ahead of me possibly made it this far without causing an accident. Good grief. You have two-foot pedals. Step on one of them, so I know what you're doing! Yet she slowed even more and was unaware there was a world around her. I'm not a hate-on-the-woman driver's kind of guy, but lord, she was awful.

I was still daydreaming when I saw out of the corner of my right eye a silver BMW. It came up alongside me in the 'slow' lane, slowed, and dropped back. It appeared to be a 325i. I rarely pay much attention to other vehicles other than for safety concerns. The way the car was being driven seemed unsafe, or maybe it held someone I knew, so I slowed down to get a look. The other car did too, long enough for me to see it had a front license plate, but I couldn't clearly see the letters or numbers in my side mirror. Which states require front license plates? I knew Connecticut did, and maybe Colorado. This plate looked more like California because the lettering looked like cursive writing, which I knew California and Louisiana used, but the coloring looked more like California. There were two men, maybe in their thirties. They continued in the right-hand lane, slower than me. I sped up and slowed down, not dramatically, but they kept their distance. We drove like that for maybe two or three miles until they took exit 48.

Maybe I'm the one being paranoid and not Javier. I kept my eye on the rear-view mirror and didn't see the car again. It was a little unnerving. Probably guys on a long vacation and just screwing around.

I went back to thinking about Javier, Franklin, and Langfeld. I had only seen Javier and Franklin in the same room, or, to be precise, the same resort twice. We had never been together at the same time. Odd. They didn't appear to have had a care in the world then. But now that Javier was acting the way he was, I wondered how Franklin was viewing their relationship and the organization. He had earned the management of a large legitimate company and had risked it throughout. I wondered if he had a safety net.

I knew through the grapevine that Franklin apparently wanted out of the drug business. Even though he and the dominant ownership group had set it up to walk away financially, I don't think they had ever discussed how to do it one by one. So, maybe Franklin wanted out, but Javier didn't want to quit yet. Terry would have gone years ago if he had had the chance. I didn't give a shit. I'd made more money in five years than I had ever dreamt. Javier's actions were troubling because I always thought of him as the backbone. Franklin may have had other connections which were valuable, but Javier seemed to me to be the rudder steering our ship. Adding up the facts and my speculations, as I knew them, this whole thing could implode soon.

In Louisville, I merged onto a spaghetti of roads and almost missed the interstate 65 North off-ramp but managed the exit, although there's a dude that still wants a piece of me for cutting him off. An hour and a half later, I pulled into our driveway, and Ashley met me on the front porch. We kissed a longer than normal welcome home kiss. She said Brittany was staying with a girlfriend. We sat on the porch, and we opened a few beers. I told Ashley of my concerns.

I said, "Honey, I think this thing is going to erupt, and soon. I'm aware it's a gut feeling, but the way Javier has been acting … damn." Ashley looked at me with a barren, empty sort of look, and her eyes spoke of fear.

She whispered, "What's going on now that you think is different?"

"Well, Javier is acting extremely paranoid. Terry has been standoffish and short with answers. I also saw that he had been looking into some of the banking records. Not that I think he would have connected any dots, but if he were checking on me, it would have been the first time. Secondly, Javier has visited Terry up here and at other locations twice this year, too. Very different from in the past."

"Maybe he's just showing up to make sure everyone knows who makes the decisions?"

"Yeah, maybe, but the visits aren't the same. He normally took everyone out for dinner. You know, remember when he took us out to Bohanan's in San Antonio. I bet he spent $1,500 that night."

I could see Ashley recalling the evening. I remembered a wonderful night, her sexy smile. We had had a few extra drinks, and we almost got caught in the hotel whirlpool in an inappropriate public state of undress. "Something else, honey. Javier has visited with me a few times in the last few months, and I don't think Terry knew we had met."

"Really? Why would he do that?"

I said, "Yeah, I asked if the three of us were going to go out because if we were, I wanted to let you know. But he said no reason to catch up with Terry."

"Did he tell you that each time?"

"Well, he said that the first visit, and I didn't bring it up thereafter. I could tell from talking to Terry later he knew nothing of the visits."

"What did you say to Terry, which makes you think he was left in the dark?"

"Well, I let it slip that 'we' had eaten at The Capital Grille. He asked who *we* were."

"How did you answer that?"

"I couldn't say it was you because he may have had asked you some time, and if I had forgotten to tell you about my faux pas, my goose would be cooked. So I told him I met an old friend of mine, took him out to eat, talked old times. I never thought he really believed it. One day he asked me again my friend's name, and I froze. I couldn't remember if I had even given him a name. I said it was Steve and asked him why? He didn't answer. He just stared at me for what felt like forever, and then he just walked away."

Ashley asked, "Where did you and Javier meet?"

As I was about to answer, I realized Javier had called me directly and picked the location where we hadn't met before. "You know something, honey? Now that we're talking, Javier never came to the plant."

"What did Javier say to you or ask you?"

"Javier asked if the operation was still as profitable as it had always been. He asked me to send him a secured email regarding all the assets he had, which isn't unusual. Javier had been getting more and more involved, but he normally called me about that stuff. He asked if you and I ever have dinner with Terry because he was a little concerned about Terry's state of mind."

"This is the same guy you're telling me is paranoid? Sounds like he was worried about Terry's mental health."

"Yeah, that is weird coming from him," I said, visualizing the conversation. "Maybe they're both a little on edge for something I know nothing about. Maybe someone was pulled over, and Javier was worried he or she would talk. That's always been our biggest concern."

"But you've told me a hundred times that the drivers had begun to get stopped for inspections but had never sold out. Maybe Javier is more worried about Langfeld talking," Ashley said.

"It just takes one," I answered.

Silence. It can be the loudest sound ever. It reminded me of late nights when there aren't any outside noises like traffic or televisions or radios. And the quieter it is, the less you need to strain to hear something. We just looked at each other and pictured the future. We had decided long ago that when we were free and clear of this, we would marry. But now, without saying it, we both knew marriage may be something we should think about more seriously for legal reasons—marriage spousal privilege.

"Ok, if this whole thing is about to blow up, did you set up the safety net you told me about some time ago?" Ashley asked.

"Yeah, I told you about it, didn't I?"

Ashely said, "Well, roughly. No need for me to have asked about any details before, but now maybe I should know."

"You know, I have always felt I wasn't being paid fairly in relation to my exposure and my relevance."

Ashely said, "I recall one night you talked about that, so what exactly did you do?"

I told her I had continued using my real name for the payroll with Baxter's, but I used Paul William Anderson for the safety net. The bank accounts and the condominiums are all in the name of Anderson. The land management company is in Anderson. I made automatic monthly payments to its business account from each of the legit businesses we used to cover the dirty money based on a consulting contract. The contract identified my company, 'PAW Real Estate Consultants, LLC' would provide consulting services needed to locate new properties for purchase or sales and to provide management services where needed. I purposefully used the initials in the order I had because I had noticed that a baby blanket centered the surname initial. I thought it looked professional and sophisticated. The contract also identified the fees for such services were to be made on a monthly retainer with no termination date.

Ashely asked if anything exposed her or Brittany. "No, honey. It's all separate from everyone except my alias."

I continued my description of what would be our long-term nest egg. "I set up each of the company's bank accounts for auto withdrawals for deposits to several PAW accounts and using several banks. Each company's retainer fee was distinctly different from the others, so no obvious pattern would emerge. The service fee was fairly nominal. None of the withdrawals/deposits were greater than $1,500. I could only use the car washes, and the cinemas, and one liquor store business. But that many businesses paying out $850 to $1,450 each month added up quickly. The first year garnered more than $200,000 in the various accounts; the next year, it exceeded over $225,000, and this last year it went over $240,000!"

Ashely gulped and squeezed my arm. "Are you kidding, Woody? My God, they're going to find out! That's too much money not to be missed."

I said, "No, I doubt it. It's really very well hidden and layered. Also, they're all making a ton of money, so no one is hurting, and no one seems to be concerned. They're more concerned about someone talking to the Feds."

"I hope you're right. Brittany and I would like to think you'll be around safe and happy with us."

"Well, just to be sure, I had also begun to move money from personal accounts to PAW during the last several years by wiring the money to a bank account in Belize, then back to PAW. It's now spotless money."

Over time, I had moved more than $600,000 to PAW through the retainer fee scheme. So, including monies I transferred to PAW from my personal accounts, PAW now had more than $1 million in cash in four bank accounts.

I had entered into mortgages to purchase, in my alias, several medium-sized apartments and/or small homes in locations not normally thought of as places drug dealers would live: Biloxi, Topsail Beach, North Carolina, Lincoln, Maine, and Escanaba, MI. Fairly adequate down payments were made, leaving medium mortgages which were paid on auto-withdrawal. Ashley knew about them and helped decorate a couple. Different bank accounts were also opened in the local towns' community banks in order to establish plausible stable roots where I purchased the properties. It was also a better way to rent the properties through local management companies.

"Honey, if you're good with all you've set up, I'm okay with it. I still am concerned that the missing money will be noticed. After all, you just told me how Javier and Terry have been acting."

I assured her everything was fine, leaned over, gave her a kiss, and said I'd be up in a minute. She went to bed, and I sat out on our porch a little longer. It liked the sound of that—our porch. I looked out through the yard. I had spent some of my downtime planting bushes, plants, and a few trees. I enjoyed working outside; it helped me decompress from all the crap. I enjoyed mowing the yard and mulching the flower gardens. The grass was slightly wet from afternoon rains. It glinted like fractured glass. I heard a frog croaking and a cricket chirping.

Brittany had graduated high school and was attending the University of Kentucky. Miguel's daughter was doing well. Langfeld had got him out of the trucking part and transferred him within Baxter's. Miguel was happy to be away from our operation.

I wondered what was next. I wished I had known the answer - the killings, the anguish suffered, losing an indescribable love, a punch to the gut with no mercy.

NINE

A cloud of anxiety continued to swirl around me. Was I becoming paranoid? I was sure my siphoning off hundreds of thousands of the business funds was wisely hidden. Nevertheless, I found it hard to be comfortable.

Terry Langfeld and Javier Muchido continued to worry about everything lately. I wasn't sure of their worries because they hadn't shared all with me. In a nutshell, that was the issue I struggled with daily. The two had given me a lot of responsibility regarding the moving of the drug proceeds, yet wouldn't let me in on any feasible fresh advances or other parts of the organization.

The rapport we had was waning. No longer were there open and easy talks and discussions. Short answers when answers were offered at all. Email communications were decreasing; using burner phones increased. It all created, in my eyes, two worries: one, had we been infiltrated; two, had the two stumbled onto my scheme? They owned wary eyes and provided short, quick glances. When one received a call during one of our meetings, he would speak softly or leave the room altogether. Maybe I'm the paranoid one.

The personnel closest to us, within the legitimate companies, were also on edge. Most knew nothing about the other business, but knew something had changed. Stan said, "The shit in the air is so heavy that if it wasn't for straws, we all would have suffocated long ago."

So, the day that Javier called and said he'd like to have a meeting with Terry and me. I jumped at the chance to smooth out actual or perceived issues. I also desired to detect if one, or both, was aware of my embezzling. I sent them both my reply to have a dinner meeting at my home. Ashley and I would host. They agreed, so Ashley and I began putting the dinner plans together.

Ashley knew how important this dinner meeting would be, so she jumped in with both feet. She hired a local home cleaning service to make the house sparkle. The servicemen pressure washed the outside, including the back deck and the front porch. I hired a landscaping company who sodded an area of the yard that I hadn't had time to repair and seed. Ashley asked them to plant several more annuals and a couple smaller bushes in the front yard near our red oak. The company mulched all the flower gardens and pulled weeds anywhere they saw them.

We discussed the prospect that if they called me out on my scheme, I would fess up and argue I was an equally important cog in the success of our business. We also had our luggage packed ready for a quick departure to the condo in Escanaba, the last area of the country they would think to look for us.

We set the dinner for Friday. Dinner would consist of a roast with all the trimmings; potatoes and carrots in a crockpot with some beer for tenderizing. It was a truly enjoyable and apprehensive time. I'm not a cook or a kitchen kind of guy, but helping Ashley was pleasurable. I especially liked the fact that every once in a while, we walked by each other and rubbed up against the other; we had to take a quick break for some kitchen sex. Who knew making a roast could be so erotic?

I couldn't take Friday off and had to leave for a few meetings, but went with a smile on my face. On the way to work, I thought I recognized that silver BMW again, but I only caught the rear end of the passenger side. The vehicle was outside of my subdivision, parked along the on-ramp to I-65. I didn't get a significant look. I hadn't been looking for it, so what I saw was at a glance. The only reason I had seen it at all was that it was extremely clean and glistened in the morning light. I thought the plate was the same type as I had seen on the drive through Kentucky. I took a quick second glance, but I was already on the highway by then. Paranoid? No, I'm losing it because of the stress of the upcoming dinner meeting.

At work, I relaxed a bit. I had to complete a review of one of our bigger business investments, which was only afloat because of our extra influx of capital. A cinema in a poorer section of St. Louis. We had purchased the movie complex for pennies on the dollar, and for good reason, it had lost money for years. When we bought it, we struggled to lure more patrons. We papered the community with coupons such as two for one tickets and cutting the price of some of the concessions. We never created any traction. There was too much crime in the area to attract a consistent clientele for evening shows. It was just a big hole where we dumped a lot of our money. I reviewed the finances and realized that we needed to sell the business or give it to the community for a tax write-off. If the IRS ever audited us, we wouldn't have had good arguments about why, or more importantly how, we provided extra capital that we had noted as business income. I called Jeff, the manager, but he was out. I left a message asking for feedback regarding the two scenarios.

Dinner was scheduled for six o'clock. It was a quarter to six. I was getting ready to walk out of the office but heard my telephone ring. It was Jeff's return call. Damn! I had to take this call at my desk. I explained his cinema was financially a loser. Explaining all our attempts to revive the business and wanted him to know that if it folded, we would give him a six-month severance package. I said we would continue paying for his health insurance for the six-months. He understood and said he hadn't a better plan and commented he always wondered why we hadn't folded sooner. Jeff thanked me for my assurance in helping him.

He asked if there was something we could do for his employees. I said I would check the home office. We talked about his family. He was married with one child and another on the way.

"Jeff, the entire company has many profitable businesses and a few, sadly, like your location. On the financial side, I'm okay with it because the businesses losing money reduced the taxable income for the whole. So please don't worry about the things you don't have control over. Like I said, I'll take care of you."

He seemed okay with the explanation, and we ended the talk. I cleaned up my desk thinking of Jeff, his wife expecting their second child, and his job ending sooner than later. Maybe a six-month severance wasn't long enough? I tried to remember how many months along her pregnancy was. I wrote myself a note to check on Monday. By then, it was ten after six. I rushed out of the office building and to my truck.

As I was leaving the interstate at my exit, I saw the silver BMW crossing the overpass from the direction of my subdivision. This time, I saw the plates, and they were from California.

I started to feel a twinge in my chest. I asked myself, how could this be a coincidence? The same type of car—a type of car I hadn't seen around at all. Two guys. Odd times of the day. Clearly not traveling to a job. What the hell?

Two miles off my exit, I turned right into my subdivision on Simpsonville Road. Mrs. Cordell was on her porch as always. She was sporting a mid-calf-length dress that had a floral weave and her ever-present black loafers. She waved. I waved, forced a smile, getting more and more uneasy and worried. The car. My gut. Two guys. California plates. Two states.

I followed Simpsonville around the loop and turned left onto Quarry Road. Mr. and Mrs. Peters were taking out the garbage cans for pick up the next morning. Both of them always took out the garbage. The driveway had old oak trees along the west side, providing evening shade on their front porch. Mr. Peters saw me; I waved at him again with a bit of a forced smile and followed Quarry Road down the dip past their house.

Quarry Road crests and travels on towards an old quarry load-out, where it rises and circles the rim. As you drive down into the dip, you can see our house off to the right, about fifty or sixty yards. There isn't another house until you continue around the corner to the right, about one hundred yards past our driveway.

I was already tensed up with that feeling you get when something is out of sync, but you can't put a finger on it. I kept rubbing the top of my left leg; I was squeezing the steering wheel hard, and glancing from side mirror to rear mirror to the other side mirror to the front of the car, all in one quick roll of the eyes.

My focus was intense, razor-sharp. I could see colors brighter than ever, and the world around me slowed down. I couldn't hear much around me, but I could hear my heartbeat. The feeling differed from the worry which one has attending a meeting in which you know you're going to be fired. This was something else. I had never sensed so many things all at once. It was like having an out-of-body experience.

I found myself in the driveway. Our front door was open. There were no birds on or near the feeder or in the multi-colored birdbath. It was eerily silent. I saw something on the front porch deck. Langfeld's car was in the driveway, one door ajar. No one in the driver's seat. I had parked and slid out of my car. But I don't recall those physical movements. I began walking along our sidewalk with the newly planted flowers along the entire perimeter. I found the porch. The something on the porch was a ... body!

I screamed. It was my beautiful Ashley. I screamed again, or at least I think I did. My breath ... I gasped to breathe in. She was wearing her white dress with string straps. But the dress was no longer just white; it was stained an ugly crimson and deep red hue. I saw the gunshot results. She was faced down. Blood on the porch beneath her. I dropped to my knees. I turned her over. Oh, Jesus! I clumsily searched for a heartbeat. Nothing. I held her; I hugged her; I kissed her and kept gasping. No! No! No! I was howling. I was looking everywhere, then burying my face in her chest, sobbing. I was getting sick and dizzy. I don't know how long I sat on the porch with her.

I began to breathe some, saw bright lights, streaks of lightning flying at me from every direction, much like how Star Wars aircraft are depicted transferring to light speed. Reds, yellows, orange, and blues in a kaleidoscope of flowing vivid colors ran in and out of my eyes.

I saw myself with Ashley at the Red Caboose diner the first day we met. Her wonderfully fetching smile. Her unique giggle, and how she started some sentences with ooh. Shivers ran down my body and I envisioned the two of us having that picnic under the oak trees in the park and us laughing because I had put the blanket over an anthill. Talking out on the porch on her double-swing about what our future could be. Her body was in my arms when we had made love. Her small hands in mine as we walked into the mall shopping for clothes. I could hear her call out to me from the back door, saying dinner was ready. I smelled perfume but knew it was just her. Her voice trembled in love with me after I returned from a trip. She and Brittany sitting on the sofa, watching TV, eating popcorn, and laughing at some show. I saw her crying when we dropped Brittany off at college. She cried even harder when she realized I had already paid for the first year. I remembered playing Scrabble and teasing her when I caught her trying to use a word that wasn't a word at all, her impish smile at me pleading. It really was a word. I could feel her holding me back from punching that guy at the Downtown Tavern, the jerk who had come on to her. I could hear our telephone calls when I was on the road, her crying that time when my truck broke down and I would have to stay a few more days out of town. I saw our life together the way we had hoped.

After some unknown amount of time, I finally got hold of myself. The scene before me finally registered. A hideous crime had occurred here. Who? Where is he or where are they now? I was still trembling. My heart was still beating so violently that I thought it would jump out of my chest. My fingers were shaking, my entire body prickly, like the arm you slept on all night, and awoke to numbness and tingling as the blood began to course through the veins.

I finally took cover behind the front door jamb and exterior wall. I had to contain my misery. I gathered my wits enough to hear noises or voices. Nothing. Still. Still as a crocodile floating in a swamp. I figured no one was inside, at least alive. I risked calling out for a response. No response. I looked back at the yard, the garage, the road. Our closest neighbor was around the corner a little, not a straight view from our front door. No one heard me screaming, or at least no one was coming to find the source of the scream.

I peeked into our house, down our hallway towards the dining room. I got as low as I could crouch my six-foot three-inch frame and slowly entered the house. I had no weapon other than my rage. Did I have time to go upstairs and retrieve my 9mm? I realized there weren't any other cars in the driveway except Langfeld's. So, probably no one else in the house. Probably.

I continued slowly down the hall, hugging it like I had seen in movies and thinking about what I would do if confronted. Oh shit! I heard something. Calm down Woody, it's just the radio, the song "Get Back" by the Beatles. I considered it for a moment, but continued and made it through the foyer and hallway. I saw no blood at all. The fuckers had shot my baby in the back as she ran. I had to stop. I was seething. I was swerving, dizzy again. Inside my brain, I was hysterical and probably incoherent. Is this what cops feel when confronting a gunman? Could my blood pressure rise any higher? Don't know how long I stood there. I eventually moved far enough down the hall to see into the kitchen and dining area.

Looking left into the kitchen, I saw Terry. He was laid over our kitchen island. Blood streamed down the side of the cherry cabinets below the island, making a pool on the hardwood floor. To the right was the dining area and Javier. He was sitting in one of our captain's chairs. His head was tilted forward and to the side. His arms were at his side on the outside of the arms of the chair. A knife stuck out of his chest.

I could smell the roast. Odd, it was the first and only thing I had smelled since turning into our driveway. I saw that the sliding glass door at the back of the house was broken and open. The bastards came in through the back. That's why Ashley had the chance to run.

It took me a few moments to start putting together the horrible picture of events. Langfeld or Javier must have told someone that we were all having dinner together. We. We, … I was supposed to have been here too, and dead too!

Think. Think, I kept telling myself. What do I do? I continued visualizing what I had just walked through. Why was Terry's passenger door open? I went out the back. I didn't want to walk past Ashley's body. I couldn't. I looked out over the backyard and beyond. I don't know that I had ever noticed, but you couldn't see any other homes very well from here. I walked slowly, or as slowly as I thought would exhibit a regular gait to anyone who might be watching.

I became more coherent. I couldn't call the police. What would I tell them? Hey, my girlfriend and my drug trafficking partners were murdered. Oh, no, officer, it wasn't me. I looked down. Blood all over me. Explainable, but I didn't want to answer those questions. That would open up way too many issues and not easily explained.

There were some papers thrown, or dropped, around the front seat of Terry's car. Business records? I couldn't tell what was missing. Was there something missing? Were they looking for something before going into the house afterward?

I heard something for the first time other than my heartbeat. Muffled. Subdued. Muted. A voice maybe. Then I saw movement out of the right side of my eye. A woman in a blue dress, its blue top patterned. She was holding one of my garden rakes, not the plastic wide-fan rake, but a metal tined rake off of my garage wall. I froze, but then … I recognized her.

"Michelle, is that you?" I whispered.

"Yes, sir, it's me, Woody."

"Are you hurt?" I asked as I held out my arms to her. She stepped into my hug and we held each other. We were silent for some time. Only our breathing and heartbeats were noticeable.

"No," she said, "I'm pissed, I'm fuming. Jesus, look at me, I'm trembling. Are they, they ... gone?"

"Yes. What the hell happened here?" I asked her, "What are you doing here in the garage?" She could not speak without gasping and wincing she carefully recounted what she knew.

"Terry asked me to go to your dinner party with him because he knew Ashley would be the only girl. He thought my being here would be good for her," she said, struggling to contain her pain and anger.

"How did you get away?" I softly inquired, still holding her.

"I didn't get away. Ashley had asked me to get some beer from the garage refrigerator. I walked out the front door and saw a silver car in the drive. I wondered who else had been invited. I had seen no one else. I continued to the garage. About the time I opened the fridge, I heard several pops; I think there were four shots. I knew in an instant they were handguns with silencers. I took cover, tried to listen, to see who was here."

I stared at her, both of us hurting and immobile. Michelle was gaining strength and let go of me and leaned against a garage wall. "Something you should know, Woody. I've been much more than his right hand for years, and, yes, I know exactly what has been happening; I know exactly what your role has been. Terry and I have been dating for several years. I know he's older, but we're in love."

I was flabbergasted and stunned. "You knew about the ... other stuff? I had no idea you and he were ... lovers."

She continued, "I'd been doing the books for Terry for years, but it had become too difficult for me. I don't have a financial bone in my body, so Terry helped me and always followed up on my work. That's why when he told me his idea to move you into that role, I was all for it."

"Geez, Michelle. I didn't know ... any of this."

I could see the more she talked about Terry, the more upset she became.

"Those motherfuckers," she said. "If I had had a gun, I would have at least taken out one."

I did a double-take hearing her speak in a way I had never heard her before or ever imagined she was capable of.

"Did you see the license plates?" I interrupted.

She stared at the ground. "What ...? License plates? I can't remember. I was at the front of the car, anyway."

"Some states require front plates too. Think. Think hard."

"I think there were plates on the front, but I'm not sure. Why is it important?"

"I've seen that car twice during the last several months. First in Kentucky, and then several times recently around here. Have you ever seen it before?"

"I don't think so. Did you call the cops?"

"No ... we can't. You must understand, now that you've told me about your involvement."

She was aching, like me, but she seemed more in control than I felt I was. Yet, I realized her hurt was deep. It was cutting, wounding her stomach. My stomach, too, was in knots, and I still felt nauseated.

I didn't know what to do or say, so I just hugged her ... tight.

Through tears she said, "I know what your ... our predicament is. I have the same issue. I'm on a bunch of joint bank accounts, and one of his cars is registered in my name."

"We need to get out of here as soon as possible. Do you have family here or anywhere nearby for you to go to?"

"No family anywhere, and by the way, that's why I encouraged Terry to hire you when he did—no known family."

"You were involved in my hiring?"

She continued while I was picking my jaw up from the floor, "I was adopted; my parents have both passed. They were older when they adopted me. Mom couldn't have children, so they thought an adoption would fill a void. I hope it did. They were wonderful parents, but they died within a year of each other about five years ago. No other family at all. They were both only children too."

"Children. Brittany! Oh shit! I've got to tell her. Oh, Lord, Michelle, I've got to tell her somehow. I have to go back to the house for some things. I've got to change out of this shirt. Stay here, I'll be only a minute."

I ran to the back to avoid the front porch. I couldn't bear to step past Ashley. I ran upstairs, two steps at a time, to our bedroom. The king-size bed had a blue and white decorated quilt as a cover. The drapes matched. I almost lost it again. I gathered my senses and opened the safe in our closet. Got out my wallet with all my other identification. Grabbed the Paul William Anderson passport. I checked the wallet for cash; I had about a thousand in it. I changed my shirt; stuffed the bloodstained shirt in a Kroger grocery bag, grabbed my already packed luggage, and ran downstairs. Habit took me out the front door and past Ashley. I mourned for a moment, but this time I developed a severe sensation of fury. I made it to the car and asked Michelle if she would drive. We had to figure out what she and I should do. As we approached neighbors, I leaned down below eye level. My car was fairly well known in the area, but maybe not discernable if an unknown female was driving it.

Michelle didn't move, not one step. She gaped at me with unblinking eyes. She was lost in thought. "I have no reason to stay here. I have the same obvious reasons as you to run. I want to kill those pricks who did this and those who ordered it. Let's go together until, or if, there is a need to split up." She turned to me and took my keys and walked to my car.

Her skin flushed red, her eyes widened. Her grip on the wheel was unbending, and her focus appeared to be unwavering. I said sternly, "Absolutely, Michelle. We will need each other for as long as it takes. I've got to stop and drop off something at Mrs. Daniels' before we hightail it out of here."

We drove over to Mrs. D's place. She wasn't home. Damn! What I had to tell her should be face-to-face. My note, hastily written, reflected what had occurred did not involve me and what she would be soon reading and hearing about. I left her a $10,000 check from an alias account, instructing her not to ask questions about the name on the check and not to deposit it for at least a week or two. At some point, I would contact her to explain. I underlined the fact I was supposed to have been home too and would have suffered the same fate had I been there. I wrote I was on the way to tell Brittany and provide instructions for her, too. I wrote and underlined it, please burn this note when finished signed. "W".

We drove to Michelle's house through the same beautiful countryside I had seen many times, but that was now blurred through wet eyes. We switched at Michelle's. I drove my car, and she drove her Honda Pilot. There was no reason to believe, at least initially, that the police would have known Michelle had been at the house. We drove to Baxter's, where I left my Highlander in a rear lot where we didn't have any security cameras.

She asked me to drive her car. The further we drove, the madder and madder she became. I heard her say under her breath, "I'm going to kill those motherfuckers."

TEN

Michelle and I drove straight to the University of Kentucky in Lexington. It's a wonderfully attractive place, but not that night, it wasn't. Michelle and I had listened to various radio stations on the way south, waiting for breaking news, but heard nothing. It was late when we arrived at her dormitory. I knocked on the resident manager's front door and asked for Brittany. The manager, a sweet young upper-class student, looked at me like I had 3-eyes. "It's Friday. No one is in except me because it's my turn to pull weekend duty," she said, rolling her eyes. "But let me check just in case. I don't know her. This is my first time at Freemont Hall."

She called Brittany's room, and of course, she wasn't in. She would be out with all her friends enjoying a wonderful evening, as everyone should be doing. I asked if I could leave a note. She said sure and showed me Brittany's mailbox. Again, I had to relay news that should have been delivered in-person. I left a note similar to the one I left with Mrs. D. I left a checkbook to my checking account which I had added her name. Brittany wasn't aware of the bank account or the amount of the balance. I wrote she would have to pay her tuition until further notice, adding, "I don't care how you use the money, but I hope you will stay in school and graduate. That's why you're on the account, anyway." I explained in my letter I would be talking to her soon. I noted I was going to find out who had done what had been done. I warned her not to tell the police I'd written because they would make her life hell. I apologized for telling her like this. I wrote ... burn the note.

Michelle and I took off East on I-64 for no other reason than just to go somewhere. The highway East from Lexington is pretty desolate. We didn't talk too much about the events of the evening. We were both almost catatonic and emotionally exhausted, literally now just going through motions. I drove, changing lanes when needed. Slowing when required. Passing when obviously needed. None of which were conscientiously completed. We got as far as Huntington, West Virginia, before I started to fall asleep. We stopped for the night. Paranoid, we slept in the car in the parking lot of a Holiday Inn. We weren't sure if we should risk getting a room, so we stayed in the car. It was late Friday, and we hoped Michelle's absence would not be known until Monday.

I woke up with a determination I hadn't felt before. Somebody was going to pay. I caught myself squeezing and re-squeezing my fists until they became sore. During the drive towards Charleston, an hour east, Michelle awoke. We stopped and had breakfast at a Bob Evans. I ordered the mush, something not usually on their menu, but I knew most of the locations could make it, so I asked. Michelle ordered the French toast and a side of bacon. We both drank coffee. We began to decompress and could now discuss somewhat rationally what our next moves should be.

"Michelle, my fingerprints at the house are to be expected, but not yours."

"I don't think I touched anything that would be dusted for prints. Terry opened the door for me, and I never sat down. We weren't there but five minutes. After greetings, Ashley walked me down the hallway. She was showing off the downstairs. She then asked me if I wouldn't mind going to the garage for a couple beers."

She opened the front door. I never even opened the fridge because I heard the gunshots."

I told Michelle that Ashley and I had purchased a place in Topsail Beach, North Carolina. It was almost winter now, so the vacationers would be gone, and the permanent residents would be the only ones until early spring. Michelle was agreeable to traveling there because what was she going to do? She felt she had lost everything. I could have suggested we fly to the moon, and she probably would have agreed. During the drive, we discussed again what the authorities would find and what they could put together of the links to Ashley, Terry, and Javier. We agreed I was the number one suspect.

Getting to Topsail Beach from where we were in West Virginia wouldn't be easy. It would take nine hours with the usual stops. I had to destroy all of my real identification and begin only using my alias. Michelle did not have a second identity, which might have to be resolved.

Even though I had a packed suitcase, I still needed a few more items. Michelle grabbed a few things when we picked up her car, but she still needed more clothes. We found a downtown mall in Charleston. Michelle spoke to a nice middle-aged salesperson, "Yes ma'am. I need two full outfits. My luggage was delayed." She would purchase the clothes with cash. She needed several pairs of jeans and a variety of shorts; casual shirts and a blouse; two sets of workout clothes; two pairs of shoes, both sport and casual types. I bought a few shirts in the Macy's there too. We had to locate a general store for bathroom items. It was mid-morning by the time we finished shopping, so we ate lunch early. We found a downtown restaurant with a Wi-Fi connection. We again checked to see if there was any news back home. News outlets in Indiana showed us nothing had been discovered.

Outside of Bluefield, West Virginia, as you roll into Virginia, there is a tunnel through the mountain and an emergency pull over for trucks or others too wide for the tunnel. I stopped and found an empty soda can which had been changed a little to be used as an ashtray. I placed my proper driver's license, credit cards, and bank cards in the can. I lit it up and stayed long enough to make sure the cards were destroyed sufficiently. I kept the driver's license for my new name, Paul William Anderson, with a credit card and bank debit cards and about a thousand dollars in cash.

We had left Charleston early in the afternoon, and except for the stop at the tunnel, we didn't stop again until we were at the outskirts of Greensboro, where I-40 and I-85 intersect. We began to gain more and more composure. Over dinner, we began to determine why and who had designed the plan to murder us.

Near Greensboro, over a dinner of spaghetti and salads, Michelle told me she had been in the Army for six years; most of her service was in the Middle East. She had been in the 160th Special Operations Aviation Regiment, known as SOAR and more commonly known as the Night Stalkers. I had heard of the Night Stalkers because I had read a book reliving some of their actions in several wars. They were a highly trained unit. I was impressed that Michelle had been a member and a little jealous. I said, "I'm not surprised you were in the military. I assumed so because you converse with men as sir and women as ma'am. But certainly am shocked by the Nightstalker duty."

Her military training began at Fort Campbell, Kentucky, and continued elsewhere. She said it in a way that I knew not to ask. I'm pretty sure my jaw was still near the floor, and my eyes were probably fifty-cent pieces. "Yeah, Woody, she said, eyeing me. I was a bit of a badass. I saw the best and worst of mankind. I saw drugs were prevalent throughout the military because it was available. There were so many depressed soldiers far away from loved ones seeing things they weren't ready to see. I really don't think the regular Joe knows what we saw, smelled, and touched. It's an awful emotional and mental scarring that takes place. I saw corruption at every level; I witnessed investigations thwarted to accommodate generals and politicians in D.C. and in-country."

She continued, "Early on, during one of my first assignments, I complained about an issue and asked for justice, only to be looked on as a troublemaker and given shit details. Because I complained, I got the more dangerous operations. It was to expose me to wounding, or worse, just to get me out of the unit. Our military was far superior to others. Most of the major countries boasted elite fighting units as capable as ours, but they lacked the resources and the continuing training needed. Because of my 'assignments of punishment,' I gained a lot of battle experience. By the time my last tour was ending, some superiors actually wanted me to re-up because I had proven myself. They really pressured me. They received permission to offer me cash incentives to stay."

"But you didn't re-up," I remarked.

"No, I told them to stick it in their collective asses, and I walked out."

I felt somewhat obligated to give her a little of my life story. About halfway through it, I realized I never really had done anything productive, and I said so.

She looked out through the glass front of the restaurant and said, "You still have time to correct that, Woody."

The house Ashley and I had bought after my name change was a block off the ocean and near the public beach access on the south end of Topsail Beach Island. I had never visited there without sensing the sea and being drawn towards the sandy link. We bought there because it hadn't yet been overrun by tourists. Probably for several reasons: one, the beach was narrow with places full of seashells; and two, it was difficult to drive or fly there without going through Wilmington, North Carolina, which provided its own beaches. There wasn't anything remarkable about Topsail Beach that stood out except for the anonymity. We had rented it out most of the time through a local land management company.

We arrived at the land management company office. I picked up the keys and explained I wanted to take the house off the market for a while.

"Of course, Mr. Anderson," the middle-aged lady said as she handed me a few documents to sign legally removing the property as a rental. "Just sign at the X's."

"What? Oh yeah, thank you. You too." Anderson. I had to get used to that, too.

The house was white, vinyl-sided and had three bedrooms. Two were medium-sized, probably only ten feet by twelve feet each. The master bedroom held a king bed and measured probably fourteen feet by twelve feet. It had two exterior walls. The home faced the southeast enough so that the ocean was visible out our kitchen and dining-room window. All the bedrooms were on the west and southwestern sides of the house, so the rising sun allowed for longer sleep time.

Michelle never hesitated in choosing one of the smaller bedrooms close to the hall bathroom. The décor of the house offered typical ocean furnishings. Seashells in, or on, various frames, glass vases, and tables. The living room provided the usual sofa and love chairs, all in white, or off-white, colors, with flamingo and watermelon hues spiraling throughout. It was nothing extravagant, which was what we had wanted. The kitchen was tiled; the laundry room, which was off it was large enough for a side-by-side combination washer-dryer. There was a garage, not a carport like many others in the area used for parking.

As we entered, it was obvious the entire house smelled of a bit too much sunscreen protection. However, coconut is a scent I enjoy. Per the guest book, it was last rented a few weeks prior by a family from Boston. They noted their stay was everything they had hoped for, adding that the kids enjoyed the local turtle habitat.

I wanted so much to contact Brittany, but knew better. The police would soon be talking to her and I just couldn't let my emotional attachment to her place myself or her in jeopardy. I still didn't know why I was on a hit list. I hoped the letter I had left her at UK would be sufficient until I could talk to her.

Michelle agreed with me we would have to ditch her car. She said, "I think we could get rid of it down in Wilmington since it's a large city." Wilmington is a cool seacoast port town, and a hidden jewel.

"How do you propose we destroy it or ditch it so no one can trace it?" I thought out loud.

"I don't know. Let's just drive that way and figure it out," she said.

"I'm going to have to buy a new car too." I said.

"How are you going to do that, Woody, I mean Paul?"

"I can write a check as long as it isn't too large, which might draw some unwanted attention, I said matter-of-factly. Let's find a used car lot on the way. By the way, call me Woody unless we're in a group."

It was Sunday, so I figured we might have a good chance of some anonymous car buying. We drove south on Rt. 17. Along the way, the view was "southern country" with sandy shoulders, scrappy trees, roadside retailers, and then a slew of used car lots emerged. We walked into A to Z Used Car dealership and were almost run over by two overeager salesmen.

"Hey, guys, Michelle said. Don't run us over for a sale and you'll probably get one."

I saw the military side of her now and the guys stopped pretty damn quickly. She turned to me immediately and seamlessly changing her tone and inflection, "Honey, I think I would like a small SUV like we used to have, okay."

I was a little taken aback by the quick turnaround of her persona, but turned to the salesmen and said, "We're looking for something with less than 80,000 miles, maybe four to five years old but in good condition. You got anything like that?"

After convincing them we were going to keep Michelle's Honda, we agreed on a green Ford Explorer XLT that had some back-quarter panel damage, possibly a glancing collision, but damage all the same. Not bad, but I knew they had paid little for it. It had 64,000 miles, which I did like. They were asking for $20,500! Good grief!

"I don't think you have but fourteen in this, and with that damage—I don't know. Also, the tags on this are out of date for almost a year, so it's sat here some time. I'll write you a check for seventeen-grand, which is more than generous."

Our guys tried to wrangle some. "You know it has low mileage. How about $18,500?"

I had already begun to write a $17,000 check, but stopped and said, "$17,000 or no deal."

Defeated, but with a sale insight, they made some calls to verify the funds but eventually came out with the sale documents. It took some time to sign all the papers and once started to write the wrong name. I didn't put Michelle's name on the paperwork and they didn't seem to notice or, if they had, they ignored it. They made a sale. It was a good day.

We now needed to find a junkyard. We drove both cars down the road a little way and I turned into a McDonald's with Michelle parking on the other side of the lot. She went into the dining room and asked about any junkyards nearby. She stepped out and gave me the thumbs up and walked to my car with two coffees and the name Wilmington Auto Salvage, with directions. We discussed how we might convince a salvage yard operator that her car needed to be crushed. Especially since it was an out-of-state car with no obvious damage.

Michelle said, "Let's drive both cars back to the house and think this through. There isn't a hurry because I doubt anyone has yet figured out that I'm missing." I agreed, and on the way back I began thinking we could start removing parts to cause damage to her car while it would be parked in the garage.

When we arrived, I told her what I had been thinking, and she said she had thought the same. Over the next couple of days, we destroyed the interior in various ways: throwing trash, including beverages throughout the interior; breaking the console cover; and cracking the rearview mirror. We scratched the body, dented the roof, broke one taillight, and etched other small marks.

"We won't be able to convince any decent junkyard guy that the damage we just caused suffices to have the car crushed. The engine is going to have to be unusable. We're going to have to ruin it," I commented.

We ran the engine in the garage after draining the oil and dripped some on the garage floor below the oil pan. It took some time, but we finally seized up the engine. The garage stunk like hell, so we cracked the windows enough to let some sea salt air in to diffuse the burnt oil and engine stench.

A couple of days later, Michelle called a local wrecker service to tow the Honda to the closest junkyard, thinking it would be the location we were told at the McDonald's. However, it ended up the towing service and junkyard was the same place. The serviceman asked her to provide the title when the driver arrived. Michelle covered the phone and said to me, "Woody, he's asking me for the title. I don't have the title with me. Who drives around with their title?"

"Just tell him we, you, have it, and we'll figure it out when he gets here."

A driver showed up about two hours later and said his name was James, but we could call him JJ. If he had wanted the vehicle title, he didn't ask about it. We started, or tried to start, the engine, and it was clear it was shot. I recognized he viewed the car as worthless except for some parts, and no matter the owner, no one would be coming to claim it, anyway.

Just to be sure there wouldn't be questions later, Michelle cozied up to JJ. She put a hundred-dollar bill in his front shirt pocket. "This piece of shit was my old boyfriend's, JJ. I don't want it to survive, you know what I mean, honey?"

He smiled with all the teeth he had and said, "I'll crush it right quick for you ... sweetie."

"Yes, JJ, you do that. That's what I want," Michelle purred.

As he drove off, Michelle turned to me and said, "Terry bought me that car. I hate those motherfuckers so much. Let's get to work on figuring out what we're going to do to them besides cutting off their balls."

It was becoming abundantly clear that Michelle and I would be a team for the time-being. We hadn't discussed splitting up and going on our own. Without it being said, we needed each other.

We located a local grocery store, bought some ground beef and a few other items. I sliced a tomato and an onion. The table was set with cheese, mustard, and the normal condiments. We had bought no bacon, so we made a note to get it the next time we ventured out. Michelle made a quality tossed salad. We ate out on the porch with a few beers to down the meal. We could see enough of the ocean to begin the healing process, if that was even a possibility. Cool winds blowing in, causing us both to wear long sleeves. She curled up on the porch chaise lounge. I sat in the rocker. We spoke very little, trying to forget the last few days. We went to our separate bedrooms, and for the first time in a few days, both of us slept through the night.

ELEVEN

"Okay, who wanted us all dead," I muttered the next morning over a cup of coffee. "Who knew we would all be there at the same time?"

"I don't know if Terry had told anyone that I was going to be there."

"Do you think you know all the players in the entire organization?" I asked.

"I'm not sure about the entire organization, but there is, of course, Javier, Terry, Franklin, and Peter Tarant."

"Who's Tarant? I never heard of him."

"I think Tarant is the principal owner of Rotten Tomatoes. He has dual citizenship, Mexico and here. I'm not sure how he rose to become an owner in Rotten Tomatoes. I think the other principals might be from Mexico. I remember Javier speaking Spanish to Tarant and others using a speakerphone in Terry's office once. I don't speak Spanish, but by virtue of Javier's responses he clearly was not the boss in the conversation."

I added, "Ok, what about Schmidt? As far as we know, he's alive. Does he have the balls to orchestrate what happened Friday? And what the hell benefit to him would there be?"

"I'm not sure, Woody, but don't forget: Franklin has partners too, and I don't know how much they know."

I said, "Maybe there is a coup of Franklin underfoot. He's never appeared to me to be much of an imposing guy. It's possible, they thought, he might cave to them. This all feels like a professional job, or at least one by those that had done it before."

I thought of the papers in Langfeld's car. "Did you and Terry take any paperwork or documents of any kind to my house?"

Michelle thought for a moment. "Yeah, I think he brought some papers in a manila folder. I'm not sure what they were about. I didn't really read them. Why?"

I said, "When I arrived Friday, I walked past his car and the passenger side door was open. Later, before I found you, I saw papers with writing that made no sense to me. I left them because I heard you in the garage. I never went back to look. What type of writing did you see? Typed or handwritten?"

She thought, "They were handwritten in pencil and spelled out letters and numbers, not in cursive, I think, Woody, I mean, Paul. I don't think I'm going to remember Paul. Do you think the numbers were larger than the letters?"

"Don't worry about how you refer to me as while we're alone. What do you mean the numbers bigger than the letters?"

"Terry had a funny way of always writing his numbers a little larger than the letters. He told me once it had started when he was younger. He felt numbers equaled money and letters equaled dreams. Dreams didn't always come true, but numbers never changed."

"The numbers were to the right of the letters, and I think they were larger. And, now that I think of it, they may have represented amounts or quantities, you know, not telephone numbers or something like that."

"Were the written letters complete names or more like initials?"

One thing that helped me through school and living on the street was an uncanny ability to visualize events and items. I closed my eyes. "It was a column of two letters so, yes, probably initials of some person or place. To the right of the letters were numerals in two or three digits."

Michelle kept questioning me, "How many rows do you think there were?"

"Maybe eight on the page I saw, but I think there were also dates on the top of the pages, you know, written with a / mark."

"Well, that's like how Terry wrote his dates."

"I think I remember seeing HTF on the bottom of one page. Mean anything to you?"

"I don't think I know anyone with the initials HTF."

"What about a place?"

"No, I don't know any places generally referred to with 3 letters."

We both took a breath and a pause, searching for any clues to help us. I finally asked, "How long do you think you had been in the garage before I arrived?"

"Only ten minutes. I held my breath to keep from being heard. I knew what had happened. I heard the pops and then soft voices near the garage. It sounded like fractured English/Spanish. I thought they were looking for me, but they must have been going through the car. They left quickly thereafter. I wonder why they would have left the papers you saw?"

"I doubt they meant to. The pages probably fell out of the folder you said Terry had brought. Did you ever see the entire group of papers Terry had with him?"

"I don't think so. It couldn't have been very thick. I saw him holding it with his thumb and forefinger; I teased him that his other three fingers were raised like he was smoking a joint."

We had been busy the last few days and hadn't checked on news reports. I said, "Okay, the guys I saw in the BMW appeared to be Mexican, or at least Hispanic. We need to see if the police have been alerted to the crime scene and if they're publicly providing anything about the murders."

Michelle grabbed the computer and began searching the

Internet for news in Bartholomew County. A few keystrokes. Breaking news:

"On Sunday evening, three bodies were discovered at a Columbus residence owned by Ashley Thompson. Thompson was the lone female murdered. The two other murdered are males. Terry Langfeld, a fellow county resident, and an unknown Hispanic male. A Paul Woodford, a resident of Thompson's, is missing. The Sheriff's Office is still in the early stages of its investigation. If you have any information, please call the 800-number noted below."

Michelle kept searching and found an updated article:

"The Bartholomew County Sheriff's Office has requested assistance in locating Mr. Woodford. His car was not found at the house. Area residents stated they saw him driving into the subdivision around 6:15 on Friday night. If anyone has any knowledge of Mr. Woodford's whereabouts, please contact the Sheriff's Office."

A telephone number, in red, for anonymous tips was provided at the end of the article. I reached for the phone in the house but stopped short. "We can't use our phones. It's possible they would trace it—anonymous or not, I believe they use caller ID," I said as much to myself as to Michelle.

"We need to give the police some facts. We need to do it without letting on its us. We certainly need to let them know about the BMW."

Michelle said, "Okay, so tomorrow we'll buy one of those phones dealers use."

I said, "Burner phones. That's what they're known as on the streets and by the cops. You can buy them almost anywhere. Let's make sure when we buy one, we're not on any cameras."

The next day, we drove US 17, again to Wilmington, and found a Harris Teeter grocery store. We strolled in and to the front register area. There was an end-cap display of gift cards and charge cards. No phones. Michelle pointed toward the Customer Service desk. In the area's rear was a locked cage with the advertisement for 'TracFones' and prepaid phones. There was no way to stay out of the security recording area.

Michelle went out to the car and let her hair down. She wore a blue winter hat pulled down close to her eyes. She bought a prepaid phone with a two-hundred-minute plan. On the way back to the house, we stopped at a Publix grocery store where she bought a second phone with a similar plan.

On our drive back to Topsail Beach we knew again, without saying it, we were beginning an unknown journey to avenge Ashley and Terry's death. Little did we know how extensive a journey it would be.

TWELVE

Albert Harris had been a Bartholomew County Deputy Sheriff for nine years before earning his detective's badge four years ago. He had lived in the county most of his adult life. The Harrises had moved to Columbus, Indiana, when Albert was eleven. He was of average height but lifted weights and looked like a small Volkswagen. He had short and early graying hair, a disarming smile, and also was a bulldog when it came to solving crimes.

Harris had been assigned as the lead detective for the Friday night triple-homicide with a Sunday evening call from the Sheriff after the bodies had been discovered. He had been given the entire office's resources although he was not yet a senior detective. Those that were senior to him recognized the fact he was a good cop and a true bulldog. They also knew the investigation meant Harris wouldn't have a normal family life for months. He didn't seem to mind he had caught the triple murder. He combined his tenacity with a high level of the new investigative tools they were teaching at the FBI academy and at other nationwide law enforcement schools.

Harris asked detective Scott Manna, an eleven-year veteran,

with six of those years as a homicide detective, to join him as his first assistant as they worked the crime scene.

When they arrived at the scene, the scene wrapped them in the typical gloomy and sullen atmosphere as all murder scenes had. However, the atmosphere at the scene was worse because the crime had occurred several days before. It appeared to the detectives that the initial responding deputies had properly controlled the area and had kept the news crews at a distance. Al found the senior deputy at the scene. "What do you have, Corporal?"

"The bodies are one female and two males. They're on the porch and in the kitchen area. All white. GSWs to them all. The crime scene team has already started gathering evidence. Photographs have been taken, and I kept the camera guy here in case you wanted more. Here are my notes where I wrote the EMS and the LEOs on-site and the names of the deputies canvassing the neighborhood."

"That's a good job, Corporal. If everyone is out of the house, we'll begin our walk-through," Manna complimented.

Scott took out a recorder; Al and he began walking up to the house. Al spoke loudly enough for Scott's recorder to hear, "Okay, the woman on the porch was shot in the back. Two rounds close together in the upper portion of the back."

Al asked the closest EMS, "Hey, can we move the bodies yet?"

"Yes sir, I believe you can roll them on their side as long as they are rolled back to the original position. Detective? I'd mask up before you go in. They're pretty ripe."

Scott rolled Ashley onto a side and Al continued, "Looks like small caliber GSWs but probably high-velocity rounds noticing the damage at the exit. It looks as though she may also have been moved or that she lived long enough to roll a little and onto her right side. The front door is open, as is an interior door. Neither of the door windows are broken, nor is the door jamb damaged; no forced entry here. Let's make a note to check with the first responders to compare notes on whether the doors were open when they arrived."

Scott said, "Yeah, Al, I'll talk to their supervisor before we let them leave."

Continuing on, Al said, "The entryway and hallway do not bear any signs of a struggle or blood spatter. Pictures on the walls and on the side-tables appear to all be of family photos. The furniture was all upright and no signs of any physical activity. Doesn't appear to have been a robbery gone bad. It also supports my initial impression that the female victim was shot on the way out of the home."

They continued into the kitchen. Scott picked up the narration. "The dining room table was set for four people. Not three, Al. There is a male at the table sitting in a dining room chair facing the kitchen and the entry hallway. He suffered a GSW to the head. Specifically, the left side of his face. There doesn't appear to be any defensive type wounds or other obvious types of physical evidence suggesting he was in a defensive posture. He may have known the shooter or shooters. A large knife is in his chest. I would believe it will be suggested to have been post mortem and referred to as overkill."

Continuing on, "Another male is in the kitchen and is draped over the granite food island. One GSW to the right side of his head."

Al interjected, "There was a roast … in the crockpot. Probably good that it had stayed on cooking without causing a fire, otherwise the smell in here may have been exceedingly worse."

"Thank you, detective Harris, for that important piece of news," Scott said with a wry smile. He continued, "Let's check to see if the knife was a kitchen knife from this location. Several rounds have entered the kitchen and dining room walls. Just eyeing the angles, they could be the killing rounds. Let's make sure they're checked too."

Harris and Manna walked throughout the entire house, noting that nothing appeared to be missing. "Scott, the house hadn't been tossed. Everything was in its place. This wasn't a robbery gone bad. This was a stone-cold assassination."

Scott noted, "The glass door in the rear was shattered and open. That's the entry point. He, or they, came through here quickly, shot these two, ran the woman down, and shot her as she was exiting the front door. Quick. Disciplined. Professional."

"Hey, Scott, we need to make sure any tire tracks are noted in case we can order some plaster molds done. They didn't walk away from here."

"Al, are you convinced there was more than one shooter?"

"I think so. Seems like it would be awful hard for one person to break the glass door, open it, enter, be able to fire at least two fatal shots off at two different subjects in two rooms, and chase the woman to make a killing shot down a fifteen-foot hallway. No, I see it as the breach guy breaks and opens the rear door out onto the porch. He stays out of the way while a shooter runs in. He gets off at least two quality shots. We'll need to compare the bullets in the males to the female. I suspect they're different. I would think the breach guy followed the other in and saw the female running down the hallway where he shot her twice."

Scott said to no one in particular, "Has anyone begun to gather up shell casings?"

Al said, "No, they've waited for us to do the initial walk through. The coroner wants to do his thing, so let's let him in do his thing too. We'll also have the evidence team finish their chores."

Walking out the back door, Scott asked, "Do you think the victims knew the killer or killers?"

"For sure. Nothing was obviously taken. There was food ready for a dinner. The killers must have known that the victims were going to be here. Yeah, they knew, maybe even planned the dinner."

"Hey, detective Harris? The car in the driveway comes back to a Terry Langfeld, which corresponds to the ID in the male's wallet in the kitchen. He's a big shot over at Baxter's. The battery in the car is dead. The passenger door was open since whenever."

Al answered, "Okay, make sure forensics dusts it for prints. Let's get someone on the phone at the plant that knows this guy. Whose car is that in the garage?"

The corporal answered, "It belongs to the female on the porch. Ms. Ashley Thompson."

Al asked, "Does anyone know anything about her?"

A voice from the other room, "I think she works as a waitress at the Red Caboose."

Scott exclaimed, "Really? Pretty nice ride and home for a waitress, don't you think?"

Al yelled, "Sergeant, take a couple more deputies and continue your canvass of the neighbors."

"Got it, Luey."

Later, in a never-ending dreadful evening, a deputy found Harris. "Hey, boss, there's a lady, a Mrs. Cordell, who said she saw a Mr. Woodford driving home that Friday night around six-fifteen. He lived here with the deceased female. She said he was driving his new Toyota Highlander."

"What did she know about him?"

"Nice guy. Works at the plant. Been seeing Ashley for several years."

"Ashley, our victim?"

"Yes, sir."

"Did she say anything else that may be helpful?"

"No, but another neighbor, Mr. Peters, said he saw a silver car he hadn't seen in the subdivision before. He thought maybe around five-thirty or a little later."

Al turned to Scott, "Would you get a hold of someone at the plant that we can talk to about Langfeld and now this Woodford guy too."

"Copy that. Hey, Al, who called this in any way?"

"It was a neighbor, Mr. Baines, walking his dog this afternoon.

The dog kept trying to walk up the driveway. Probably caught the smell. Kind of sad, the lady here was well-liked."

"Okay, let's talk to Mr. Baines." They drove around the subdivision until they arrived at Mr. Baines's home. He wasn't surprised to see the detectives. "That Ms. Ashley was a doll baby. She had had it rough, you know, being a single mom and all."

Al looked at Scott and then at Mr. Baines. "She had children?"

"Oh yeah, Brittany. She's off at college somewhere in Kentucky. Nice kid. She's going to be devastated. At least she'll have Woody to ease the pain."

"Woody? Who is Woody?"

"That's Ashley's boyfriend. He's lived with her for a few years. Don't really approve of that shacking up without being married, but I guess this generation lives differently than mine. He's a great guy. He wasn't one of those killed there, was he?"

"We don't think so. Can you describe this, Woody?"

"Sure, maybe thirty-five. Dark hair not over his ears that I recall, and no beard like these other young kids have these days. Square guy, I mean not short but wide. Maybe six-four. I'm not an excellent judge of someone's weight, but he's a big boy. I think he works out at the 'Y' and boxes, too. He's always been a good neighbor. He helped fund the entrance marker to the subdivision. Big money, that was."

"Is he white or black?"

"Oh, he's white."

"You haven't seen him since last week?"

"No, but we went up to the lake Saturday and just got back today around noon. I didn't see his car around, so I figured he was out of town. He travels some for his job."

"What does he drive?"

"A Toyota. Don't know which type."

"Do you know what he did at Baxter's?"

"He drove a semi-truck for some time, but I think that ended a couple of years ago."

"Anything unusual or out of place about him when you saw him last week?"

"No, seemed the same to me."

"Ok, thank you, Mr. Baines. If you remember anything, call me. My number is on this business card. Okay?"

"Yes sir, sure hope Woody is ok. A shame about Ms. Ashley. Damnable ... business," he muttered, holding back tears.

Less than ten hours later, and four hours sleep, Al and Scott drove to Baxter's Engine Plant. On the way, they discussed that the other male victim in the dining room had no ID on him. Al said, "That's weird, and suspicious. I'm profiling, but who runs around without a driver's license these days? I'll answer for you ... criminals."

They met James Winger, the plant president. He was about fifty-five. He wore jeans and a long-sleeve shirt. Obviously shook up. A little perspiration on his forehead. His shirt armpits were damp. Winger's office wasn't quite like either detective assumed the president of a large company should have looked. Another man was present too.

Al started out, "Mr. Winger, thank you for meeting with us. This is an awful mess we face. Our condolences for the loss of Mr. Langfeld." Turning to the unknown male, he asked, "Is this your attorney?"

"This is Steve Lawson. He's the company's lawyer, and thank you for the compassion. I didn't know what to expect, and I'm nervous as hell. I just asked Steve to sit in."

Lawson interjected. "I'm here as a friend. If the questioning is ... ah ... more accusatorial, we'll stop the interview and have Mr. Winger get personal legal counsel."

"Ok, that's fair. No problem. Just wanting to get some background is all. No one is a suspect yet. Don't yet know what the hell we've got except for three dead people."

"Mr. Winger, can you give us a thumbnail sketch of Baxter's and Mr. Langfeld's role in it?"

"Sure, Terry has been with the company for ... must be thirty years. He's worked in several departments and at several locations. He worked himself up to the Chief Financial Officer for this plant and is on the Board of Directors, in one of the employee member slots."

Al asked, "Locations? Where, how many?"

"The company is the third-largest of its type in the world. We primarily manufacture diesel engines, which are sold globally. We have three plants in the US: McAllen, Texas; Mobile, Alabama; and here in Columbus. We have two in Mexico, one in Canada, and one in Germany. I don't know what else I know that's helpful."

"Has someone associated with the company, or outside the company, ever threatened Mr. Langfeld?"

"No, I think he would have shared that with me or our Security Department and they would have notified me."

"Is Mr. Langfeld married?"

"No, he's been divorced for a long time. I'm not even sure he speaks to anyone in the family. I think he has a son but no idea where he or his ex-wife lives."

"Do you know a Ms. Ashley Thompson?"

"Not that I'm aware of. Does she work for us?"

"No, Mr. Langfeld was found dead at her house. No idea of why he would have been there?"

"I don't know Ms. Thompson, nor why Terry would have been at her house."

"Was Mr. Langfeld seeing anyone romantically?"

"No, I don't think so, but he was pretty reserved about his private life. I don't even recall him taking any vacations. He just worked and went home except those incidences he had to travel for us. He was hurt awful bad with the divorce and all."

"Mr. Winger, are you familiar with Paul Woodford?"

"Yes, he worked in the Transportation Department under Stan Eddy until a few years ago. He's a junior accountant/bookkeeper in accounting now. Stan runs the domestic transportation portion for this plant. Mr. Woodford was a driver until the move to accounting. I'm not sure who his supervisor would be now, but I can get that for you. Why do you ask?"

"He lived with Ms. Thompson and we're trying to locate him."

"Oh, is he a suspect?"

"Well, we don't know who is or who isn't."

"Do I, or any of us here at the plant, need to be worried? Steve, I think this should probably be sent to the Board, don't you think?"

Larson answered Winger but for all to hear, "Yes, especially if this Woodford is a suspect since we don't know the motives for the murders."

Al said, "I don't know how to advise you or if I should. Your attorney certainly can. We're just now beginning the investigation. Because Mr. Langfeld was murdered and an employee of his is missing from the same location doesn't bode well, but it could just be a coincidence. We don't know whether Mr. Woodford is a victim or a suspect, or on vacation. Would it be okay to get the personnel files for Baxter's?"

"Steve, I can give him that information, can't I?"

"Detective, we want to help, but would it be okay to provide you the requested data for specific persons without handing over the entire personnel file? There are more than 180 employees."

"Well, I would like the entire file. I don't know what I don't know, so there may be something in the files of importance. But I do understand. How about the files for Langfeld and Woodford to start with?"

Lawson said, "Not a problem. Jim, I'll call HR and get copies of Woodford's and Langfeld's over to detective Harris as soon as possible and have them copy the other employee files."

Scott, looking over at Al, but speaking to Winger, said, "Yeah, that would be helpful, guys. Get us those two files now, and if there is a need later for others, we'll get back to you then. No reason for extra work for no reason. Okay?"

Lawson answered for Winger, "That's very kind of you guys. I'll make sure you have those files before the end of the day."

As we drove away, Manna said, "Al, does it make any sense that this Woodford dude would be one of the shooters? Think of it. We agreed there were probably two shooters entering through the rear door of a house ... he lived in. The neighbors stated he waved to them on the way into the subdivision that night. Why would someone intent on murder allow himself to be seen by those that knew him? Why would he break in through the back door? Although, I know it's early, this guy was well-liked."

"I agree. He looks to be more of a victim or maybe even a hostage." Looking out through the bug-spattered windshield, Al sighed, "What the hell do we have here, Scott?"

THIRTEEN

Harris and Manna kept copious notes on a shared computer file. The examination of data continued; Ms. Thompson's cell phone was located, but the battery had died. It didn't look like anything of value would be recovered. The home had been searched, but no letters or telephone lists were found. There weren't any bills or invoices identifying where the daughter attended college. Woodford lived there, but nothing of consequence was located, which showed a light on him as a suspect or a victim. His Toyota was found later in the back part of the plant's parking lot.

"Mr. Winger, this is detective Harris again. I understand that Mr. Woodford's vehicle was found today."

"Yes sir, in a part of the parking area seldom used."

"Do you know if he normally parked there?"

"No, no one parks there. It's an area used only by the maintenance group when working on the large trucks. But even they don't park their personal vehicles there because the large trucks need space to maneuver. That's actually why we found Mr. Woodford's car. A driver was making a large turn to check out stabilizers in an older truck and almost ran over the car."

"I'm going to have it towed to the county garage so our

forensics team can go over it. Would you please let your security people know that Mason's Towing Service will be arriving to tow it?"

"Of course, sir. Did you get the files on Woodford and Langfeld?"

"Yes sir, tell Mr. Lawson thanks." Al hung up and immediately received a call. "Harris here."

"Officer, this Mr. Baines. You asked where the Thompson girl was attending college."

"Yes, Mr. Baines. Do you know where?"

"Yes, she's going to the University of Kentucky," Mr. Baines announced.

"Thank you very much, Mr. Baines. A big help, that is."

Harris said. "Scott, please contact the University of Kentucky Security Office and see if they can locate Brittany Thompson. We'll need to call her, tell her about her mother and then go down there and interview her."

A few phone calls: "Hello, this is detective Scott Manna from the Bartholomew County Sheriff's Office in Columbus, Indiana. We've had a triple murder here and one victim has a daughter there at your school. Brittany Thompson. We need to talk to her and … you know … let her know the news. Do you have a number and an address?"

After obtaining the needed information, Al called the number, but Brittany's roommate said she was on a school trip at Cave Run and there wasn't any cell service there because she had tried calling earlier. Brittany would be back Friday and her roommate wanted to know if there was a message she should give Brittany.

Al instructed the roommate to have Brittany call him as soon as she returned while trying not to make it sound serious. He then telephoned the Security Office again and explained the conversation he had just had. "We've got to get hold of this girl before she finds out on the radio or, worse, is in danger."

The security officer said they would take care of it. He said, "This kind of news should be face-to-face."

"I know," said Harris. "Okay, thanks. That's really going to be a crappy conversation. If you guys have anything up this way, please call me. I owe you big time."

"Hey Scott, the security officer said the officer would get a state trooper from the nearby detachment to go with one of them to ensure she is okay and to make the proper notification. Also, Winger called yesterday while we were out. He said Langfeld's assistant manager, Michelle Freeman, hadn't shown up to work yet this week. She hasn't been seen since last Friday."

"Are you kidding me?! Who reported her missing?"

Winger said that Langfeld's secretary told him that Ms. Freeman hadn't come up to work Monday and everyone just figured she didn't go to work because of what happened to Langfeld. But when she didn't show up today either, they got to checking, and she hadn't been seen or heard from since last Friday. Someone at the plant went over to her apartment and conveyed to Winger that Freeman's Honda Pilot was gone too.

"This is spiraling quickly and hopefully not out of control, Scott. Call the State Police and ask if they can assist us. Put a BOLO out for her car too."

Michelle and I discussed what we wanted to accomplish by calling the anonymous tip line. First, we hoped to provide enough plausible evidence that would exonerate us. Second, we wanted to elicit some information, if possible. We talked through several stories but hadn't yet settled on one.

"Why don't we just send a letter?" Michelle suggested.

"I don't think so. It would take too long, and the postmark would be suspicious. Why would someone a thousand miles away know any of the detailed evidence?" I argued.

"Okay, fair enough. How about one of us just happened to have seen the murder, but we were too scared to talk."

"I don't think so. They would say we're fruitcakes even if we gave them some details. Unless the details were too good. Then they might think we're the suspects."

"Okay. Do you have any ideas?"

I suggested a scenario and Michelle agreed on the story.

"Hello? Yes, is this the tip line for the murders the other day? Ok, Mr. Harris, I want to tell you I saw a BMW leaving that subdivision last week. I think it was gray or silver. No, sir, I'd rather not give my name. I don't want to be the next one dead. I think the car was from California. I used to live in San Diego, and the plate looked like a California plate. No, I don't remember the plate number. No, I had never seen the car before in that area. What time? It must have been around six on Saturday … no, it was Friday night. Yes, I'm a little nervous. I was in the area too, ah, I'd rather not say. I'm married. I hope you find out who did it soon." Michelle hung up and breathed a sigh of relief.

"Any gut feeling about how that went?" I asked.

"He seemed excited, especially about the car. He stated back to me my words as if to make sure he had written the facts as I gave him."

"What's his name?"

"Albert Harris."

Al called out to Scott, "Take a listen to this hotline call I took today."

"Why were you taking the tip line calls?" Scott asked.

"I wasn't. I was in dispatch when the call came in and Judy and I answered by speakerphone until the information seemed important. I picked up then."

"Alright. Let's hear your summary."

"Hmm, a gray or silver BMW. Didn't Mr. Peters say he saw a silver BMW earlier the night of the murders?"

"Yeah, he said he hadn't seen it before in the neighborhood."

"Any idea of the caller's identity?"

"No, she used a non-traceable phone that didn't allow caller ID."

"Wish she had let us know how she knew about the BMW."

"Well, she kind of implied she was having an affair," Al said.

"Have we gotten any surveillance cameras in the general area that may have picked up on the BMW?"

"Not sure, Al, let me call upstairs."

"Hey, Sylvia, he cooed into the phone. Would you run the State Police License Plate Identification Recordings on the interstate in our general area Friday morning through that evening?"

"Hey, Al, Sylvia said we should get the LPIR data in about ten minutes."

While they waited, Al asked, "What day is this? I'm trying to write up some of these reports; I'm confusing the interview date with today's date and the written date."

"Wednesday, buddy."

"Hey, Scott, downloads complete. Let's look and see if there is something that helps."

"I'm always amazed how long an hour of recorded surveillance video takes to review."

"Yeah, seems like a three to one ratio." For the next twenty-five minutes, they watched; reversed, watched, and sped up.

"There, right there! Back it up."

"I see it. A BMW northbound on I-65 near Bannington's Truck Stop. Can you zoom in? The plates are ... shit, they're fuzzier than ... no wait, that's better. T65RTE3 California, Al yelled into the dispatch room. Sarge, we need that run right now!"

"Hey Al, the plates come back stolen, as reported by Jackson Dynamics, Inc., in Fremont, California. A search of the business shows it as an investment company. They reported the plates stolen three weeks ago."

"You put the BOLO out on it, right?"

"Of course, I did, Al, and I also went through the Woodford file. Nothing much there."

"Scott, do you think that this Woodford and the Freeman girl could have done the killing? It doesn't feel right, but where are they? If they had been kidnapped, we don't have any communication from the kidnappers."

Scott answered, "We also don't have any bodies. Al, why would the killers not kill those two? Makes no sense. What do those two have in common?"

"I don't know, buddy. Did the forensics establish anything else?"

Scott, skimming a report, answered, "Well, the GSWs to the girl were from a different gun than the one used on the two males, as we figured. The knife was from the kitchen and was post mortem. Woodford's Highlander only had his fingerprints. We haven't yet found out who the John Doe victim is. We have gotten nothing back on credit cards or other banking transactions of Woodford or Freeman woman."

Al said, "So, we don't have any answers … just more questions. Wonderful."

FOURTEEN

The sun rising over the Atlantic was a picturesque vista from the side porch view. We were drinking our usual morning coffee and hot tea. The last several days and nights had been spent discussing the who-fors and what-fors. We were also incorporating ourselves into the local community by walking and talking to almost anyone we met on the beach or in the stores. That's how we met our next-door neighbor, Jim Fleck.

Jim was a retired cop from Michigan. His wife had passed away that last summer and their children had long ago moved out of Michigan. Topsail Beach had become more of the Flecks' home than a vacation home years ago. He was the stereotypical movie actor depicting a retired cop. Square shoulders. Crew cut. No glasses and no facial hair. Thick upper arms and a chest that looked though it was cut out of a fifty-five-gallon drum. He wore an American Flag T-shirt much of the time and the other days the T-shirt that read Home of the Free because of the Brave. He moved like a cop, unfazed, with purpose and confidence. When he answered a question, he often cocked his head a little and squinted one eye as if he was trying to figure out why you had just asked him the question. But he was genuine. He was the real deal.

Since Michelle and I were younger than nearly all the other residents, we had come up with a logical reason we were living in Topsail Beach, seemingly without a job, yet wealthy. When asked, I gave whomever the name of one company I had started for investments and consulting. We would then explain that Michelle was my girlfriend, and she worked for me at the company. Since it was an investment/consulting company, I explained we could work from home most of the time. However, from time to time, we would have to travel to client locations. It gave us a plausible reason for living in Topsail Beach, but also for why we might be gone for extended periods.

Mr. Fleck was very talkative, maybe a little lonely too, but very proud of his career. He enjoyed his career and all of whom he knew in various law enforcement agencies, including the FBI. We invited him over for dinner because Michelle liked to cook and it was a great way to foster the friendship. Jim truly had enjoyed an interesting career. He said he was eventually promoted to homicide detective in his county. He got his "high three" and pulled the plug when the new sheriff made some questionable changes to the department like he wanted the police force to kowtow to the perpetrators. The new guy seemed to promote the bad guys and not the cops. He said it was a liberal doctrine across the country that made him sick. He then apologized for banging the drum.

"Yeah, the new boss wanted us to be more feely feely with the accused. He also wanted us to do more community outreach events to promote the good of his office, which literally took cops off the streets. Well, shit, Paul, our agency did that long before he became sheriff, but he wanted the homicide group to be part of it. We had never done it before because we always had to cancel because we invariably would be called out to a homicide or an assault. It was hard to follow leads on a working homicide when you were required to be in a kindergarten class. He didn't care what I thought, so I had enough and left. Rita and I stayed in the area for a while but eventually the winters caught up with us and we landed here."

I was indeed interested, so I kept his story going. "Homicide detective, hey. That must have been a helluva career. Were there many murders that your office got involved in?"

"We had seven or eight a year, which sounds pretty low, and it is as a statistical number. However, for a detective's squad of four homicide detectives working all the rapes and aggravated assaults too, it kept us busy all year round. It's not like on TV where the murder is always resolved in 48 hours. Often, it might take two months or more for one murder, and that doesn't include all the bullshit court appearances. Oh, sorry about my language. I forget I'm no longer in the squad room."

Michelle answered for us both, "Sir, we're adults. We've heard them all and used them all too. No reason to apologize."

"Maybe not, but I need to watch my tongue, and you needn't be so formal." Mr. Fleck said.

Michelle answered, "Yes, sir. I mean I'll try to be more civil. I was Army, so it was drilled into my soul."

I wanted to delve into the homicide part for obvious reasons. "Are the TV shows close to real life?"

"Some are fairly close, but you know they have to do it in a thirty or sixty-minute block. They definitely don't illustrate the time spent writing up reports and dealing with lawyers. I know the lawyers have a job to do, but hell, it always seemed like our own attorneys were working against us."

"What do they do right?"

"Well, the investigative process usually televised is accurate. You know, roping off the area, interviewing everyone in the immediate area, contacting family members, speaking with employers, locating telephones, conducting searches at the residences and in the cars, looking through the databases for strange searches, and some of the cop-speak too is spot-on. The activity that isn't shown is the vast amount of investigative time the detectives end up conducting surveillance after a prime suspect is identified. Often, there are just a few pieces of evidence lacking for an arrest, so surveillance, follow-up interviews of witnesses, or even revisiting the scene is helpful. Those actions take hours, sometimes days and weeks. We were pretty lucky that all the murders we investigated were resolved and prosecuted. We only had one multiple-victim homicide. They're somewhat harder for obvious reasons."

Michelle chimed in with, "Does it change any of the dynamics if the victims were unrelated, sir?"

"Well, if they're not family …"

"No, I meant, the victims didn't know each other."

"Oh, well yeah, that would make it harder. I didn't face that situation, but I would think the specter of a serial killer would have to be considered. Those are obviously the hardest to resolve. When there isn't any obvious link to the victims, then it's like looking for the needle in the haystack. Glad I never was dealt that hand."

After Jim went home for the evening, we started discussing again what we could do to learn about the investigation. Michelle suggested using the hotline again for clues. We knew that her name and mine had been acknowledged through the press as persons of interest. I had already begun to grow a beard and cut my hair shorter. Michelle had cut her hair a little, dyed it, and was wearing it differently.

"Okay," I started, "If we called the hotline again, what could we offer them?"

"What if we gave them Javier's name? That would be huge for them?"

"It would also put us at the scene, or at least in their circle," I said.

"Yeah, you're right. What about if we said we saw you or me somewhere?"

I said, "I'm not sure. I'm exhausted. Let's sleep on it and talk again in the morning."

The next morning was a classic sunrise and blue sky start for Topsail Beach. Wonderfully bright and ... well, cheerful, if the weather can be so described and if Michelle and I allowed ourselves such a description. We sat out on the patio drinking our usual and eating a donut this morning. We resisted the discussion of last night until it could no longer be ignored.

"I think it might be worth the risk for a call again."

"How about the thing I said last night? You know, about having seen one of us."

"Okay, I'm good with that, but where? It's got to be close to home or it wouldn't make sense," I answered.

"How about the county where Jim used to work? Michigan isn't that far and, who knows, maybe it would be helpful?"

"Yeah, yeah, that might work, and if calls were made, maybe Jim would get interested."

"Where did he say he had been a cop?"

"He said he lived in Adrian. I remembered the name because when he said the name, it reminded me of my girlfriend in high school. Can you look that up and see what county it's in?"

"Okay, here it is, Lenawee County. Okay, and the map shows that if we were driving from Toledo to Lansing, we would go through Adrian. That may be enough to get their attention," Michelle noted.

"I agree, but this time it can't be you dropping a dime. Too much of a coincidence that the same female calls again from a few hundred miles away, just coincidentally having seen the missing girl. No, no, I better make the call this time."

I had to have another coffee to wake myself up, and I figured if I was going to have more coffee, I should also eat one of the no-bake cookies Michelle made last night; the donuts were gone anyway.

"Hello, is this the Bartholomew County Sheriff's Office?"

"Yes, you called our tip line. Did you mean to call this number?"

"Yes ... yeah, I ah ... ah I think I may have seen that girl," I said.

"Which girl are you referring to, sir?"

"The one in the newspaper and on TV the other day. I don't know her name. I just think I might have seen her."

"Ok, are you referring to the woman referred to in the murders recently?"

"Yes, sir."

"Okay, where do you think you saw the woman?"

"Well, I was driving from Toledo to Lansing and I was at the Marathon Truck Stop on Rt. 223. I'm pretty sure it was her cause I had just seen the TV with her picture. I'm a sucker for good-looking women," I said as I looked straight at Michelle, who blushed.

"What was she wearing?"

I described the clothes Michelle was now wearing in front of me but described her hairstyle as it had been. "No, I don't know if she was with anyone else. I saw her at the back of a blue Pilot getting gas," I answered. "My name? Ah, I'd rather be kept out of it. I'm just a passerby. If she was kidnapped, I hope you get the creep." I hung up and breathed out a sigh of relief.

Michelle looked at me and said, "Kind of laid it on thick about me, didn't you?"

I looked away as I walked away ... "Nope."

The next day offered another beautiful day, but Ashley and Brittany were still on my mind, so the visuals were clouded. The person or persons that set up the murders must be wondering where I was. I wondered again if they were worried or felt secure knowing I had run. Hopefully, the latter.

driver's written test and if she passed, the DMV would schedule her for the driving test. He said if everything went well, she should have a permanent license within the next two months.

We walked out, leaving Mr. Horny confused and gazing at her backside. Michelle just smiled knowingly.

FIFTEEN

Harris turned to Manna and mentioned, "No one has seen either Woodford or Freeman or her Honda Pilot during the last week and a half?"

"No bodies either," Scott said.

"Someone, somewhere, knows something."

"Hey, Lieutenant, got results back on our John Doe. Comes back as Javier Muchido. Mexican National with dual citizenship. Address given is in McAllen, Texas."

"Okay. Scott, let's call down there and get someone on the horn and see if they've got anything on this Muchido."

Finding a number for Hidalgo County, Texas Sheriff's Office took longer than expected, but they finally found the correct number. Al and Scott called and put the call on speaker.

"Hello, Hidalgo County Sheriff's Office. This is Sergeant Lopez. May I help you?"

"Hey, Sarge, this is Lieutenant Harris up here in Columbus, Indiana."

"Columbus, Indiana? Are you sure?" Lopez laughingly retorted?

"Yeah, I know we get confused with that other town all the time."

"Yeah, I know. I had a cousin that got on the wrong bus once. She was really confused after leaving for Charleston, South Carolina, and stepped off in Charleston, West Virginia. She never saw the ocean either."

"Sure, gets confusing sometimes, Sarge. I wish the rest of this conversation would be as funny, but it's not. We're working a triple murder up here, and we just found out our John Doe is Javier Muchido with an address in your county."

"Are you sure it is Muchido? He's a big deal down here. Owns a trucking company—Dos Amigos Trucking. I think he's involved with other companies too. They freelance work for anybody needing transport. The company donates thousands to some of the local schools and churches. Man, I hope it's not him."

"Well, our coroner sent off fingerprints and the FBI Center got a positive hit and reflected that he had been given citizenship some years ago, which is why he was in the national database."

"Damn. I hate to hear that. I don't know what else to tell you. I'm not familiar with him from a law enforcement angle, just from word of mouth and what I've read in the news. You said a triple homicide?"

"Yeah, Muchido and two others from this area. They were gunned down in one of the victim's homes. There wasn't anything taken from the home or the people. Looks like an assassination."

"Damn, Lieutenant, a triple murder! Your office has got their hands full for sure. Are the Feds helping?"

"Yeah, it sucks, and, no, the Feds haven't yet been brought in. We may have to ask them for resource issues, but you know them, they'll swoop in and we'll never know what's happening until it's over."

"For sure, that seems true every time here too."

Al, getting back on track, said, "Anyway, since he has dual citizenship, do you know if he had family in your area?"

"No, I doubt it. Any family would probably be in Mexico, and I would have to check around to see where exactly. He spent a lot of time in Mexico. I have a telephone number for the trucking company here in McAllen if you want it."

"The phone number would be great. I would assume someone there has a family member's name and number to contact regarding the death."

"What office did you say you're calling from again?"

"The Bartholomew County Sheriff's Office in Columbus Indiana."

"Man, this is tough. Good luck."

Scott called the Dos Amigos trucking phone number and again used the speakerphone.

When the call was answered, Scott explained to Pedro why he had called. He was put on hold for a few minutes.

"Hello, this is Don Hanson. I'm the lawyer for Dos Amigos. Pedro just told me that Mr. Muchido was found murdered? How can that be? When? Are you sure it's him?"

"Yes sir, Mr. Hanson. I'm Lieutenant Manna with the Bartholomew County Sheriff's Office in Columbus, Indiana. I'm sorry to be the bearer of bad news. He was found murdered at a residence up here. A lady by the name of Thompson and another male, too. Do you know why Mr. Muchido would have been up here in Indiana?"

Hanson squeaked, "I don't know for sure, sir. Our company subcontracted with Baxter's up there and we shared hauls. They're in Columbus, but I'm sure you know that. I'm not sure exactly when we started making hauls for Baxter's. You could contact Mr. Langfeld up there at Baxter's. He would know."

"Ah ... Mr. Langfeld was killed, along with Mr. Muchido. It was actually a triple murder. They were killed at Ms. Ashley Thompson's house."

"Oh my God! Why? This is crazy. Have you any leads or anyone you're looking at for the killings? Geez, this is crazy. Mr. Muchido ... murdered. I'm at a loss. Damn, I can't believe this ... Javier," Hanson squeaked again.

"It's an awful mess, I agree. We're just now getting started on the investigation. I'm sure as an attorney you'll understand that I can't reveal too much information. I can tell you it appears to have been a setup by someone because they were all at the Thompson home for dinner. There isn't any evidence that either male victim knew Ms. Thompson. We're still trying to figure out that connection. Do you know this, Ms. Thompson?"

"No, sir, I've never heard the name, but I've also not traveled to your county either. What can I do to help?".

"Is there family I can contact with this awful news?"

"This is awful ... family ... Oh, they're all in Mexico. It might be better that I tell them, anyway. They don't trust Federales, if you know what I mean, sir."

"Sure, I understand, but I'll need a name and contact information in order to write in my report. At some point we're going to have to talk to at least the wife, surely you understand."

"Of course. His wife's name is Isabella. I don't have her number readily available. Why don't you give me a fax number and I'll send the information to you?"

"That will work. Please let me know as soon as you can. Like I said, she will need to be interviewed."

"Yes, sir, I understand. Detective, was there anyone injured along with the murders?"

"Injured? No, three people, three dead. If there is anything else you think of, please don't hesitate to call me here."

"I will, sir. This is just awful."

Michelle and I were sitting at a local restaurant sipping on some cold drinks and listening to Bon Jovi's It's My Life. The waiter brought over some barbecued chicken wings. I said to Michelle, "I'm missing, and there isn't a body." She countered, "eventually they're going to realize that I'm also missing."

"Yep, and sooner than later, they'll have identified Javier. How long will it be before they connect Langfeld to Javier and drug trafficking? Not long, I bet. And when that happens, how long before I'm linked," I grumbled.

Michelle pondered, "Of course in my mind, all of that leads back to the person, or persons, that arranged for the hit."

"Exactly. That's the key for us. We need to figure out those connections. I wonder about Tarant: is he higher up the food chain than Javier; could he have found out something that made him feel threatened and ultimately resolved to cut it all off at the source?"

"Who would know, and would they talk to us, or would they go to Tarant?" she added.

"I wonder if I dare contact Franklin Schmidt. I seldom, if ever, spoke with him outside of Terry's presence. Do you think he could have been responsible, Michelle?"

"Could he and Tarant have run the whole thing without Terry and Javier?" Michelle asked and added, "I don't know him well enough to answer that."

I repeated, "Since they know I wasn't killed and also that you had been there too, how would they be reacting? I have to assume that Brittany is safe. And you have no living family members, so you're safe as long as we're smart."

Michelle questioned, "Who would they be reaching out to for information, and do we reach out for similar information?"

I answered her, "I can call the only person I trust right now other than you."

"Who's that Woody?"

"Miguel."

I called Miguel and thankfully; he answered.

"Mi Amigo. Oh my, are you alright? I've been worried so much about you. Where are you?"

"Hey, slow down, my man, I'm fine. Has anyone talked to you yet, you know, the cops?"

"No. No one."

"Can I trust you to forget we've talked?"

"Si."

"Miguel, you know I didn't do this, and I don't know who did, but I've got my suspicions. Do you have any ideas?"

"I know you didn't do this. You could never have hurt Ms. Ashley. I think it may have been Mr. Tarant because Mr. Schmidt has been lying low. I know someone at Rotten Tomatoes said there was a lot of talk that someone talked and Mr. Tarant was going to take care of it, you know what I mean?"

"That's what I was thinking, too. Whoever it is had to feel threatened, and I don't think Mr. Schmidt would have contracted a hitman, but it makes sense that this guy Tarant may have that ability. Any idea who he might have contacted?"

"No, but my friend there might have the chance to figure it out. You want me to ask?"

"Well, not directly, Miguel. You need to protect yourself first, understand?"

"Si."

"If you talk to him about the murders, you need to let him offer the information first, or it'll look like you're interviewing him. You know what I mean?" I instructed.

"Yes, sir. How is Brittany?" Miguel asked.

"I don't know yet, but I'm going to know soon. Do you have a pen, Miguel? I'll give you a phone number you can call me on. No text messages. Don't let anyone have this number. Understand?" I again directed.

"Okay, my friend, be careful. I've heard that Tarant is ruthless." Miguel answered.

"I will, and you too. If he finds out we're talking, you won't be safe either."

"Woody? Have you heard about Ms. Freeman? She's missing too."

I was conflicted. I had to trust Miguel, but should I tell him everything? I decided I had to, or at some point, he might not trust me; I needed his full loyalty and trust.

"Yes, Miguel, she's with me and she's ok."

"That's good. We were scared she was dead and buried somewhere."

"Don't tell anyone, and I mean anyone, she's with me or that she's okay. It's the safest thing right now that everyone thinks she's just missing. It will help keep her protected. It's her life, understand?" "My lips are sealed."

SIXTEEN

"Hey, Al. The guy from Texas is on three."

"Hello, this is Detective Harris. May I help you?"

"Sir, this is Sergeant Lopez. I talked to several of the deputies at a couple of roll calls and it looks like Muchido's trucking company could have been involved in drugs, specifically trafficking meth. I never had heard anything about that earlier. I'm sorry."

"No need to apologize. Tell me what you found. Sounds like recent news," Al said.

"Yeah, that's a shock to me, too. I had never heard squat about him. Well, the deputy assigned to the local drug task force said they've heard inklings about Muchido for years, but no one here could make a buy. No one pinched ever rolled up on him, either. The scenario the boys here figured used was they were running meth from Mexico through a business in the States and distributed somehow, somewhere. The guys said he never had his hands on anything, so our guys could only speculate, but there wasn't any hard evidence—hear me?"

"Yeah, loud and clear. Did anyone ever hear the name Baxter's or Langfeld?"

"They knew of both. It was my understanding that they felt

Baxter's would make a haul for another business here, Schmidt's Distributors, on their return trips from their plant here in McAllen. The thinking was that was how Muchido was moving the drugs. By chance, one of Schmidt's trucks was stopped by Texas highway patrol some time ago. The truck was headed for a hog farm up in Arkansas. The highway patrol had called in the stop for a broken rear taillight, and one of the task force officers heard the call; he told the patrol officer to slow roll the stop so he could get there. When he did, he asked permission to search. The driver had no problem and gave consent. So, they did a consensual search and found nothing. Well, that's not quite true. They found rotting food and nothing else, so they let him go. The officer told the task force, and as far as I could tell, Muchido just found his way to the back-burner. Remember, I said he was a big donator in town."

Harris told the deputy he had called Dos Amigo Trucking and spoke to their lawyer, Don Hanson. "I had asked him to contact Muchido's wife and to send me contact information. Do you know about Hanson?"

"Sure, he's a well-known lawyer here. I didn't think he did any corporate work. I thought he just did defense work."

"What kind of defense?"

"Generally, for drugs and guns. We have a major problem with that down here. I'm sure you're aware. There are a lot of lawyers making a bundle defending that type of representation. Hanson isn't a stereotypical defense attorney." Lopez said.

Harris asked, "What kind of attorney is he?"

"Well, I mean. Drug dealers are, by nature a rough lot. Hanson sounds as though he is still in grade school. He has a squeaky tone ... as if he was going through puberty," Lopez said.

"Squeaky. You're right. I wouldn't have described a drug attorney as if he was still in junior high. So, does any of this make sense to you, Sarge? I mean, a trucking company owner fifteen hundred miles away is found murdered by two others, one of whom he had a business relationship with. His company's lawyer is also a defense attorney, primarily for drug dealers. The local task force has heard his name and allegations of moving shit by our other guys' company trucks. Really?"

"I'm tracking you. I'm going to talk to the task force captain and have someone detailed to poke around a little more now with Muchido's murder. Maybe someone here will now remember things they forgot before his murder ... which tends to wake people up and talk."

"Copy that."

"Hey, also, Hanson asked us a strange question. After he had learned about the triple murder and the names of the other two victims, he asked if anyone had been injured."

"Injured? That's weird. Wonder why he asked? It's almost like he wondered if others were at the scene."

"Exactly what we thought too."

Miguel called me later, but I didn't want to let on about the time difference because it would reflect we weren't in the same time zone. I had to be cautious no matter what.

"Mr. Woody, I talked to my friend at Rotten Tomatoes. He said that Tarant has been silent lately, but his closest associates told someone that the job was almost finished. I asked my friend what that meant and he said someone in Indiana had talked to the police."

"Did he mean before the murders or since then?"

Miguel answered, "I'm sure he meant before."

"Did he know who or when?"

"He said that Langfeld had talked about Muchido being paranoid and thinking someone had squealed. Don't know when. Don't know who. It wasn't me, amigo."

"Who up there started driving for you when Terry took you off the road?"

Miguel answered, "Ah, it's now Gary Stewart. He was hired

recently to replace the other guy. I don't know his name, but he was okay, just had to quit because he needed to be home more. I don't know Stewart well and I don't know why Mr. Langfeld picked him to do the driving. I can probably find out though."

"Be careful, Miguel. If he's dirty, then anyone asking questions is going to be a marked man. Did you get the impression that someone had talked to the cops up there or in Texas?"

"I don't think it was the local police. I think my friend meant the Feds."

"How well do you trust him? Does he know what you and I did?" I asked.

"Yeah, he knows what I did. We were close. He knew about Elizabeth's medical problems, so I told him how I could afford everything. I guess he might think you know because we drove together, but he's said nothing about you. In fact, he's never mentioned you at all because you're missing."

"Make sure he's trustworthy; I was on the target list, which means you could be too. So, for you, your family, Michelle, and Brittany, we've got to be sure of who our friends are, comprende?"

"Si amigo. I understand. I'm already thinking of sending Stacy and Elizabeth to her folks for a long vacation. They've been wanting to go visit the grandparents for months, so this works."

"That sounds like a splendid plan, Miguel. You should do it, soon, and I hung up." Again, I thought of the organization and how many levels there were above Langfeld and Muchido. They were all responsible for Michelle's and my heartache.

Michelle had listened to the conversation and put two and two together. "Are you sure you can trust him?"

"I, we, have to. We need to have some ears on the ground at Baxter's and in the circle. Do you have any suggestions of someone else you can think of we could trust?"

Michelle said, "I've been racking my mind, but I'm not yet convinced of anyone. I'll let you know if I remember someone we could trust."

I was still swimming with questions and scenarios that would explain the murders. I had been racking my brain for some time on how to develop the needed intel on Tarant and others. Changing the subject, I asked, "You ever been to Dallas?"

"No, why?"

"I want to look up someone who might help. But we need to ask Jimmy for a favor first."

"Okay, what's the favor?"

"Hello."

"Jim, this is Paul from next door."

"Well, hi Paul. What's up?"

"Are you busy? Can we come over for a minute? I've got a favor to ask of you."

"I'm not doing anything. Come on over." Jimmy said.

"Great, we'll be right there."

As we walked across the yard, I explained to Michelle that Tawon would be a safe contact.

"I appreciate your taking some time for us, Jim. So, this is the story of a hard-luck kid in Dallas I met years ago. His name is Tawon Phelps. We became friends through our ... let's say similar lifestyles. Anyway, I've thought about him over these years. I was lucky to have made it out with no harm done and become successful. I've wondered how he has fared. So, my request is would you know how, and would you help me, to locate him?"

"Sure. Do you have any other information, like an approximate birth year?" Jim asked.

"No, not really. I'd say he is a couple of years younger, so maybe around thirty, thirty-two. I don't know too much about his family, either. I'm pretty sure they all lived in that area. I know he was arrested a few years ago. By the way, he's black if that matters."

"Okay. Was he arrested in Texas?"

"Yeah, Jim. I think it was probably on state drug charges."

"Ok, let me make a call and see what I can come up with. I'll call you if, no when, I find something."

"Thanks, Jim. I appreciate it. If I can help him, it would mean a lot to me."

Walking back home, Michelle asked again about Tawon.

I answered her, "I was in Dallas when one day shortly after arriving, on the south-side, I think it was, I came upon a group of guys a little older than me. They had circled Tawon, who was obviously in a predicament, not the least of which he was in a darkened alley. I hate bullies, so I didn't turn and walk away. I don't look for trouble. It just sometimes finds me. Anyway, I sauntered to the circle around Tawon with only five or six feet separating them. They were all just taunting him, but it was escalating and I could sense that someone in the circle was going to take a run at him."

Michelle nodded at me as visualized the scene, as to say, and then what happened?

As I neared the group of five, one of them saw me and said, "You need to leave if you know what's good for you."

I answered, "I never have known what was good for me. Maybe you should tell me."

That stopped their circling of Tawon. I had now become the focus of their attention. I assumed Tawon would run like hell as soon as he saw the opening, but he didn't. So, the group of all white kids now approached me with the usual street threats I had heard for years. There was one guy, probably twenty-three, a bit more aggravated that I had broken up their party. He said, "You really don't want to be here asshole."

I saw Michelle sporting a startled look. "I wasn't scared, Michelle. I never was when I was ready for a fight. Back then, I was only worried when I slept in a park or under an overpass and couldn't be on guard. So, as they got closer, I just stood my ground and figured I was in for a good brawl. I figured the older guy would charge me and the dude to his left, my right, might be next. I told him, 'When pigs fly asshole'."

As I was telling Michelle the story, I began smiling because this was a side of me she knew nothing about, or at least in this much detail. It was kind of like her military service I hadn't known about.

I kept grinning and continued, "What I wasn't ready for was for three of them charging me at the same time. Damn! My street instincts and pure I-don't-give-a-damn, took over my senses and reactions."

"I hit the first guy with a left and swung my right arm to the side of the guy on his left so I could throw him, or at least could deflect him, towards the third guy who was on my left—their right. They crashed into each other and rolled onto the sticky, wet alley. It stunk like most of them did - piss puddles along with rotting food and, for good measure, maybe a pile of shit. Them falling allowed me to get in a second left hand crushing punch to the first guy's stomach, dropping him to his knees."

"One of the other two guys came in behind me. He drilled me with a quality punch to the right side of my head. He landed it between my eye and my ear. It stung like hell. I dropped to a knee. Had to shake my head to clear it. He threw a quick jab off my chin. Whew! Okay. What am I doing? That's two quality blows. I never gave a rat's ass about being hit. I turned around and saw he was shocked I hadn't given up. I smiled at him and laid him out with one of my better straight arm jabs to his jaw. I heard bones cracking. He was out before he flopped on the sidewalk like the sack of shit he was," I said, smiling, thinking back to that day.

Michelle began to ask me a question, but I was reliving the day, and found myself excited and kept jabbering away.

"I grabbed one other while his friends were reeling and trying to get away. I kicked him in his balls and dropped him with a blow to the back of the neck. A really vicious crunch, if I say so myself. I hadn't killed before, so I was worried I may have just joined that group. He dropped next to the first guy, who was still trying to get his breath. Those that could move turned and ran. I started walking away, thinking that Tawon had already run away. Nope. He just looked at me with a truly bewildering expression, kind of like your look, Michelle. But his look was more like, Who the fuck is this white boy helping me."

"Tawon told me he owed me. But he didn't owe me anything. Anyway, that's how we met and became close friends for several years."

"Wow! I mean Jesus, Woody! You were really into telling the story as if you enjoyed the fight. That shocks me to think you're a badass like me too," Michelle giggled.

"That's why Tawon is trustworthy and my guess is that he's probably still slinging if he's not in prison. Know what I mean?"

"Yes, but how is that helpful to us?"

"Well, two things. I really want to help him get straight and start a new life. The other is to see if he can find out something about Rotten Tomatoes, Schmidt, Tarant, or anyone else. He was extremely good at finding out information. So, I'm just hoping he can help us. But if he can't, I still hope I can help him walk on the straight and narrow."

"Sounds good to me. When do we leave?"

"Hopefully, Jim comes up with some good information that will help us track Tawon down."

Well, Jim found Tawon, but not exactly where we would have liked.

"Hey, Paul, Jim yelled to me from his porch to me on mine. I found your buddy. He's in a small county jail in Texas for stealing some drugs from a pharmacy. The amount wasn't significant enough for the DEA to care, so the county prosecuted in order to seize a Toyota 4x4 he was driving."

"Thanks, Jim. What county is he being held?"

"It's Rains County. Are you familiar with it?"

"Yeah, Jim, it's east of Dallas, but not too far. Thanks again."

"No problem, Paul. Good luck."

On the flight to Dallas, Michelle and I sat quietly. So quietly that she fell asleep leaning on my shoulder. I've got to say I was uncomfortable and conflicted so soon after Ashley's death. After we rented a car, she asked, "What are you going to do about contacting Brittany?"

"I've thought about that. I think we should stop in Lexington on the way home."

"Yeah, you need to talk to her sooner than later, even though I know why you haven't."

At the Rains County Jail, we had a bit of trouble convincing the jailer that I knew Tawon since we were kids. Then twice, when asked if he was expecting anyone by the name of Paul, Tawon declined the visit. The third time, I asked the jailer to tell him it was Big Cracker. The jailer eyed me up and down, switched his well-used toothpick from one fat jowl to the other; and strolled away confused, but we were allowed into the internal waiting room where we were properly searched for any weapons or contraband.

The Rains County Jail was typical of many county and city jails across the country. Sorry to say, I've seen my share of them when visiting dad or bailing him out. They're all usually small and smelly. Very little privacy and too small to separate prisoners based on their crimes. So, a murder suspect might be held along with a drunk, at least until the first appearance. We were led to a small room with enough space for only two chairs, so I stood.

"Hey brother," I said, "So ... you do ... remember me."

Tawon had a big smile and said, "Yeah, Cracker. What are you doing here? It's been a long time. How did you find me, bro? This your main squeeze?"

"Slow down 'T', you're rattling on a mile a minute. I know I left before saying bye, my man. I'm sorry. I had to get out of town back then. Too hot. No, this is not my squeeze. This is Michelle, and she's just a very good friend. And you don't need to know how I found you."

"Sure, Cracker, sure. You look good, man. You working out ... lifting and boxing?"

"Yeah, some, it comes and goes, you know?"

"I'm with you. In here, I have to for protection. There's a dude in here bigger than a fucking car and so I've been spotting for him, and lifting and talking to him enough he's watching my back."

We talked for thirty minutes or longer. His record was actually pretty clean. He was due out in twelve days after serving four months. He had nowhere to go at this point. I explained to him a little of my life since we last saw each other, avoiding some details ... all jails have ears, but laid it on thick enough he knew I was now successful.

During our talk, I learned he had dabbled in moving crank, but only through some coded language. He didn't like the buyers because they were crazy half the time. He knew a bunch of the dealers in the area.

I finally whispered to him, as low as I could go, about the murders and about the fact Michelle and I were planning on seeking revenge. The light bulb went on for him. He knew why I was there. He didn't even flinch.

"Ok Cracker, I'm in. What do you want me to do? How can I help you both from here?"

Michelle gawked a little when Tawon said he'd do whatever for us with no questions asked.

"Let's talk with the prosecutor and maybe the probation officer. Let's see if they can have the judge release you early. Did you have an attorney?"

"I just had a public defender. Man, you know me, I didn't have no bread to pay anyone. I did it so I just plead guilty."

"Ok. Let me try to figure out what we can do. We'll be in touch."

I had to tell Tawon of my alias before leaving. We then tracked down the Assistant District Attorney who had handled Tawon's case. She was a really attractive woman. She wore a sharp-looking gray blazer over a white blouse. I think the skirt was blue, but it could have been black. Professional indeed. I was surprised she gave us the time of the day. Looking at her desk, she had to be overworked.

I explained that Michelle and I ran several investment and real estate companies. We gave her a business card. I explained I had known Tawon years before and just learned of his predicament. I offered my belief that it might be good for Tawon, and the taxpayers of the county, if Tawon could be released to me and Michelle.

"Mr. Anderson, that is an interesting offer. One might think there are ulterior motives. Are there?"

"No, ma'am. I really just want to help him. I got lucky and turned my life straight. He hasn't had that break yet. I'd like to give him a chance at a break that I got."

She made the call for Tawon to the probation officer, who said he would sign off on anything she offered to the judge regarding an early out. She then called Judge Muriel, turned to us, and said, "Our jail is so overcrowded I think he'll go for it."

Judge Muriel was also intrigued and rightfully quizzical. He must have asked the ADA questions because she repeated my comments to him. She listened to him, wrote some notes, and gave us the thumbs-up sign. She hung up and began the paperwork. She explained it would have to be faxed to the public defender for his review and signature, which she stated was just a formality. He would gladly sign and get Phelps off the books. She said to come back after lunch. The paperwork should be completed by then, and Tawon should be allowed to go free. She said he would still have to abide by the original sentence, which included two years of probation. By the end of the day, Tawon, Michelle, and I were walking out the door.

"I owe you, Cracker, big time."

"No, you don't. I truly want to help you. So, here's what I'm thinking. I want to set you up with whatever you need to be financially secure. I want you to ask questions, not to deal, and keep your ears to the ground, and your eyes to the sky. I need you to search for anything to do with the players in the organization and especially the bastards that killed Ashley and the others?"

"Of course, man. But how am I going to explain my new found money and new shit?"

"I don't know. You've always been a good bullshitter. I have all the faith and trust in the world. You'll figure out something."

Michelle chimed in, "Why don't we make him an employee?"

"That's a great idea, Michelle. He wouldn't have to be a college graduate to identify properties that might be good buys."

"What do you say, Tawon? You think you could bullshit enough if asked about your job as a real estate investor?"

"Hell yeah, let's do it. I'm excited to help and do something else in my life."

We drove down to a local bank here and opened an account for Tawon just before they closed the doors. I used a check from one of the investment accounts. I gave Tawon a couple of business cards too. I figured $20,000 would be enough to get things rolling for him. He stared at the check, then at me, then back to the check and finally nervously signed his name. I saw a tear in his eye and he knew it and turned away.

We drove to a local apartment complex in a much better neighborhood than he had ever lived in. We were lucky again when an onsite manager could show us a two-bedroom and bath, one-level apartment. A parking slot was assigned to each apartment so that when Tawon got himself a ride, the parking space would already be taken care of. After explaining to the building manager I was setting up a new division and Tawon was going to head it, he became comfortable with me writing the first month's check and deposit from my business account.

"Tawon, you need to find some new casual clothes that fit a more business-like guy. You need to rent a car until we can create the employee records reflecting that you've been an employee for some time and something on paper noting your salary. When that is done, we can buy you a used car."

There was one of the national rent-a-car businesses down the street. We bought Tawon a car on a thirty-day rent to own plan.

The way Tawon hugged me when Michelle and I left him at his new apartment told me he was more than appreciative, which checked off one of my bucket lists of things to do.

Now, to the University of Kentucky and Brittany.

SEVENTEEN

"Woody, let me approach Brittany first. It might help her process everything if I explained to her my part in this, too. She's going to be excited, angry, relieved, mad, and nervous to see you, so maybe I can calm her a little. That okay with you?"

"Of course, that sounds like a perfect plan, and thank you for thinking of her."

We drove on the tree-lined streets in Lexington and approached closer to Brittany's apartment, hoping to spot her. Not much of a plan. I recalled a diner she had mentioned once that she enjoyed, so we tried it. We found Brittany there. Michelle entered, not looking much older than the waiters and the college kids getting meals. Michelle was wonderful. I could see through a glass window Michelle walking up to Brittany at a table in the restaurant. During a brief discussion, Brittany showed restrained excitement; and painful emotion as she looked around fervently. She excused herself from her friends and almost skipped out of the diner with Michelle. Michelle was still talking; they stopped twice and hugged and cried. I got out of the rental car and Brittany ran to me and jumped into my waiting arms; we cried together; I put her down but didn't want to.

"Oh, Brittany, I'm so sorry for this. It's killing me that mom isn't here. There was so much I wanted to do with you and her."

We hugged and talked and hugged some more. She said she was really confused and hurt when she read the letter. The cops found her a day or two later with the official news. She said she still hadn't processed it all, so when they told her, she broke down again. I had not considered how she would react to the news of her mother's murder two or three days after having already been told. Had she not reacted as one would have expected, I assumed a good detective would have looked deeper into why she hadn't.

I explained that Michelle and I were using aliases, which we would not tell her. We didn't want her to be in the uncomfortable position of explaining our new aliases to the police if they came around again.

She understood and said the police hadn't had too many questions for her. They, of course, wanted to know where I was and if we had spoken. She looked at me slyly and said, "I told them the truth: we hadn't talked."

Michelle looked at me then said, "She's as smart as you said she was."

Brittany continued and asked, "I'm confused about the checking account with my name and your name on it, but not Mom's. Why?"

I explained, "I opened up the bank account when I got the job at Baxter's. Later on, after the three of us became more comfortable as a ... family, I knew you would be going to college. I knew Mom didn't have the resources so ...." Brittany cried again and hugged me again. Her embrace felt sincere and natural—a good feeling. "If the police ask you, you can tell them the truth: it was to be used for college and general expenses."

"What about the other people, Woody?" she asked. I started to answer, but Michelle interrupted.

"Honey, like I told you earlier, my boyfriend, Terry Langfeld, was killed, too. What you don't know is that he had basically forced your dad, I mean Woody, and others, including me, to operate as part of an illegal drug organization. He and the other man killed at your house, blackmailed us, and others, for years. Your mom was just in the wrong place at the wrong time. Woody was late in coming home for dinner that night or he would have been killed too. I was lucky. I was in the garage when the bastards went into the house."

"My God! Did mom know about all this?"

I wanted to deny it, and I tried to come up with a story, but before I could answer, she knew. She just looked down, trying to process everything she'd just heard. I felt so fucking guilty I could hardly speak, so I didn't. Thankfully, Michelle came to my rescue again.

"Brittany, please understand that when I say we were all blackmailed, we were but weren't aware of the extent of the organization until we were too far in. For years, your dad and I felt we were doing a good job for Baxter's and were paid well for our service. When we found out what we were involved in, it was too late to reverse ourselves. Trust me when I say your dad and mom probably had the same devastating conversation that Terry and I had when I discovered the truth."

Brittany looked at me and then back at Michelle. "Thank you, Michelle. I think I understand. Is the money in the checking account from ... drugs?"

"No, honey. It was my payroll checks. It's all legitimate. I'm so sorry about ... everything. Your mom and I wanted to safely get away from all of this, but we never had the opportunity. We just never had the opportunity."

Before we left each other, I told her, I've got to continue to stay away from her for everyone's safety. I asked for her phone number so I could call. I said I'd be using different cell phones and not to be surprised if a different number showed up.

"Keep on working hard at school and someday we will be together. I hope you can forgive me, honey. I love you."

"I love you too, and, Michelle, I always considered him my dad."

I practically broke down with both affection and guilt for having brought Ashley and Brittany into this mess.

As we drove away, I glanced at Michelle and said, "Thank you for making this easier on her and me. I wish I could have done something, anything, to have made things easier on you. You've gone through it too."

"Just being here for me, Woody, is all I need. I know our goals are the same. I want what you want too."

"Hey, Scott … phone call on two. It's the Feds."

"This is detective Manna. May I help you?"

"Hello, Detective. This is special agent Burke with the FBI up here in Indianapolis. I've got some information for you regarding meth trafficking through your county and possibly about the murders. Can you come up to my office?"

"Of course. Is this afternoon too early?"

"This afternoon is good for me."

"Can you give me some details, like how credible is the intel?"

"I've got an informant that has fed me some information."

"How did your informant come up with this?"

Burke hesitated. "Why don't you come up here? We can sit down and talk it through."

"Well, okay. I'm going to tell the lead detective, Al Harris, about this, so both of us will be driving up. See you in an hour."

Scott found Al at his cluttered, but cop-organized, desk. "Al, we need to take a ride. I'll fill you in on the way."

On the way to the FBI office in Indianapolis, Scott relayed the information from agent Burke. "So, apparently, the Bureau has been getting information about a large meth ring in the area and they have cultivated a source. The source probably heard about the killings and hopefully has some names for us."

The FBI office was the typical government building. High granite walls and higher windows. The building is surrounded by deterrent obstacles creating a modern-day moat between the good guys and the bad guys. All types and shapes of antennas and satellite dishes dotted the roof with a catwalk encircling the entire structure. A long series of steps and ramps zig-zagged from the sidewalk up to the front entryway. No obvious rear entrance and the obligatory wrought iron fencing encircling the property at various heights, depending on the grade of the land.

Harris and Manna were escorted to the visitor's conference room by a young female. She noted Agent Burke was on his way and asked if either of the detectives wished for a cup of coffee. Neither did, so she excused herself and left. Agent Kurt Burke walked in and immediately introduced himself. In return, "I'm Al Harris, and this is my partner Scott Manna. Thanks for calling us. We've got a mess south of here."

"No problem, our source isn't here. Hopefully, he's out working, doing what he's being paid for. I'm sure I can relay the information I know as of now."

Al said, "Okay, but we understood we would have the chance to talk to your guy. It is a guy, isn't it?"

"Yeah, a guy."

"Okay, how has he learned anything about our murders?"

"A little background first. He has been working for us over the last few months. The other day he said he heard the killings down your way were done by a couple of Mexicans from Texas. They had been hired to do the job. He said he hadn't yet heard who made the contract."

"Who did he hear this from?"

"I don't know if we know that yet."

"Okay, who's your guy so we can talk to him?"

Hesitation and a change in Burke's body position. His shoulders tensed some, and he leaned back in his chair. "I can't tell you his name. He's a numbered informant."

"You can't allow us to interview him for a murder investigation? Since when?"

"I know, I know. It's … ah … FBI policy. You know, following the US Attorney's orders not to reveal informant identification until necessary, generally only at court proceedings."

Al looked at Scott and said, "That's news to me. I thought there were exceptions. So, how are we supposed to use the information you've told us?"

"Let me talk to my boss again and see about an exception."

"Before you make the call, can you at least tell us why you think your guy's information is even credible?"

"He's given us some information that has been good, and so we feel this is too."

"What do you have on him? He's working for you?"

"He was picked up by the DEA, transporting a truck with meth in Louisiana. They interviewed the guy, and he turned his bosses in and then said he had grown up here, so they introduced him to us, which is why I'm not sure we can divulge his identity yet. I think he may still also be on DEA paper."

"When did this all happen?"

"Several months ago, maybe three months now."

"Okay, not much more we can do until you get the go-ahead to let us talk to him. What's your Resident Agent in Charge's name in case our Sheriff wants to call him?"

"Kevin Wunderland and, guys, I'm just following his orders."

"Sure, talk to you later."

As they walked away, Scott said the obvious. "That was as big a tease as ever. Nothing we could use in court or even to secure a search warrant if that opportunity arose."

"Well, some things never change, Scott. The Feds are so full of themselves they won't, or can't, help real cops on a murder case. Ain't that some shit."

"Yeah, but think of the few things he told us. A trucker pulled over in Louisiana with meth a few months ago. A coincidence that two of the three targeted for murder held jobs at an engine plant that trucked engines and parts to the southern states."

"I never believed in coincidences in a murder case."I

"Me either."

"Let's get with Winger at Baxter's again and find out if any of their drivers have been stopped recently."

Agent Wunderland's office telephone line 7 lit up. This was his direct line few knew. He answered, "Hello."

The caller said, "Continue to keep the investigation under wraps."

Wunderland hung up and sat back in his chair. He had no decision that he could make without dire consequences.

They drove south to Columbus and their office. There they settled into individual four-foot-high cubicles. Manna and Harris sat caddy-corner of each other. The office was open and noisy. All police offices are similar, yet different too. Each one has its own unique atmosphere based on geography and ethnic makeup. Most have the usual posters like DARE and other anti-drug program posters; some may have child abduction flyers. The normal banter includes gutter language; inappropriate jokes; observational views of the public with no filters, so any officer with thin skin has a very rough time until their skin thickens. So, asking the squad to be quiet to make a phone call generally results in screw you or up your ass remarks, but this investigation was brutal, unique, complex, and mesmerizing. When Harris picked up his phone, stood up, and waved a hand, the entire office fell eerily silent.

"Mr. Winger, this is detective Harris again. Ah, yes, the investigation is still ongoing. May we come by to talk with you again? No sir, just more background stuff. Sure, you can have Mr. Lawson sit in. Give us a couple of hours. Is that okay? Good, we've got a few things to do before coming over. Thanks again."

Miguel called me late again. "He doesn't know we're a time zone earlier than him, I told Michelle." We had been sitting watching TV in our living room and enjoying a beer or two. Michelle had decorated the house. I knew she wanted to make it a little more like a home since we had been displaced in the worse possible way imaginable. Her apartment in Columbus was going to have to just fade away. It would be too risky for her to get in and remove any personal items. Even if she was not seen, the results would look like a flashing red light to the police. They certainly would have by now searched her apartment and cataloged the contents.

She had placed fresh-cut flowers in vases on several end tables and on the coffee table. Michelle was an excellent cook and, like me, struggling with being thrown together as a pseudo couple. She was respectful to me and me to her. But the arrangement was simply a necessity and not one of any romantic interest.

"What's up, Miguel?" I said, answering.

"I think I know what happened, my friend. The guy that took over for me, Gary Stewart, got pulled over near Baton Rouge a few months ago with a return load, you know? My guy said that the stop was very lengthy, and the trailer was searched. He never spent a day in jail, Woody. Not one day. He's got to be working for the feds."

"Well, if so, why would Tarant or whoever have targets put out on us? Why not Stewart?"

"Not sure, Woody. Isn't it possible that Tarant put the hit out on you all before Stewart?" Miguel answered.

"That's possible, but quite a coincidence, don't you think? Tarant gets the feeling or information that someone is talking at or near the same time that Stewart is picked up and begins talking with the feds?" I said.

"You're right, Woody. Almost has to have been that Tarant was told Stewart was talking."

"Well, Stewart is a walking dead man. Tarant can't allow him to continue to breathe. What makes little sense is why the feds have arrested no one?"

"I know, but you know something, Woody? He's not around here anymore. No one has seen him lately. He may already be dead."

Michelle was listening to our conversation when she chimed in, "Miguel, do you know who referred this dude to Baxter's? Terry always relied on trusted referrals."

"Oh, hi Michelle. It's sure good to hear your voice. I'm really sorry about Mr. Langfeld."

"Thank you, Miguel, that's nice of you to say. I appreciate it," Michelle answered.

"I don't know how Stewart got the job. I never really talked to him."

"How long had he been running your old route?"

"I quit a few years ago, Michelle, but I don't think he started running my old route right away. Is that important?"

"Everyone that was involved in this mess was known to Terry and me, but I don't recall this Stewart guy. Of course, when Terry was promoted to CFO, I went with him, so I wasn't privy to everything at Transportation. Can you find out how he was introduced and who hired him?"

"Ok, senorita."

EIGHTEEN

"Thanks, Mr. Winger, for seeing us."

"Not a problem. Has there been any good news about this affair?"

"No sir. Nothing we can divulge to you now. You can refer to either of us by our first names if you so choose. We've both been referred to by worse names."

"Sure thing. What can I do for you guys?"

"We're not sure if you have this information directly, but we assume you would know who to ask. Have you had any truckers stopped or arrested in the last several months?"

"I don't know. Stan probably knows."

"Stan?"

"Oh, I'm sorry. Stan Eddy, he's in charge of the Domestic Transportation Division for this plant. Hey, Julie. Call Stan in here, please."

While they waited, Al nudged Scott to look at the diploma on the wall for Winger. He had graduated from Yale.

"Stan, these detectives are with the Bartholomew County Sheriff's Office. They're investigating the murders."

"Hello, Mr. Eddy. I'm Scott Manna and this is Al Harris. He's the lead detective on this case, but I'm going to do most of the asking today. He did the last few, so his voice is a little hoarse."

"Sure, officers, what do you need from me?"

"How many truck drivers do you have?"

"Well, let me think about it for a minute. Do you mean long haulers or short local runs?"

"Long hauls for sure."

"Ok. We have four long haulers with one short route driver that fills in when needed."

"What states do you operate in that require long hauls?"

"We have plants in Texas, Alabama, and here so the long hauls are generally to those plants in Texas and Alabama."

"What do you mean ... generally?"

"Well, sometimes the loads going out include an engine or two owed to a dealer, and it makes sense to drop them off on the way when it isn't too far out of their normal route. But most of the time, the engines still need some work done at the southern plants."

"What cargo do the drivers return with?"

Winger interrupted, "Okay, like I was saying before. We send a truck full of engines and/or parts a few times a month to McAllen, Texas, or Mobile, Alabama. The Alabama plant has only just recently geared up to full production. It's only two years old. Anyway, it's cost efficient for truck transportation because we wouldn't have enough cargo to meet the train minimum weights for a better deal. The cargo we send by train goes to Mexico. The truckloads are distributed out of McAllen to dealers or the end-users in Texas and Mexico. Not all the plants build the same type of engine. So, often we ship engines for distribution through Alabama now. Sounds inefficient, but the costs to have retooled Alabama for just a few engines had been too expensive in the past. We have closed a plant in California because of the taxes, and so it had to be done."

Stan picked up the conversation. "When Mr. Langfeld transferred from McAllen to Columbus, he began to use our empty trucks on their return trip to haul for other businesses. It's all a pretty good financial arrangement."

"Okay, so we asked Mr. Winger if any of your drivers had been pulled over during their hauls in the last few months. Are you aware of any issues?"

"Yeah, we had one issue. Ah ... it was Gary Stewart. Before you ask, he quit shortly afterward, and I don't know why. I don't even recall why he was pulled over. I think he was near Baton Rouge, but I'm not sure the reason they stopped him. We never were told by him or the police. It wasn't an accident or the insurance company would have reached out to us by now."

"Who is ... was his partner?"

"Well, he didn't have a partner. Mr. Langfeld let him run alone."

Winger looked shocked. "Terry allowed that, Stan?"

"Yeah. We were short-handed for a short bit. He let Woody do single driver hauls once or twice too."

"Woody?" Winger asked.

Stan turned to Winger. "Oh yeah. Paul Woodford also drove to McAllen for him for several years."

"Who was his partner?"

"Stewart never had one, but Woody's partner used to be Miguel Cortino."

"Who is Cortino's partner now?"

"Well, he's not driving anymore, either. He still works here, but he's doing maintenance now."

"Why the change, if you know?"

"Well, his daughter had been diagnosed with brain cancer several years back. Mr. Langfeld let him move over and stop driving when the medical treatments were closer together and more painful for her. After several years of treatment, she beat it and was told she was symptom free. Although I think she still takes a lot of medicine."

"Okay, so back to this Stewart guy. Any idea where Stewart lives or went after quitting?" Scott asked.

"We have his personal residence address in HR, but no, not sure if he is still in the area. He told me once that he had a sister or an aunt in Walesboro. I'm pretty sure her last name is Oliver."

"Okay, please get me the addresses and phone numbers for both locations, please? And, thanks, guys," Scott said.

Leaving the plant, Al turned to Scott and read from a six-inch by nine-inch steno pad, "Eddy just confirmed some things."

Langfeld is linked to both McAllen and Columbus and was over trucking at Baxter's for a while.

Paul Woodford was hired by Langfeld and drove for him to at least McAllen.

Miguel Cortino worked for Langfeld as a driver to McAllen and was paired up with Woodford. Cortino is no longer driving but is still here at the plant.

Stewart drove the route to McAllen, but alone, and recently quit. We don't know why he drove alone.

Javier Muchido is a suspected drug dealer in McAllen. He operates a freelance trucking company.

Muchido was associated with Schmidt's Distributorship and so was Langfeld per Lopez in McAllen.

A return haul of Baxter's had been stopped with rotting vegetables, but no drugs as far as Lopez knew. But the FBI said that Stewart was the driver and there were drugs.

Langfeld's assistant manager, Michelle Freeman, is missing.

If Woodford had been home, three of the four known connections between Columbus and McAllen would have been killed.

Stewart is also missing, or at least hasn't reported to Burke.

Cortino is the only known Baxter employee who connects McAllen and Columbus and who isn't missing.

Scott asked, "What has changed or happened that someone thought they needed to silence this group? The answer has to be Stewart—right? And, is Cortino a probable suspect?"

"Obviously, someone they worked for, or with, got spooked. Let's talk again to Lopez in McAllen, who told us about their task force information and if they're aware of Stewart. We also need to talk to Cortino. Scott, would you set that interview up please? I've got to finish some reports?"

"Sure thing, Al. I'll get it done."

Scott contacted Winger and Eddy to line up the interview of Cortino at the Sheriff's Office.

"Hey, it's me. Can you talk?" Miguel asked as soon as I picked up the telephone.

"Of course, Miguel. Are you okay?"

"Si. The cops asked to interview me. Just wanted you to know."

"When are you meeting with them?"

"Tomorrow. Do you have any advice?"

Michelle interjected, "Miguel, what you need to do is tell the truth, except for speaking to us. Everything else can be told truthfully, understand?"

"Well, I guess so. I think I understand. I just don't want to go to jail or say something that hurts either of you two."

I said, "You'll be fine Miguel. They're not investigating for the drugs, just the murders. Call us when you can to let us know how it went."

Miguel drove slowly to the Sheriff's Office, thinking of what the cops would ask him. He had slept poorly, imagining all the things they might ask. He was no longer concerned about the hauls anymore. Elizabeth was well, and that's what most mattered. How do I protect Woody and now Michelle? Should I protect both? Of course, I must. Should I hire an attorney? Oh, man. If I do, they'll know something's up. He took Michelle and Woody's advice and tell the truth, except for their contact.

Miguel walked into the Sheriff's Office and asked for detectives, Manna and Harris. He was walked down the light gray tiled floor hall to the interview room. A metal-colored door with a small window was opened by a deputy. The small, square concrete-walled space had one door and only the small window in the door. One mirror. He had wondered while he walked down the hall if he was going to his doom. He sat in the uncomfortable chair he was directed to take and was asked if he wanted a beverage of his choice. He wanted a beer but asked for a diet soda. He waited two minutes. It seemed like an hour.

Harris and Manna entered and introduced themselves.

"Thank you, Mr. Cortino, for agreeing to this request," Scott said.

Miguel nervously asked, "Is this important?"

Al said, "Yes, Mr. Cortino, this is a very important interview. We're hoping you can help us understand some workings at Baxter's."

"Sure, Detectives. Glad to help if I can. I'm not sure I know much, and you guys can call me Miguel," He said as he took a quick drink.

Al, as the lead detective, began the interview. "Okay, Miguel. Give us the story of Miguel Cortino at Baxter's. Just tell us from when you started and include your different jobs. By the way, your English is very good. Did you grow up in America?"

Miguel said, "Yes, I was actually born here in Indiana. My parents spoke Spanish, so I grew up bilingual from the start. I've been with the company now for eighteen years. I started in the maintenance division working for Frank Hall. He's no longer with the company. He retired several years after I started. I stayed there for seven years when there was an opening in transportation. I applied for it because the pay was better and I was tired of the maintenance job. Scott Crosby was my boss then, but he retired soon after I started. Terry Langfeld then moved here from the McAllen plant and took Crosby's position. Sometime soon after that, he found out about my daughter."

"What about your daughter, Miguel?"

Miguel took a long drink. "Elizabeth was diagnosed with a unique brain cancer, one that is treatable at only a few medical hospitals. Mr. Langfeld gave me permission to drive a different route. That allowed me the opportunity to take her for the treatments."

"What was different about the route?"

"Well, I normally drove with Jorge Taylor to the McAllen plant and then straight back. We drove that route about every ten to thirteen days, depending on a lot of factors I wasn't part of. The alternative route was only every three weeks. I got paid for forty hours a week, but only had to show up at the plant on the days we drove. The entire round trip was generally six days and accounted for up to 120 hours, so each trip equaled three weeks of work and then the fourth week we would run again. I drove that route for several years with Jorge and later with Woody."

Al interrupted, "Tell us what you know about Mr. Woodford please."

Miguel drank again and thought about his answer, "Well, he started driving with me when Jorge was deported, about five years ago maybe. Anyway, I know little about Woody. He never talked about family much. He liked to read, so the long hauls were perfect for him to read. I think he read almost anything. He read a bunch about accounting and stuff like that. He and Ms. Ashley dated, and then he moved in with her; they were thrilled. Then Mr. Langfeld transferred Woody to the accounting department, so I didn't have a partner for a little while, but then Mr. Langfeld allowed me to transfer back to maintenance."

"When was that?"

"When my daughter started having more treatments closer together. I couldn't drive her there, so Mr. Langfeld allowed me to switch jobs. It was maybe two years ago."

Harris asked the sixty-four-thousand-dollar question. "Do you know anything about the murders at the Thompson home?"

"No sir, no idea, and I am worried for Woody's safety." This he had practiced making sure not to mention Michelle's name.

"Miguel, do you have any idea where he is?"

Miguel drank the last of the soda. "No, I don't have any clue. Like I said, he never told me much about family. I think his dad is in prison, but I don't know where. That's why I'm worried about his safety."

"Would your friend Woody have been able to have committed the killings?"

"Oh, no way. He loved Ms. Ashley."

"You obviously know Mr. Langfeld, but did you know the other male victim?" Manna interjected.

"I read in the paper, or saw on TV, his name was Muchido and that he worked at a trucking company named Dos Amigos. That's all I know."

"Is there anyone that Woody trusts to protect him if he's running from the killer or killers?"

"I can't think of anyone. I'm really worried now because your questions lead me to feel he hasn't been found."

"Miguel, we understand that on your return trips from Texas, Langfeld had planned with another company to haul other items for other businesses. What stuff, and where did you go?"

"Terry, ah Mr. Langfeld, and a guy that owned a Food Distribution company realized that if we trucked their old fruits and vegetables to a couple of other locations, or directly to hog farms, both of them could make a little of money from the rotting crap," Miguel gleefully said.

"That's really an interesting pact. Why would they move their rotting vegetables rather than just dump them?"

"I think they sold them to the hog farms. You know hogs eat almost anything."

"How did you load and unload the rotting ... food?"

"We didn't. That was done by others. We just drove. No big deal."

"What was the name of the company, and what about those other locations?"

"Schmidt's Distributors & Parson's Fruits and Vegetables, and we dropped off in Atlanta, a place near Alice Texas, Biloxi, New Orleans, and Kansas City. Various hog farms too."

"Were you ever stopped by police or by any state Weights and Standards officers?"

"A few times for minor infractions, like a busted taillight. Our logbooks were always spot on and we never drove over the time limits. The weights we hauled to Texas were much heavier than those we returned with."

"How was the rotting food crated or boxed?"

Miguel wasn't ready for that question. "I don't know," he fumbled. "I said they were loaded and unloaded by workers at Schmidt's. I never saw how it was boxed or crated."

Scott and Al both were quiet and reflective. "Thank you, Miguel. We appreciate your help. Please contact us if you think of anything else and especially if Woody contacts you. He hasn't contacted you, has he?"

Miguel was surprised a little, but quickly recovered and answered, "I don't have any idea where he's at." Which didn't answer the question, but nothing was said.

Miguel exited and took a deep breath at his car. The day was cloudy and looking like a storm brewing. He hoped it wasn't an omen.

NINETEEN

Alonzo Morelo sat on a white pool chair at the Aruba Marriott Resort & Casino, looking westward at the sundown. Dark red lines encircled by burnt orange peeking through a distant gathering of clouds on the horizon. It reminded him of his youth when he looked out over the Pacific Ocean from his homeland in Costa Rica. The colors always were optimistic no matter their hues. He was flanked by several bodyguards ... or at least bodybuilders, and a couple of gorgeous bikini-clad girls. Even though it was in the nineties, the guards wore long beige pants and Hawaiian type three-button-down shirts. Morelo called out to one of his guards and asked for a phone. The guard dutifully handed him a cell phone and backed up to his prior position.

Morelo hit a button on the phone and raised it to his left ear. "Hello, my friend. Have our problems in Indiana been taken care of?"

Peter Tarant jumped when the call came through because he knew what was going to be asked. He answered on the second ring. He was dreading this call and from whom it came. "No, amigo. One target was not at the dinner," Tarant answered.

"That's not good news," Morelo said sternly. "How are you going to fix the problem?"

Tarant shivered a little, took a quick breath to calm his nerves. He answered, "I learned of a mole we have up there at the same time the main problems were supposed to have been taken care of. We hadn't the opportunity to fix both ... but it needs to be handled."

"Let me make it perfectly clear, Peter. I don't want any loose ends ... do you understand?"

"It will be taken care of," Tarant tensely replied.

"You and I are expendable if 'he' finds out. I'm relying on you because you told me there were problems. I trusted that whoever or whatever the problems were, all would be dealt with."

"Yes, sir, I understand, and I will take care of it personally if need be. Sir, if I may, what happened that ... all of this was needed?"

Morelo considered the question and weighed an answer, "Higher-ups than you know want to get out of the business and switch to, ah ... something else. Something that I am very keen on. It was decided that if Javier, Terry, and the Woodford kid were stealing money, they were the three most involved in the business; a complete scrubbing would cut all ties with suppliers and buyers. That is all you need to know."

Tarant breathed a sigh of relief. He hadn't been involved in the scheme. He had knowledge because of a few meetings where details were shared, but his hands were clean. "Thanks, boss. I understand now the urgency."

"See that you do. I expect word before the end of the week." With that, he threw the phone to the guard, who took out the SIM card and then stepped on the phone, crushing it. The phone was then discarded into a trash bin.

About two thousand miles away, Tarant looked at his phone and thought about the money man, Woodford, who hadn't been found and, therefore, not taken care of. Tarant himself wanted Woodford taken care of because he was close to Langfeld, and he was sure Woodford had been pocketing the money, his money.

Morelo had specifically told Tarant to make Langfeld and Muchido no more. He never said why exactly, but Tarant had the feeling it had to do with missing money or drugs. The fact was the mole Morelo referred to was Stewart and had most likely talked to the Feds in Louisiana. Obviously worrisome, but that could be fixed. The bigger picture was what Stewart may have found out about the Indiana/Texas connection and told to the feds. The information Tarant had garnered from his sources, which suggested the Feds hadn't yet responded to anything Stewart might have imparted. The problem as he saw it was the damn Bartholomew County Sheriff's Office detectives reaching out because of the murders; that was going to be an issue. Nothing he could do about them now. Hanson needed to wall off the investigation at his end. He grabbed his phone and punched a speed dial digit.

"Hello, this is Peter Tarant. I need to speak with Don ... Hello, Don. I'll make this quick. What can you tell me about the investigation into Javier's murder up in Indiana?"

Hanson responded, "I was telephoned from one of the detectives handling the case, a Detective Manna. He didn't tell me too much. He wanted to know about the family and who to contact regarding Javier's death, but I explained Isabella is in Mexico and it would be better that I relay the news. He was okay with that."

"Okay, nothing else?" Tarant asked.

"He said that Langfeld was killed, along with a female by the name of Thompson. I don't know who that is, do you?"

"She's the broad that Woodford lived with. Where's he, by the way?" asked Tarant.

Hanson nervously squeaked, "I don't have any idea about him. Who is he?"

"You haven't heard of him?"

"No, should I have?" Hanson answered, somewhat alarmed.

Tarant thought about this response and then answered, "Never mind, then. Just keep your eyes and ears open. Call me if something unusual happens regarding the investigation. We don't need them cops sniffing around."

"Ok, Mr. Tarant, will do. Am I supposed to check around down here for this Woodford guy?"

"No, just keep your eyes and ears open for now."

Michelle and I were trying to take it easy on the side porch in Topsail Beach, wondering how Miguel's interview had gone. The ocean view was as splendid as ever. A golden orangeish hue with a blue border and sunrays spreading out from the center. Seagulls swooping, landing, and taking wing as coordinated as any trained marching band. A true postcard moment. But we were on edge. So many things could go wrong for us. So many things had already gone ... bad. I didn't know how I would react if more went to shit.

Michelle had brought me a piece of toast with some strawberry jam and sat down on a lounge chair. I saw she had a bowl of brown sugar oats. The phone rang. I jumped. I saw it was Miguel and breathed a sigh of relief. "Hello Miguel, we've been wondering how yesterday went and if you uncovered any more info on Stewart?"

"Well, the interview went okay. They were just looking for general background and how the hauls were done. No big deal. They wanted to know anything about you, Woody, and I truly know little about your family, so all I could tell them was that you liked to read a lot. They know Javier owns Dos Amigos."

"Did they ask anything you weren't ready for?" I asked.

"Not really. They asked if I knew how the rotting food was crated or boxed. I wasn't sure anyway and told them I never loaded or unloaded, which was the truth."

"Did they ask about me and Michelle?"

"About you, yes, but not about Michelle, which I thought was strange. I think they were baiting me."

"What did you say about me and where I am?"

"I answered honestly."

"What!?"

"Hey man, I said I didn't know where you were, which is the truth," Miguel smirked.

Letting out a sigh, I said, "Oh, that's just rude man. You almost gave me a heart attack."

"No, I wouldn't give you up. I know what you did for me when you spoke with Terry."

"Sounds like it went well. Did you ever dig up any more information on Stewart?"

"Yeah, he's holed up in Walesboro with his sister, a Mrs. Oliver."

Miguel added, "It sounded like he was scared, so he must have talked to the Feds. My guy at Rotten Tomatoes said Tarant and others are not using the regular phones anymore too. They're only talking on burner phones."

"There are powers higher than us, and they are out of control. They're pissed off and killing anyone they think has knowledge of them. You be careful, Miguel."

"I will, and you too," Miguel said.

I turned to Michelle, "We need to make a road trip back to Indiana."

"Are you sure, Woody?"

"Yeah, we need to talk with Stewart to find out what he knows and what he's said to whomever, and we have to do it without the Feds knowing."

Michele noted, "Let's fly instead of driving. That's a long haul. We can also get out of dodge quickly if we need to."

"Okay, would you call for the tickets? I'm going next door to ask Mr. Fleck a couple of things."

As I walked next door, I recognized that the beautiful sunrise had nearly vanished. A storm was developing quickly to the south. It appeared to be moving inland. The winds were out of the south too, so it wouldn't be long before we would get some rain. I knocked on the door.

"Jim, are you busy?"

"No, come on in, Paul. Nice day, isn't it?"

"So far, Jim, but it sure looks like rain is on the way. We've grown fond of the weather here, but we need the rain too. The skies and the sunrises are gorgeous. And now that I just said how much we love it here, I wanted to let you know Michelle and I are leaving for business. Before we go, I want to ask you a strange question about your career."

"Sure, what's up?"

"Well, I'm curious about informants. Michelle and I were watching TV the other night and the cop show dealt with an informant who wasn't working so well. When you had informants, how did you make sure they were safe from … you know, the bad guys, and still telling you the truth?"

"Ha! They were bad guys before we made them informants, Paul! They were good at keeping safe because their livelihoods depended on their survival techniques. Now the authentic part. That's a whole other matter."

"Well, I'm a little embarrassed. I know nothing about that dichotomy," I responded.

"Nah, don't be. Using informants sometimes is like beating your head against a cement wall. They seldom are reliable for keeping on-time appointments while you're wasting time away from your family. However, we usually worked our way through it. It changes a little as you get closer to court dates because you have to make sure your informant is ready to testify. Why the curiosity?"

"Well, again a little embarrassed. Like I said, we were

watching one of those cop and robber TV shows the other day and the cops lost, or rather, couldn't locate their guy, and they were really scrambling. The show made them look more concerned for the guy's safety at the same time they were worried about the case. Were we reading too much into that? I always thought that cops cared little for the safety of informants."

"Well, it's a little complicated. You need to understand that informants, generally, are defendants that got caught but have not yet been charged. Their crime is much less egregious than that of your major target or targets. They are informants because the cop feels they can lead to those targets. So, you encourage them to work for you as an informant, hoping once everything is over and the informant pleads guilty to the charges, the judge won't sentence them as strongly because of their cooperation and assistance. It evolves into an employer-employee relationship. The informant usually only wants to do just enough to get his get-out-of-jail card stamped and then go back to the environment he was accustomed to."

I said, "Okay, I think I follow."

"Remember, most cops want to use the informant as long as it is practical to do. The cop needs to get credible intelligence on as many investigations as possible. You're somewhat correct about the low concern a cop has for an informant's health, but that changes as the informant becomes more and more valuable. Also, remember, the informant is paid for information. That is a big motivator for many informants to keep somewhat on the straight and narrow. Some informants make it a job, so they're much more aware and cautious about getting caught by the bad guys. The cops also begin to get closer to the informant and sometimes develop a strange friendship. Sometimes covering years."

"So," I queried, "if the informant wanted to get out from under the thumb of a cop, he would have to disappear because he still could be charged with an earlier crime?"

"Exactly, that's why some will do as little as possible and call a lawyer to help them out of their situation."

"Okay, cool," I said. "I know it's corny for me to ask, but law enforcement is such an interesting subject. I hope you don't mind my stupid questions."

"No, not at all, Paul. It gives me a chance to relive some old, but good times. Have a safe trip."

"We will, thanks."

So, of course, just off his porch, it thundered and began to rain cats-and-dogs. I was drenched by the time I reached my back porch door. "Hey Michelle, did you get the tickets?"

She came out of the bathroom, obviously after a shower. She had on only her pink bathrobe. She looked good. Looking longer than I had expected, I felt embarrassed. Ashley had been gone a short while but ... I guess human biological desires don't get time-off for compassion. Michelle looked like a weight-lifting athlete. She noticed me hovering.

"Yeah, we're on the two o'clock to Louisville. I'll drive to the airport. You drive like an old lady." I laughed because of her comment, but also to hide my staring. I rushed to my room to shower off the rain and begin to pack. It felt oddly good that she had needled me.

The flight from Wilmington to Louisville stopped over in Charlotte. It was a fifty-five-minute layover, so we ordered a quick bite to eat. We sat in the usual airport food garden with every type of person you could think of. I'm normally always interested in "watching" the crowd, visualizing their lives away from the airport, or imagining their conversation. I don't know why I do, but I do it in any large gathering of people. I've always assumed it's a defense mechanism, due in part to the wariness my dad instilled in me.

In Louisville, we rented a dark green Ford Ranger pickup. It's every bit of an hour and a half drive north on I-65 to Walesboro, and on the way, we discussed again how we wanted to approach Stewart.

Michelle said, "How about me approaching him one on one? I don't recall ever meeting him. You know, I can say that I used to work for Terry and I understand he did too and see where we take."

"Maybe," I said, thinking out loud. "If he's lying low from Tarant, he might not talk to anyone, anyway."

"I assume we will have to lure him away from his sister's house somehow," Michelle said. "I don't know how we can do it though."

I said, "We may have to just knock on the door and hope. Not much of a plan, but if he lets us tell him who we are, he may give us the chance. He's got to know there's a target on his back and know there is one on mine too."

"Okay, we'll ad-lib it," Michelle said.

TWENTY

Mrs. Oliver's house was a small cookie-cutter type, seemingly on the same street where some family TV shows were filmed. It looked a lot like the Thirtysomething house of Hope Steadman. A Chevrolet parked in the driveway, no less. Sidewalks too. Yep, American as apple pie.

I rang the doorbell; the ring was that of echoing church bells. Michelle and I waited, but no answer. No sounds at all. It was approximately eight in the evening. Sundown had been thirty minutes earlier, but there was a three-quarter moon peeping through a slim cloud cover. We had parked a block up the street and had walked along the sidewalk on the other side of the street. No cars drove by, and no one had been outside, no children playing.

"Hey, Woody, look at this," Michelle said, pointing to trampled coneflowers and lamb's ears under the large front glass window on the left side of the house.

I couldn't see in the window because of the closed drapes. It had sprinkled in the day. It was clear someone had walked on the flowers recently. We put on our gloves. We walked together around the left side of the house and away from the garage, which was on the opposite side. On the left side, there were several windows. A side entry door about halfway down the length of the house. The neighbor's home looked to be about sixty feet away, and a four-foot-high walnut-stained fence ran the entire length of the property line, obviously to keep a pet inside, not for privacy. No movements in or out of either house.

As we crept slowly down the left side of the house with Michelle in the lead, she groaned. "Oh shit! No ... look in the window, Woody."

I peered into the window, which looked into the dining area of the house. A white male lay on his right side on the floor, covered in blood. There didn't appear to be anyone else near him. We crouched down and duck-walked past the next window to the side door, which entered the kitchen. I pointed towards the door jamb so Michelle could see it had been jimmied, splintered jaggedly. She responded and avoided snagging her clothes.

Michelle eyed me and gave me hand signals I should go in first and then veer off immediately toward the body; she would follow straight in behind me. Neither of us brought a gun. If someone was still in the house, we were going to have to be on our toes.

As I entered and approached the male, I could hear him gasping, choking, wheezing. "He's still alive," I whispered.

He was red-headed, but now a much darker red was strewn through his scalp. He was alive, but it would not be long before he would take his last breath. Michelle turned to me after she had looked down the hallway and said, "There isn't anything we can do for him even if we had an onsite trauma team. He's almost bled out."

I got close and asked, "Hey man, we've called for an ambulance. Just hold on, okay?"

"He choked out a 'thanks'."

"Who did this to you?" I asked.

His eyes darted around and were glazing over. I didn't think he could answer me, so I leaned further over his chest. He barely could see me for the damage to his face and head. His chest looked to have been severely beaten in, and one arm looked to be broken. I turned away and took a deep breath. He stared at me with concern and fear. He croaked, "Tarant. Are you the FBI ... with Burke?"

There was no doubt this dying mane was Stewart. I answered, "Yes, I'm working with him. He's on his way too. The ambulance is five minutes out. When did this happen?"

He gurgled, spit, and struggled to speak. "My notes ... are at ... the drop site."

Michelle quickly asked, "Which drop site, Gary? Burke uses over one secured spot."

He turned towards her voice, just now noticing someone else in the room. He gurgled, "Under the 9th Street ... Park ... bench ... corner."

"Okay," Michelle said, "I know exactly which one you're talking about. I've used it myself."

He began to speak again, but he exhaled a muffled sigh and gurgle; his eyes rolled up and back, and he was gone. We just watched him for a moment. "Mrs. Oliver! Jesus, is she here?" I said out loud, but in a hushed voice.

Michelle was thinking the same, already on her way down the hardwood-covered hallway. I saw she was glued to one wall, sliding down the hall. A bedroom door towards the end of the hall was opened a little with a light showing. She glanced in, and I heard a gasp. I went down the hallway on the same side as Michelle.

Mrs. Oliver had been bludgeoned repeatedly with a baseball bat which had been left next to her on the floor. It was a terrible sight. It was hard to discern what color hair she had or the correct shade of her blouse. There was blood spattered all over the bedroom and on the inside of the window. The mattress where she lay was darkened red. Her arms were contorted and had been struck many times in her vain attempts to defend herself. She had only one shoe on, and the other was lying on top of the dresser five feet away.

Michelle said, "This looks like the Taliban tortured and killed her. Pure hatred."

The room had been tossed. Same as the rest of the house. I told Michelle that the murderers had to have been here for some time in order to have done what we were seeing. Another bedroom converted as an office was trashed. Someone had been looking for something that Stewart hadn't told them about, but considered having been secreted there. If it was Tarant or his soldiers, would they have known, or suspected, there were notes?

I told Michelle, "Look at the floor. Anything of interest?"

"No bloody footprints. That's why I stepped the way I had."

"Right. How can that be possible? Mrs. Oliver's room's walls are covered. How could there be no footprints?"

Michelle paused. "Would the person or persons have brought a change of clothes?"

"And shoes. That's … just … scary wrong. I was dumbfounded. Damn, Michelle, that's careful planning or reflects past deeds."

We walked out the way we had come in, making sure nothing had been disturbed, nor had we left any bloody footprints. The living room had been searched. Furniture, table drawers were thrown around, doors had almost been torn off their hinges. We had accomplished what we could; we knew it was Tarant who so viciously killed these two. We walked back to the rental and drove straight to the ninth Street Park.

We sat in the car looking at the two benches on the corner for ten to fifteen minutes. It was ten p.m. "Most assuredly. We need to talk with Stewart to find out what he knows and what he's said to whomever, and we have to do it without the Feds knowing."

"Woody, how long before you think the cops are going to be notified?"

"Unless Mrs. Oliver had an appointment with family last night or today, I'd say not until sometime tomorrow. Is there a Mr. Oliver?"

"I don't think so. The bedroom didn't have any male shoes or clothes."

"Let's find a hotel room. We'll try our luck in the morning to find the notes Stewart spoke about. I think we both have changed our looks enough to rent a room in the area for one night, don't you think?" I wondered.

We found a low-rent motel on the outskirts of town. I said, "I'll sleep on the couch." She went in and booked the night for Mr. and Mrs. Beyer with a six o'clock wake-up call. Neither of us slept well. We both were awake by five-thirty.

We showered, cleaned up, and walked next door to a service station with a diner attached. Neither of us had been at either before and requested a couple of coffees to go. We discussed the obvious. Stewart said it had been Tarant. He didn't say Tarant sent someone. He said it was Tarant. Specific. Direct. Resolute. Nothing more to say.

I asked Michelle, "What about the Fed, Burke? Why would Stewart make notes for him rather than just tell him the information he had found?"

"I don't know. I don't know," Michelle said. "I would think it would have been much easier, and not the least of which better secured, to just pick up the phone or meet and tell him face to face."

We drove to the ninth Street Park. On the way, I stopped at a local coffee shop I had never frequented. According to Michelle, she hadn't either. She went in and bought two more coffees, which proved substantially better than the service station's brew earlier. Hers was an espresso and mine with half and half creamer.

We found the park to be without kids. No adults either. Nothing happening. Too early. Michelle walked over and sat down on a bench. She drank some of her espresso and leaned down to set it on the ground; as she did, she searched underneath the bench as far as her arms allowed. She had to stand and walk over to the other bench before feeling a brown eight-by-eleven sealable envelope, and brought it up to her chest and slid it under the jacket, then walked back to our rental. She slid into the medium-sized Ford truck. We drove off and out of the city.

We stopped at a rest stop five miles south toward Louisville.

Michelle read the notes. We were astounded by how much Stewart had learned. "I don't think he has briefed the Feds on this yet, Woody," she said. "And I don't think it's just drugs that are being moved. Stewart wrote, referencing various types of handguns, Sig Sauer, Glock, Berettas, and some foreign manufactures. Most had quantities next to the brands."

"I doubt anyone will connect Tarant to Stewart, do you?"

"No, I hope not. I want Tarant for myself," quickly, looking at me and adding, "I mean for us."

"I know what you meant," I said, gritting my teeth. "I still can't get the picture of Mrs. Oliver out of my head. We need to warn Miguel, and I need to make a second stop."

We drove over to Mrs. D's house. I parked in the alley that ran the full length of her street, splitting the back yards on all the houses on her block. Several of the homes had maple trees and one oak that shaped the alley like a bowling lane. We waited alongside a maple for her to leave through the back door as she had done for years. Around seven o'clock, as was her routine, she walked out her back door towards her car. I rolled down my window and, trying not to scare her to death, whispered, "It's me."

She did jump, but then, seeing me, she beamed and bolted to the car. "I just knew you'd come back, honey," she cried.

"No, I'm not back. I'm just riding through. I got caught up in something big and awful, Mrs. D. I want to explain, but I don't have enough time to do it justice. Just know that I haven't lifted a finger towards anyone. I'm going to fix this. You use that money I gave you wisely," I instructed.

She said, "The police haven't talked to me yet. I figure it's because Brittany is an adult and I haven't babysat for years even though I always came by to help Ms. Ashley."

"Have you talked with Brittany yet?" Michelle asked.

Mrs. D sort of did a double-take when she saw Michelle. "Yes ma'am, I have. She knows the score. She's a strong young lady."

I said, "Mrs. D, this is Michelle Freeman. She was a guest at our house when Ashley and the others were killed. She only escaped because she was in the garage at the time. We're putting together the pieces of what happened and are going to make amends together. When it's safe, we will go to the police."

"Okay honey. You two be careful."

I said, "You keep tabs on Brittany and remember the phones have ears, okay?" I said.

"I understand, Woody, I love you. Be careful."

We drove back to I-65 and then south on the way to Louisville when my phone rang. It was Tawon.

"Hey, bro, what's shaking?" I asked.

"Hey, Big Cracker, I gots some news for you. You know that old white dude we used to deal with by the overpass on County Line Road by the airport?"

"Yeah, sure. Why?"

"He knows about your boys. They've been moving that meth shit for some time through a trucking company out of McAllen. Not heavyweights, but consistent and high quality. He also said there may be some metal, too. And, get this, homeboy, guess what the name of the trucking company is: Dos Amigos Trucking. Your Javier is, was, an owner, but the lawyer dude has a lot of pull too. My guy didn't know his name, at least not yet."

"Tawon, you're awesome. Why is the white dude talking to you about this?"

"I told him that someone in their organization killed my

brother's wife. It's all he needed to hear. He said that there's another dude up the ladder who provides some muscle when needed. He thinks his name is Peter or Paul, but he wasn't sure."

"Yep, Peter is right. His last name is Tarant. He just killed a snitch in one of their distributor's businesses up in Indiana. Killed the sister too. Bashed both of their heads in. A real piece of work."

"Ah man, that's fucked up, bro. What else can I do to help?"

"Kind of hard to ask you to do anything more. But if you happened to get eyes on this Tarant guy, that would be ideal. Do you have anyone down that way that you can trust with your life because that's what's necessary?"

"I think so, Woody. I'll check around to be sure. What are you thinking?"

"Just thinking, my man. Just thinking."

TWENTY-ONE

I hung up with Tawon and turned to Michelle. "We need to exchange the tickets from Wilmington to San Antonio. We'll drive from there to McAllen. I'm going to assume that Tawon will have gotten with someone by then to help. If not, we'll just have to make do. We're close. I can feel it."

The flight change was seamless, but we had to wait until the next morning. We drove to Louisville and lodged near the airport, again as the Beyers.

The following morning, Michelle said on the way to our boarding gate, "Okay, we're going to need to score some guns ... I'm not walking into this man's neighborhood with just my hands, you know?"

"We'll do it in San Antonio, which shouldn't be too hard."

As we waited at the San Antonio baggage claim, Michelle called the Bartholomew County Sheriff's Office hotline:

"Yes, I've got information for you regarding those murders a month ago. You've got two more in Walesboro, and you need to call the FBI and ask for Burke." She hung up. She then took out the Sim card and threw the phone in the closest trash bin.

"Agent Burke, you have a call on two," the voice came over the intercom.

"This is Kurt Burke. How can I help you?"

"This is Harris again with the Bartholomew County Sheriff's Office. We just received a call on our hotline regarding the triple murders last month. A female called in and said we have two more dead; we needed to call you, so we are. Now, do you think maybe you, your boss, and the FBI procedures could help us investigate five fucking murders in my county!"

Burke instantly knew who was dead. He stammered and stuttered, finally saying to Harris, "I'm pretty sure one body is that of Gary Stewart. I don't know who the other person might be. Stewart is ... was our informant. He went off the grid about two weeks after the first murders. I wasn't sure if he was, or is, connected to your case, so I wasn't sure what to say, and my boss had advised me to sit on it until a link was made. Your hotline caller puts them together."

"How could you not know there was a connection? Baxter's is the link to all the murders!"

"I don't know how to answer that," he weakly muttered. Burke was defeated: not by the detectives, but by his own boss and policies. He began spilling the beans as he knew them.

"Stewart was picked up in a DEA sting in Louisiana a couple of months back. He was a truck driver for Baxter's returning with a subcontracted haul of produce going to Arkansas. The DEA had had a source to tell them the load included meth and guns. I'm not clear of all the probable cause evidence that produced the warrant, but there was some meth found in the trailer—not the cab. It wasn't a lot, but enough to make Stewart convinced it was better to work for the government rather than against them. The DEA didn't want to work him because they were concerned he might unknowingly burn the original snitch, so they got with the local FBI office, who referred him to us since Baxter's is located here and where Stewart lived."

"Go on," Al said.

"He made one more run to McAllen, but just up and quit after he returned. I had initially debriefed him about what he knew. He connected Langfeld to McAllen and Schmidt's Distributors. Langfeld had set up some kind of contract for the return trip to haul loads for Schmidt's. Stewart said he didn't know what he was hauling except to say it stunk to high heaven."

"He was supposed to meet with me two weeks ago and provide me with more information. That's all I know, and I'm sorry. Sometimes the FBI protocol, and the bosses, are our own worst enemy."

"As pissed as your agency has made me, Burke, where should we be looking for Stewart?"

Burke relented. "He's not at his residence in Columbus. You probably should go to his sister's in Walesboro. He's called me from there once. Burke gave Harris the needed information and said, I'll tell my boss, Wunderland, as soon as I hang up. I hope he'll do everything to assist your office in the murder investigations."

"Damn nice of you," Harris said and slammed his phone down, almost breaking the outer shell box.

Scott leaned over his desk and squinted through the sunlight streaming into the squad room, "Hey Al, think maybe the high and mighty Feds might have got the hint that murder investigations are more important than one of their fucking sources?"

"I doubt it, Scott. They're so wrapped up in their own world most of them don't understand that street cops are important too."

"Stewart's the guy that Langfeld allowed solo trips when in the past they worked as two-man teams—right?"

"Yep, and they did not know why he just up and quit. They clearly wouldn't have known he was working with the Bureau." Harris got on the phone to dispatch, "Mary, would you have a couple of units respond to the address for Mrs. Oliver. Tell them to secure the house; it's probably a crime scene."

Mary said, "Sure honey."

"Dispatch to Deputy Rowley?" When Rowley answered, she advised him what Harris wanted.

Al and Scott stood up from their respective desks and started down the hall. Al asked Scott, "You care to drive? I want to make some notes."

"Sure, no problem, Al. Do you care if we stop at my place? I need to change this shirt. I spilled half a pot of coffee on it this morning."

"I was wondering if you bought the shirt at the Goodwill Store."

They began their fifteen-minute drive, but five minutes after they left Scott's house, Deputy Rowley broadcast, "This is a 10-100. No suspects located. Need backup."

Harris telephoned dispatch and had Mary connect him to Rowley. Al said, "Deputy, are you at the address given?"

"Yes sir, two bodies, one male one female."

"Control the location. We're on our way." Scott had already been in contact with dispatch to rush EMS, the Coroner, and at least three other units to the address ASAP.

At the crime scene, scanning the interior of the house and the blood spatter over what seemed like the entire home, Scott said, "Jesus Al, look at this. What's the probable time of death?"

"I'm guessing in the last two days."

"This is worse than the Thompson house. There it was, clean, or as clean as a triple-murder scene can be. Gunshots and nothing else. Here ... just an awful beating with a damn baseball bat! Good Lord!"

For the second time in several months, the detectives began a murder investigation, shaking their heads with grief, despair, and wonderment. "Al, look at this, pointing to the flower beds at the front of the home."

"The flowers have been trampled on and by over one person,

too. Look at the different sizes of shoes. Scott, this one over here looks more like a child's footprint."

"No, I think it's more likely a woman's foot. It reminds me of my wife's. But there is only one print, and it looks like it may have been made before the other prints because those prints stepped over the top."

"Scott, the deputies that canvassed the neighbors are ready for an update, are you?"

"Yeah, Al, let's get that done."

Scott called over one of the officers at the scene. "Let's hear what you've found, deputy."

"Yes sir. We've spoken to most of the area residents and no one recalled hearing or seeing anything. In fact, they're not sure when they last saw Mrs. Oliver at the house. Several noted her brother had visited recently but didn't know if he was still in town. The car in the driveway is Mrs. Oliver's. Several neighbors said that Mr. Oliver hadn't lived here in years but didn't know if they were divorced or just separated. There wasn't any inkling that there may have been issues between them, at least to this degree."

"Okay, officer, thank you. Have you all begun to identify family members for notifications?"

"Yes sir. Trenton is making those calls."

"Okay, make sure the evidence team has full access but not so that it prohibits the coroner."

Al and Scott stood, taking in the scene before them, and almost in unison, shook their heads again. Al finally said what they both were feeling. "This is a mess; it's too big for you and me. We're going to have to call for more help and the FBI since it's their informant. Damn hard to call Burke after those bastards already screwed us once. What do you think?"

"We're probably going to need to approach them and ask. Maybe the Sheriff will make that call?"

"The hotline caller was a female—right, Scott? Could the footprints of the female here be our mystery caller?"

"I doubt it. Not unless the killer and she were playing games with us."

"But how else would she know about the murders and this address within a day of the murders?"

"Maybe she's just a neighbor or someone not willing to identify herself. Probably for her own safety."

"Could be. You're probably right, Al," he said as his phone rang. "Hello, Manna here. Oh, that's good news. I'll tell him. He's standing here next to me."

"Hey Al, the forensics team got enough of a fingerprint off the back-porch railing at the Thompson residence. It came back to a Pedro Lopez. There's paper out on him in Texas for assault and battery."

"Finally, a quality break," Al said. "Maybe someone will pick him up soon."

"I wonder if a call to Hanson at Dos Amigos Trucking would be of benefit. Also, what do you think of putting out a person of interest flag through a news report for Woodford and Freeman?"

"Yes," agreed Al. "We need to start shaking the trees to see what falls out. Let's do the news report before reaching out to Hanson. I'm not yet convinced that Dos Amigos isn't a bigger part of this mess."

In San Antonio, Michelle turned to me in our hotel bar and asked, "Do you think you've ever met Tarant?"

"I don't think so. I would think Terry or Javier would have introduced me to Tarant, and I don't recall that happening."

"They should be looking for you, Woody, or at least logically, they should. But, for me, they might not even know I had been there. I think we should try to maneuver somehow to put ourselves in an inside position. It's the only solution I see to get intel on Tarant and whomever. Maybe Tawon, through his friend or contacts, could get me close."

We sat at the hotel bar. We assumed we'd be staying for an hour distracted by Wheel of Fortune playing on the back wall behind the bar. The counter displayed photos, magazine covers, and newspaper clippings, under a Lucite finish. We drank our last beers and strolled outside on the patio. No one else around. I called Tawon and put him on speaker. "Hey, little brother. Do you have someone down there who can make an introduction for Michelle; maybe to one of the businesses?"

"Yes. Me bro," he answered.

"You? What do you mean?" I asked.

"Well, my big Cracker, it's a small world. I used to sell to a dude who now works for that trucking company you told me about. He thinks I'm looking for a job, so Michelle can be with me and I can introduce her if you want me to, or you can let me go in by myself."

I looked at Michelle. "What do you think?"

"Tawon, what do you mean, a job?"

"I'm pretty sure he wants to sell me some shit, probably meth."

"Whatever it takes," Michelle answered, looking out into space.

"Okay. I'll make a call or two and get back to you, bro," Tawon said.

After Tawon hung up, I said to Michelle, "I saw you look away with concern when you agreed with Tawon. If you're worried, tell me and we will figure something else out."

"I'm not scared. I was just thinking of Terry. He never wanted me involved in the drug business. I was just having a memory, Woody, I'm okay, but thanks for caring."

"Okay, if you're good with this, I am, too. We need to score a gun or two."

Although we had a rental, we took a city bus to the downtown area and departed on Broadway and Brooklyn. I had been there several times with Tawon back in the day, not selling or buying, just for visits. We walked along Brooklyn and found a tavern near the San Antonio River.

Buying a gun in certain areas of the country isn't anything like it is depicted on some TV shows. In some places, it's not any harder than just asking. However, the real issue, or key, is to know whom to ask. Once that's determined, it's just a simple, "Got any metal," a "trigger," or something real ingenious like, "You got a gun?"

We walked into the Sit N Bull Tavern and ordered two Dos Equis Amber beers on tap. The tavern was exactly what the name described. A bunch of drinkers sitting and bullshitting each other over the more important things of the day. Like, who was the best basketball player ever or how many politicians it takes to change a light bulb. A replica of a buffalo hung on the wall to the right of the bar. A Texas state flag draped on the wall to the left. NRA signs and placards everywhere. Cowboys, Texans, and Spurs banners were strategically placed near television sets throughout. A healthy young lady walked through the tables, dropping off and picking up new orders. The tavern supported a western-style motif complete with a Longhorn set of horns and a lasso dangling from one horn. A wonderful homage to the native Indians in the area, including news accounts of their plight and reports of massacres by our ancestors. There were the obligatory peanut shells on the wooden floor, which appeared not to have been swept in some time. I could smell chicken wings simmering, and there were several arcade video games of the past decades set in a side room.

I had spent many a night in bars, but taverns, true taverns, create the best form of atmosphere for all things good and bad.

Michelle was looking good. Her long black hair made her appear more Native Indian than Hispanic, as I sometimes felt. She certainly stood out as the pretty lady that she is, and especially in this location.

I had begun to notice that when needed, she could change her posture and voice sufficiently to disguise her Indiana roots. I kept having to remind myself of her military experience and realized she was more prepared than me if ever confronted by something other than a fist. And even at that, I figured she'd practiced enough hand-to-hand training to have held her own.

With all that said, thousands of years of DNA, gender bias, and the formation of traditions kept intensifying in me. I felt myself wanting to protect her.

Michelle nodded towards a white dude, maybe thirty-five, wearing a leather motorcycle jacket with colors that I was unfamiliar with. Since there are hundreds of motorcycle clubs across the country, there was no way to tell if this club was violent or not. I had seen no other members in this part of the tavern, but the pool tables and the dance floor sat around to the rear. I agreed. He looked like a possibility and nodded back at her. I stayed near a table in the rear and watched the bar.

Michelle was composed and fixated on the task. I saw she had begun a conversation. Not too direct, but allowing for his responses. Pretty soon, I noticed a body shift by both. He leaned over towards her and said something to her as he looked over her shoulder at the front entrance. Michelle nodded in the affirmative. They both got up to walk out and Michelle gave me a do not follow sign by a wave of her hand behind the back.

I sat in the bar for what seemed like thirty minutes, but I knew had been only five or ten. They walked in together. Michelle came over to my table and sat down.

"Okay, here's the deal. I told him we're together. He was cool with it and assumed I had to have someone covering my ass. He showed me two handguns, a 9mm Glock and a 9mm Sig Sauer. Neither fits my hand. He said he'd bring me a Sig P229 rather than the P226 he's carrying toting with him. If we buy both Sig

Sauer's, it would cost six-fifty. If you want the Glock in place of a Sig Sauer, it would be seven hundred."

"The Sig Sauer is right for me. How long before he can produce a P229 for you?"

"He said about the same time it would take us to drink another beer."

"How much does he want down to go get the other pistol?"

"He wants all of it now, and I said ok."

"If you think he'll be back, let's do it."

"He'll be back ... I took his wallet," she said, smiling.

I pulled out six fifty and told her to make the deal. She walked over to him and said something, and I saw him walk out the door. We ordered two beers and timed him. He came back in about the time we finished: impressive. He motioned her to come out, and so we both walked out into the street.

"Little lady, I'd like to have my wallet back before we go forth on this deal," he said with a gravelly voice that belied his age.

"Sure thing—when you show me the triggers," Michelle said calmly.

When he opened up the saddlebag on the right-side of his Black and Silver Indian and she saw the guns, she nodded to me. I took them, put them in my jacket, and nodded too. She handed him the wallet and told him, "I hope these shoot straight."

"They will, don't you worry. They've never been used, so they're not linked to anything the law would be interested in."

He drove off, and we walked back towards the bus stop. No one there, so she dry-fired her P229. It was fine. We took the bus back to the hotel. We stashed our new items in the trunk of our latest rental.

It was a quiet and dry winter evening. We walked around the downtown area until we went back to the hotel. We stopped at a local clothing store; we bought a few items and carried them in the oversized shopping bag announcing the store's name. We did reserve a room at the hotel we had stopped at earlier, a one-bedroom with two beds. We had no luggage, so the clothes we bought would be tomorrow's attire. We had been traveling a mile a minute since that day with little downtime.

"You want to have a drink? I think we both could use one?" I asked.

"Exactly what I was thinking."

The hotel had a second bar on the sixth floor. It also presented a western décor, but one stylishly different from the lobby bar. A wall of deer and elk heads. A few fish. A bear rug on the floor. It illustrated the splendor of southwestern art by Native Indians, complete with wall coverings in muted reds and oranges.

There weren't a lot of patrons, maybe ten or twelve. The bartender was an older man trying to look like Sam Elliott, wearing a cowboy hat, a Schneider's, to be exact. It wore him well —not the other way around.

I ordered a beer and Michelle asked for a gin and tonic with a twist.

I noticed she was in deep thought, so I said nothing. I just drank. Soon, I saw she was fumbling with trying to start a conversation.

"What's on your mind?" I asked.

"I've been thinking about Terry again, and whether it would have ever worked out."

"I never had an inkling you two were romantically involved. Surprised the hell out of me when you told me."

"He didn't want the company to know ... you know, fraternization and all," Michelle answered.

"He was also protecting you from the others like Tarant."

"That's what has got me thinking. He knew I was aware of the drugs you all were into. So, what else could there have been that he wanted to, or needed to, keep our relationship quiet and me safe? I mean, he was high enough up the ladder at Baxter's that if we had been found out, he could have weathered the storm, if any storm had come at all. Maybe he just didn't think we could make it in the long haul."

I said, "I've been having a lot of dreams of Ashley, more like nightmares. I killed her, Michelle, plain and simple. Had it not been for greed, mine included, she'd be alive."

We sat digesting each other's comments and long enough to order a second round. The bartender was polite enough to stay on the other side of the bar top, so we had to raise an empty glass to get his attention.

Michelle wanted to or needed to change our conservation, so she said, "You know we haven't discussed how we're going to approach Tarant. We certainly can't just walk up on him. I know Tawon says we can meet his guy, but that doesn't guarantee an introduction to Tarant."

"Let's call Tawon again and ask him just that question."

"How about in the morning? I'm tired, and these gins have taken it out of me, ok?"

"Yeah, I'm pretty beat myself."

We went to our room. Somewhat awkwardly. Some electricity, because of the alcohol, but we both knew this was a relationship out of necessity. Still, there was something we both were feeling.

TWENTY-TWO

Jimmy was enjoying his normal morning eggs and bacon with a glass of orange juice. Eggs over medium and crisp bacon. He was watching one of the morning national TV news shows, flipping channels back and forth depending on who was speaking and whether he felt that specific news was interesting to him. He toasted some whole wheat bread, which he had finally gotten used to, following his doctor's advice for the first time in years.

While the bread was toasting, he continued to eat the eggs, and he looked up at a picture of Paul there on the news!

"Paul Woodford is a person of interest in the triple murders in Columbus, Indiana, that occurred late last year," the news spokesman read.

Jimmy almost choked on the eggs. He couldn't believe it. It couldn't be Paul next door, could it? But there sure as hell was a photo of Paul. No way, just a close resemblance. Jimmy picked up his phone and dialed a number he knew by heart.

"Hey, Pins, this is Jim," he said.

"Yeah, Jimmy. Can't stay away, huh?"

"Something like that. Oh, shit!"

"Jimmy, are you okay?"

"Yeah, the toast started burning. Jesus. Hey, I have a favor. Would you be able to round up any intel on a triple murder in Columbus, Indiana, that occurred in the last six or eight months?"

"Ok, but what am I looking for, Jimmy, and why?"

"I don't know yet but, trust me, I have a good reason. Keep it on the down-low, please. No reason to raise any eyebrows, okay?"

"Sure, Jimmy. No problem. Are you sure you're, ok? Are you in some kind of trouble?"

"Everything is fine. Something about that case has me intrigued, is all. Let me know what you come up with, okay?"

Gary Pinson, Jim's old partner, hung up and did not believe his old partner just happened to feel curious about a triple murder in another state. Something was up, but Jim Fleck had taught him everything he had ever known about homicide investigations, and if Jim was asking for a favor, then who was he to question him.

Gary got to work. He called the Sheriff's Office and asked to speak to the lead detective. He was told detective Al Harris would be with him momentarily.

"Hello, this is Detective Harris. May I help you?"

"Hello, this is Detective Gary Pinson up here in Lenawee County, Michigan. I just listened to an interesting anonymous call our office received recently. The call had nothing to do with anything we were working here, so dispatch put it aside and forgot about it, and sad to say so did I until this morning. The caller, a male, said we should look into a triple murder in Columbus. I spent this morning talking to every cop in Columbus, Ohio, until one of them said there had been a triple murder in Columbus, Indiana."

"Yeah, we get mistaken for the big city all the time. What was the caller saying in particular?"

"I don't recall all the details, just that our department here should get involved because of some type of link. I'm sorry about the vagueness, but the call was deleted over this last weekend. Have you all gotten any intel linking your murders to our county?"

"Not that I'm aware of Detective ..."

"It's Gary Pinson. Just call me Pins, everyone else does."

"Sure, okay ... Pins, call me Al. I'm pretty confident there hasn't been a link, but we've gotten nowhere fast on this case. We did recently get a hit on one person who we think may have been involved. A Pedro Lopez. He hasn't been located yet. Does that name mean anything to you?"

"Lopez? No, not that I know of, but we've got a lot of Mexicans in the area. Would you mind if I stepped in a little and read some of your reports? It's possible there's a name or a link that isn't obvious. I've got nothing going on here right now, so I'd be glad to help if I can."

"It's ok with me. We need some other eyes on this. Anything you can do, like you said, to see some links we're not aware of yet would be helpful. I'll have the secretary fax them to you this afternoon, OK? Where did you say you were calling from?" Al asked.

"Lenawee County, Michigan."

"That's weird. We received an anonymous tip from a male up that way saying he thought he saw a female missing in our case. Maybe there's something to this after all," Al noted.

"That's great. Hopefully, I'll see something that will help you all."

"Jimmy, me, Pins. Do you have a fax machine or a computer with a printer?"

"Yes, I've got it all. Did you find something already?"

"The lead detective in the investigation is going to send me their reports. I gave him a song and dance, Jimmy. Don't paint me into a corner, I still have nine more years to go."

"You know better than to ask, but I would go down with the ship before screwing you. Anyway, this is just me being bored. Thanks."

Pinson waited around the precinct for the fax, but he was called out on an assault case, another domestic case. A boyfriend, drunk and high, beat the shit out of his girlfriend because he thought he saw her with another man. Turned out to be her brother. Jesus, what is the world coming to?

He didn't get back to the office until later that night. Early the next morning, he saw he had received the fax. He read through the reports quickly. He cringed, having never worked a triple homicide before and understanding what the detectives were up against. He faxed the reports to Jimmy around nine-thirty the next morning.

A little later, Jimmy was reading the many investigation reports. The forms were quite similar to his own office's reports, and also contained reports regarding a recent double murder that, according to the notes page, might be connected to the triple-murder. The reports seemed to support his feelings that Paul, or whatever his name was, just wasn't the killer. He didn't fit the mold as a person, as a burglar, nor as a jilted lover. There wasn't any obvious motive. There was no sign that life insurance could be a factor. The one caveat was Michelle. Who was she to Paul?

Jim began walking through his neighborhood with a cup of coffee and two reports. Might as well enjoy the morning air and sea breeze; the rest of the day appeared to be fraught with some sort of come-to-Jesus-meeting with Paul. There was a park bench a few blocks from his house where he often sat admiring the seascape. This morning he sat, but he wasn't admiring anything.

Jim put himself back in the detective's shoes again, ran the evidence from the reports, compared that to his interactions with Paul and Michelle. It made little sense that Paul would have killed his girlfriend in their home, along with his boss and another male with an obvious connection. Yet everyone and his brother would have him as the prime suspect. His own dealings with Paul didn't project him as a killer or a criminal. And what about Michelle?

The guy, Langfeld, had an assistant named Michelle, but he hadn't read a report of an interview with her. It seemed more than ironic, or coincidental, or erroneous why she hadn't been interviewed. That both of his neighbors are Paul and Michelle, makes them runners for their own safety. Even with some facial hair or changes to his head of hair, Paul was definitely the person he saw on the news show. He had seen no photos of the Freeman woman but, again, some coincidence. They have to be the two missing persons, but they sure aren't the killers.

But now, what to do with this deciphered information? How to approach his friends?

"Tawon, any luck?" I asked, after not waiting for his promised return call.

"He's wanting to sell some meth, and I told him about Michelle. I said she's not interested in the crank but thinking of maybe landing a job. I said I'd buy his crank, but I'm not sure about the job angle. I was just trying to put some distance between Michelle and my guy."

Michelle said, "Ok, that may work. I just need to walk in the door to see what we're up against. Would he sell you the shit at the business?"

"I doubt it, but it depends on how comfortable he is there. We'll find out soon enough. I said we're on our way there today."

I was excited, "Excellent brother. Meet us at the Sit N Bull and we'll iron out the details. It's too late today to drive to McAllen … it must be around a three-hour drive."

"I'll be at the Sit N Bull later tonight, but we're meeting in Alice," Tawon said and hung up.

We left for the Sit N Bull. As we neared the tavern this time, I saw several bikers and their rides outside. I also saw Tawon trying to calm down a crowd. We rolled up to the group. I got out and walked towards the crowd.

Tawon saw me and sighed as if to say, "I'm in trouble again." Instead, he said, "It's about time, homey. These dudes want to crack my skull for being black. Who'd ever thought white boys still want to hang a nigga," he said jokingly but clearly worried.

"Okay, boys, he's with us. No problem here. We all just want to get a drink," I said.

Michelle had parked the car and had joined us. One biker said, "Your boy there doesn't belong in this here bar."

I walked straight over to the dude. He was shorter than me. I looked down at him and said, "We're getting a drink or two, and he ain't going anywhere but with us into the bar. He's with us."

"I think you should consider your decision again," he growled.

"When pigs fly," I answered. I hit him about the time "fly" left my lips. A pretty good upper jab to his solar plexus. Where the ganglion nerves are most concentrated. He lost his breath and the will to continue. I kicked him in his left knee, flopping him to the ground, still gasping for enough air to consider if he had other options. One of his buddies took a quick step towards me, but Michelle pulled out her new P229 and stuck it in his left ear with her right hand. With her left hand, she cradled his jaw before he or his friends could move. She whispered softly but sternly, "I'm really thirsty. Wouldn't mind buying you boys a round either. I know this was just a misunderstanding. If you don't like that offer, I'll be more than happy to let him kick your buddy's balls up to his throat. What do you say?"

The others just watched and gawked. The biker with the gun in his ear grudgingly relented. Tawon, Michelle, and I walked into the bar, not bragging or laughing, just composed.

"That was impressive," Michelle said. "Have you always hated pigs that much?"

"I don't know why, but I've used that phrase since I was a kid. Me, impressive? How about you?"

Tawon said, "I certainly am down with you two being on my side. That was like old times, Cracker." Turning to Michelle, "I'd get in a spot and he'd come to my rescue." We all smiled, but not too obviously. We didn't want to rile the boys.

Over the next hour, we drank a few, and Tawon and Michelle worked out their play. They were having trouble working through introducing Michelle for a job. It just didn't feel right. The link from drugs to employment was too much of a leap.

"Okay, the drugs to job just ain't going to get it," I agreed. I said, "I think you'll just have to tell your connection you threw out the job story to feel him out about the real reason you and Michelle were here."

"Yeah, that's better. It'll be a lot easier to run the play that she is the money or has the connection to the money."

Michelle said, "Tawon, I haven't ever done a drug deal. So, I'm out of my league. What would be easier to sell, me being the money or the connection to your source?"

Tawon gazed at her a bit and then said, "You're the money. You're good-looking, and if he presses you any, you could say something like your main squeeze has the money but not the time."

"I think that works for me," Michelle agreed.

On the way out of the bar, two or three bikers stood and watched us leave. No one physically confronted us, but we weren't ignored either. Far from it. Michelle received a few cat-calls and whistles, but they were more to repair bruised egos. Michelle held up her end by raising her middle finger, which was received by more cat-calls and some laughter.

My phone started ringing before we drove away. Only five people had my number, and two of them were in the car with me.

"Hello."

"Paul, this is Jimmy. Do you have a minute?"

"Sure, Jim. Are you okay?"

"I'm fine, but you and Michelle may not be."

"Oh, ... Michelle's with me now. Okay, to put this on speaker?" I raised a finger to my lips, looking at Tawon.

"Yeah, this concerns her too."

For the next fifteen minutes, he recalled his last day or two and what he had learned from the police reports. It was sobering to hear.

"Jim, you have to know Michelle and I did nothing anyone else wouldn't have done, if given the same scenario. We would have been victims had it not been for just plain luck."

"I know you aren't involved. If I had thought so, I would have turned you in already. But I'd like to know your side of the story."

I recounted everything I could in a summary, starting with the chance meeting with Langfeld at the Red Caboose and ending with the murders. I provided enough details of my drug-dealing days to let Jim know I wasn't a saint.

Michelle wove into the conversation about her role this web found us. We explained we had determined that Gary Stewart was the FBI's source and how we stumbled onto his and his sister's murder.

With everything out in the open, Michelle and I were quite relieved. Jim wasn't turning us in, and we now had a friend we could talk to, albeit a retired cop.

"Listen, since your picture is out in public, it's just a matter of time before you're going to be noticed. I realize you've attempted to change your appearance somewhat. Nevertheless, you have to be careful. Don't get arrested. That would be the end as soon as they run your prints."

"I don't know what you two are planning but, I think I've got a pretty good idea. You need to think that through carefully, and I mean carefully. Understand?"

"Yes sir. As soon as we can, we're going to turn ourselves in as witnesses, not suspects."

"Listen up. The investigation pulled a print at your house. It belongs to a Pedro Lopez. There are warrants out for him in Texas. Have you ever heard of him?"

I looked at Michelle, and she mouthed no. I said, "No, Jim, we've never heard of him."

"He has to be one of the shooters, then. Be careful."

Hearing the name Pedro Lopez, both Michelle and I saw Tawon almost turn white. Still looking at Tawon, I answered Jim, "Will do, and we don't know how to thank you for understanding our predicament."

"No problem. You two just stay safe. I've grown to kind of liking you two."

We drove for a few more miles, not saying much but staring daggers at Tawon. I said, "Who the hell is Pedro Lopez to you?"

"He's the guy my buddy is introducing us to at the meeting tomorrow."

TWENTY-THREE

The FBI had taken over the murder investigation of Stewart and his sister because he had been their informant and the Sheriff didn't want to extend Harris and their homicide team any further. Harris had arranged for their reports and other forensic findings to be turned over, albeit a bit reluctantly.

Burke wasn't a bad FBI agent. He had been "institutionalized" as most of their agents had been, meaning they did nothing wrong, but if they did, they went to Congress and pleaded for more money so those mistakes wouldn't happen again. Burke was a well-trained agent, as were all of their agents. He was human, so he felt terrible about the events. He felt obligated to pour his all into solving the Stewart/Oliver murders and, if possible, to assist the detectives in their investigation of the other murders.

Burke noted the same interesting footprints around the flower garden. The spattering of roses and petunias coupled with the trampled down coneflowers and lamb's ears. There were six different handprints throughout the crime scene. Only a few of the prints could be identified because of smudges and smears. Ms. Oliver's and Stewart's prints were obvious. However, several prints in the home were obviously left by the killers. They were tracked throughout the house in an ugly red and now a blackening hue.

Burke and his forensic team made the determination that there was over one killer because there weren't any defensive wounds on either victim, which led them to believe it was a surprise attack. He believed both were killed at or near the same time by two killers. However, only one baseball bat was found, and it lay next to the female. A fact that would have to be vetted properly.

The coroner working with the FBI lab noted in his report the obvious cause of death was extreme trauma to the head of each victim. The crucial and most likely fatal blow appeared to be more on the left side of both victims, leading them to believe the assailant, or assailants, to be right-handed.

The house was ransacked, but it didn't appear to have been a botched robbery because the jewelry was still present on the dresser and on Mrs. Oliver. No glass breaks. No other obvious missing items. The car was in the garage. The female's purse and wallet were visible on the kitchen table. Her purse contained over two hundred cash. Law enforcement officers had run their names and identifiers for credit card usage, and none had been used since their deaths. None of their bank accounts had been emptied, either.

Stewart's apartment outside of Columbus was searched by the FBI, and nothing of great value turned up linking to the murder. However, what Burke was really looking for wasn't there either, and his search at the ninth Street Park resulted in nothing too. He now wished he had pushed harder for Stewart to phone him with summaries. He shouldn't have allowed Wunderland to micromanage this matter.

Burke called Baxter's and spoke with their attorney Larson and told him he was faxing a subpoena for all of Stewart's personnel files and truck logbooks.

A few days later, Burke at his desk, trying to make heads or tails of the murders, jotted down some summary-type notes. One, Stewart had been burned. Two, it was only natural to believe that someone above Langfeld had figured it out. Three, who, how, and when? Four, he had a feeling that Stewart had found a weapons link. He called a friend.

"Hello, Alcohol, Tobacco, and Firearms. May I help you?"

"Hi, this is special agent Burke with the FBI in Indianapolis. Is Seth Cottrell in today?"

"Yes, he is. I'll transfer you."

"Hello, Cottrell here. May I help you?"

"Hey, buddy," Burke here.

"Well, I haven't heard from the Feebs in a long while. How is the family?"

"The family is well. Thanks for asking. Hope you and the girlfriend are doing well."

"Yeah, everyone here is doing well. I could be doing better though."

"Oh, well, what's up with you?"

"I had an informant getting evidence of a drug trafficking group out of Mexico through Texas and up this way. It had just started, and he had given me the basic method of distribution and a few names. I got the feeling guns were also being dealt. I had just begun to develop a plan, but he got burned. He was murdered last week."

"Oh shit, man. Sorry to hear that. What can I do?"

"Well, let me run the names by you he gave me. Can you run them in your databases?"

"Sure, email them to me and I'll do what I can. Sorry again about your CI."

"Yeah, they killed his sister, too. Cold-blooded bastards."

Michelle asked Tawon, "How well do you know Pedro?"

"I dealt with him a couple of years ago. I bought meth and a couple of guns from him."

"Where and how did you meet him?" I asked.

"Do you remember Stumpy over by the zoo?"

"Sure, Black dude about five foot tall whether he was standing up or lying down."

Michelle giggled at the description.

"That's the guy. He introduced me one day to Pedro. By the way, Pedro's nickname is Zipper."

"Zipper? Why?" I asked.

"Because he sometimes drops his pants and hangs his junk out just for laughs."

"I hope he hangs it out for me. I'll cut it off and stick it in his ear," Michelle spat.

Tawon continued, "I never felt he was violent, or at least he never showed me that side. I don't know why he would have gotten involved in murders. He might be a little more fucked up than I thought. I think we can approach him with no issues, but if you want to go another route, I'm okay with canceling."

Michelle clearly would not cancel. I was only concerned that she'd just kill him right off the bat. Michelle interjected, "No. We go now. We don't have any other opportunities. We need to find out who the other shooter is."

"Hopefully, but one is better than none, so let's just go one step at a time."

We drove to Alice, Texas. It's about halfway between San Antonio and McAllen. We met near the Greyhound station because there were several places nearby to eat. We arrived there two hours ahead of time to scope out a few spots. Our dream was to pick the location, but Pedro contacted Tawon and told him where they were going to meet. Tawon had to agree. We split up and walked around the area, looking for anything unusual. Michelle noticed that the actual meeting location was in a very open area. A sort of sidewalk eatery. She was comfortable. She was focused. I was worried like you are when your wife or girlfriend finds herself in an unsafe spot. She wasn't my girlfriend, but those feelings were physiological. Millions of years in the making.

Tawon was cool. He was laid back and just chillin'. He had matured a lot from years back. Wore his hair short-cropped and no baggy jeans. If he were in a suit, you'd have thought he was a businessman. I guess he still is. Just not your typical business. Soon he touched his nose, which was the signal he had seen Pedro.

Pedro wasn't alone. At least two others were with him. If Tawon was scared or worried, he didn't show it. He gave Pedro a street handshake and acknowledged the others.

"What up," Tawon started.

"Same old shit, compadre," answered Pedro.

Tawon looked over at the others. "You brought friends. Are we still good?"

"Yeah, so did you, looking over at Michelle. Like I said on the phone. We ain't seen each other in a while. I have to be … ah … wondering … why we ain't talked and now out of nowhere you call me."

"Yo, I get it. We ain't talked because I was in the box. Now I need to get back into the game. I gots no other way to make any cash." Hooking a thumb towards Michelle, Tawon said, "She's doing me a favor. If things work out, maybe we all can profit down the road."

Pedro glanced over at one of his friends who walked over to Tawon with a TV remote-looking thing and held it next to Tawon. He did the same to Michelle, who hadn't yet said anything, and allowed the dude to get up close to her with the scanner. He brushed it over her and along her breasts with his hand inside to rub up against her. She glared at him and he smiled. He then nodded okay to Pedro and stepped away.

Pedro sat down next to Tawon and Michelle. The others stayed about ten feet away.

"Why did you bring her my amigo?" motioning to Michelle.

"Like I said," she's doing me a favor. "We've known each other for a few years but haven't really worked together."

Michelle felt it was time to speak. "Listen, if you two want to get a room, just tell me and I'll find another supplier."

Pedro refocused on Michelle, digesting her statement. Tawon said nothing. He hadn't even turned to look at her.

Pedro finally said, "No, we're cool. Just need to be careful is all."

"Maybe it should be us checking you out," retorted Michelle.

"I don't think so, senorita, but the boys might want to check you out."

Michelle stepped forward, and it looked as if she was going to drop him right there. She stopped short, placed her hand between Pedro's legs, and said, "You first, big boy. They get scraps if you're worth it."

I almost fell over!

"Business and pleasure. Tawon, you're okay," Zipper retorted.

Tawon answered, "First we talk business, bro. Then you two can talk pleasure."

"Okay. We're looking to move two to three pounds a week to start in your area. You're still in Dallas, right?"

"Yeah, we're both in the city."

"We lost a good customer and we need to work back up to twenty pounds a month. He bought metal too from time to time. We can talk about that later."

"You're going to have to front me, Zipper. Like I said, I ain't got any green right now."

Pedro looked at Michelle and said, "Isn't that why you're here? Half, or it's off. We need to know you're the real shit."

Tawon looked at Michelle, who then looked at Pedro. "Okay, half it is."

"Meet us in the lumberyard," Pedro ordered.

"Not all of you. Just you, Zipper," Michelle said. "I'm not walking in on a gang-bang, so the deal is you and me. Tawon will owe you his half, but the deal now is just you and me."

After a short stare, Pedro answered, "Be there tomorrow at four … alone." Later, in the rental car driving over to book a hotel, I asked what their thoughts were regarding how this was going to proceed. Michelle was pretty sure that Pedro was going to make a move on her after the deal.

"Why did you ask for a one-on-one meeting then?" I asked.

"Because when I kill him, the cops will assume it was a rape gone wrong and not a drug deal gone bad. That also covers Tawon."

"Are you good with that Tawon?"

"He killed your girlfriend and her boyfriend. I'm good with anything you two want and not worried at all about them coming after me." Tawon said.

"Michelle, we still need to find out who the other bastards are," I noted.

"That's still the plan," Michelle answered.

The lumber yard was sizable. Not exactly a rectangle, but certainly not square either. The main gate, one of two, was large enough for two eighteen-wheelers to pass each other. The yard was open to the public, but according to the sign hung on the chain-link fence near the gate, it would be closed on Sunday afternoon. There was a showroom in the main building at about ten o'clock as you viewed it from the front gate and at least fifty yards away.

The interior walls showed photos of various homes built with the timber they had supplied. The sign at the main office reflected open-and-closed times. Sundays, the showroom was open until four; the yard and sawmill closed at noon from September through February. Odd. The main office windows peered out toward the main entrance, which also looked out over the parking lot. The showroom floor was four steps above the lot.

There wasn't any obvious reason for the location of the

meeting proposed by Pedro. He hadn't said where exactly in the lumber yard we would be meeting so we had assumed it would be at or near the front entrance, but that didn't seem very safe. We split up and walked around, looking for other spots and places to protect Michelle.

The yard was a series of well-organized rows of various cuts of timber. Various lengths and widths. Different trees. The rows intersected cross-ways, making it look like a map of city streets and avenues. The lumber was stacked in what could only be described as a large honeycomb or a shoe caddy in a woman's closet. Several of the cross aisles showed holes or, specifically, alcoves containing workbenches with tools and other carpentry materials. Several sported wood awnings for work during the middle of summer and, of course, cover for rain. The rows in any direction rose to heights of at least fifteen feet. If the honeycomb only held a few boards of lumber and was eye-level, it was possible to see through to the adjacent row.

The furthest row stood about thirty-five yards from the front doors, and the closest row was maybe ten yards away. The length of the rows varied, but appeared to be about twenty yards long. I counted four rows on my side of the yard. Michelle and Tawon said there were only two rows on the other side of the office. The honeycomb was encircled by a wide space of ground so trucks of all sizes could drive the perimeter. An enormous complex, for sure. Fork trucks and skid steers were parked at various random locations throughout. None of us during our walk could see the furthest part of the yard at any point.

No buildings were situated contiguous to the lumber yard tall enough for any security we could use. There was medium vehicular city traffic and little foot traffic.

Michelle was most likely going to be on her own unless she could steer the scheduled meeting to a place within the yard we could view. The odds of that were abysmal. Pedro had done this for a long time, so we had to assume he'd used this location previously and was comfortable no police would happen on the deal.

He might have had someone on the inside, so he was comfortable here. We knew he would be adamant the meet would be at the location he picked. We decided our only option was to just watch the two entrances to make sure Pedro didn't bring an army.

Tawon had selected a room in a hotel he'd used in the past, so we decided not to meet at either hotel. We agreed to meet and eat elsewhere. We chose a restaurant that was, by chance, a block from the Sit N Bull. It had a wide menu to pick from. I requested a rib-eye steak and baked potato. Michelle ordered grilled chicken, Tawon ordered the sea bass. Apparently, I had given him sufficient funds. We enjoyed the dinner as best we could, considering tomorrow's unknown.

Michelle noted, "Okay, our plans have changed a little because Pedro is at least one killer we wanted to find. Lucky for sure. If Pedro just makes the deal and there isn't any way to hold him for intel, what do we do then?"

Tawon added, "I don't think there is any way he's coming alone, so holding him is probably not going to be easy."

I wondered out loud, "The fact that we probably won't be with you or very close anyway causes me a lot of concern. I know we've discussed this ad nauseam, but I haven't yet heard a good way to assure your safety, other than your own abilities." Michelle nodded, reached over and squeezed my hand, and gave us both the okay sign.

We drove to the lumber yard a little after eleven; Michelle stayed in the car while Tawon and I walked the perimeter of the yard. When we met back at the car, Michelle wasn't there. It was another thirty minutes before the meet time. No way to contact her. I began having that same gut feeling I had when I walked toward my house that ... night.

"Tawon, I'm going in. You stay here with the car for a quick get-the-hell-out-of-dodge."

"You got it, Cracker."

As I walked toward the showroom, I saw one of yesterday's friends leaning on a Ford 250. No need to act like I hadn't noticed. I just nodded at him to say we're here too. He nodded back. All is even, but the back gate now was entirely an unknown variable to us. I stayed close enough to act if need be. He didn't make a phone call or look around, so I felt okay. I saw no one else.

Time crawled like a 6-month infant. I thought I heard each Tick-Tock of the showroom clock. What I heard was a scream. Not from Michelle. It wasn't a long yell. Zipper's friend and I both took steps towards the sound, but we saw Michelle walking towards us at a pretty good clip from behind the second row. Her shirt was torn. She was now wearing … a backpack? Michelle walked towards us with a distinct purpose. She strode past an alcove where Pedro's friend made a quick step and grabbed her around the neck. "Where's Pedro?" he asked angrily.

Michelle's shirt was more than torn, it was cut. I stepped toward him, but he came up with an eight-inch Parryblade and walked backward, pulling Michelle into an alcove with him.

He said to me, "Back up," and then to Michelle. "I said where is Pedro?"

Michelle uttered, "If he was up your ass, you'd know, wouldn't you?"

He squeezed harder and this time a little higher up her chest to her neck. He switched the knife from her neck to a threatening thrust at me.

"Listen to me," I said. "I don't know what happened back there. I wouldn't be surprised if Pedro didn't make a move to get in her pants. He's probably back there gasping for air and trying to find his balls. Just let her be. Go back and get your boy and let's forget this happened."

"I don't think so; she's got his pack. I ain't letting her go until I know the man is all right."

"I don't think that's going to happen," I said.

"I'll cut her from her throat to her damn pussy."

"When pigs fly," I said. And, as fly left my mouth, Michelle lifted her legs towards her chest, which dropped her entire weight on the one arm holding her. She dropped about six inches before he could react and, therefore, he was forced to bend forward and down. I stepped forward with a downward-angled punch. I caught him on the left side of his throat. Quite effective. His knife-holding hand dropped a little in trajectory and I pushed it to the side. Michelle stomped on his instep with her heel and he lost his balance. Just in time for me to hit him with a left-hand cross. This time, it was even a better punch. He went down in a heap. His eyes rolled up and back. He was out for the count.

Michelle asked, "How did you know I would drop?"

"Well, you're the only person I've told my pigs' story to, so I just figured a Nightstalker would be smart enough to know what needed to be done."

"Well, it worked."

"You want to tell me about your shirt and Zipper?"

"He had roving hands. I swatted his arm away. He pulled a knife faster than I had ever seen. Scared me. He swiped at me with the knife. Cut me too. I couldn't tell how serious it was."

"What the hell did you do?" I asked.

"Well, we were so close, I bit his nose. He grabbed for me and his nose at the same time. Bad decision. He stabbed himself near his eye. I had time then. He's laid up in the back, by the first workbench. The one with the band saw."

"Please tell me you didn't use the saw," I said.

"No, but that was my first thought. No one is back there. Have Tawon drive in here."

Tawon drove up to the alcove where Michelle was standing. She had laid Pedro out with her knife. A slick stab to his neck and what appeared to be a slice down his chest. I was surprised there wasn't more blood, but then I saw Michelle had dumped a pail of sawdust onto the area. His penis was, in fact, in his mouth. She said, "I wasn't sure if we would have the chance to get rid of his body, so I made it look like he picked on the wrong girl or a jealous boyfriend who took revenge."

Tawon said, "And to think white people think we're thugs." He laughed when he saw Michelle giggling.

I asked, "Did he say anything or …"

"Nothing, but I only gave him to two. I wasn't about to wait any longer. I had moved around to his side; I pulled my knife and swung it around his neck so I wouldn't spill as much blood. I was so mad I almost cut his head off. It's a miracle I didn't stay there and cut him up into little pieces. I might have if I could have lifted him onto the band saw table."

I turned towards Tawon. "Give me a hand with Pedro's bodyguard. We need to drag some information from him."

We loaded both without so much as anyone coming to the area right there, two rows behind the main building. Pedro in the trunk and his buddy in the back seat. As we drove away, I saw through the showroom window and saw a Dallas Cowboys football game on the big screen TV. Everyone was facing the TV, which was angled away from the exterior window. Hmm, I used to hate the Cowboys … and now; I knew why the odd open-hour schedule.

As we drove away from the lumberyard, Tawon asked, "Do you want me to drive towards San Antonio or McAllen?"

"What do you think, Michelle?"

"Let's go north. We need to make some space and find a place to drop Zipper."

"Agreed. Tawon, north as far as we can until we need gas or see a place to drop him."

As Tawon drove, Michelle and I climbed in the back and began to tie our passenger up so he was sitting up but couldn't alert anyone. Michelle used some sort of military knot which transformed our quarry into a sleeping passenger. She said they used the technique in Iraq to decoy the enemy sometimes.

An hour later or so, our passenger began to wake up. He quickly realized he was a captive. We didn't ask him questions.

We let him stew. We spoke to each that Pedro was dead and in the trunk.

We had almost reached San Antonio when I read on a large wooden sign, *Morrison's Hog Farm*. It would be the perfect place to drop-off for Pedro. I felt it would also be a perfect way to convince our friend to talk. Since I had trucked rotting fruit to hog farms for Baxter's, I had learned that hogs eat almost anything. If properly motivated, they will do it quickly too.

"Turn here at this farm, Tawon."

"What, this is a pig farm, Cracker? What the hell are we going to do here?"

"Well, my city man; hogs eat almost anything, and I mean anything. More importantly ... everything."

"Oh, man, you've gotten hard, Cracker."

"Oh, yeah, and let's make sure dick breath back there can watch too," Michelle said.

Tawon turned off the interstate and followed a frontage road. Turned up a winding one-hundred-yard driveway. About halfway to the farm was a split. The split to the right was hidden from the farm behind a stone wall and a thicket of briarwood trees. The split to the left was in the open air for fifteen yards, but it was all below grade at the split. At the split, you could see the roof of the farmhouse. The driveway circled from the split and, therefore, presented entrances to the farmhouse from either direction. Michelle had held our backseat passenger's head up so he could see out the back of the car, and, specifically, so he could read Morrison's Hog Farm.

Tawon took the left fork, pulled over and turned the car around so the trunk was hidden from view of the farmhouse. We hadn't yet seen the barn or a hog pen, but could see hogs roaming around inside the fence.

Tawon and I dragged Zipper from out of the trunk. The rental company had not cleaned the trunk very well. A box containing Yard & Lawn trash bags had been left. We had laid out a bunch of them back at the lumber yard so hopefully it had captured the remaining blood. Zipper plopped to the ground like a sack of shit, which he was. Deadweight. I never knew how accurate that saying was until then. Damn, he was heavy, or maybe he was just awkward to get a hold of. We started to drag him instead of trying to carry him.

"Aw, man, what's that smell?" coughed Tawon.

"Whew, that is pretty bad," I returned. "It's the hogs. That's about as bad as I ever have smelled. I always knew they stunk, but shit, it took our breath away."

The left-hand fork, although initially below-grade, soon rose back up the knoll and began a slow turn towards the right and a barn I could now see, and a hog-pen also now visible. The farmhouse was visible from that point.

We continued to drag him and took him down a slope to a dry ditch line. It was easy dragging downhill, but we had to go to the upper bank on the other side of the dry creek bed to reach the farm fence and gate. Pull. Drag. Breathe. Start over again. We were dripping wet and not much closer to the hog fence. We gained the upper part of the bank; there, the land leveled off for about five feet until meeting the fence. He was too heavy to have tried to throw him over the fence, which is why I had Tawon park there in front of the gate.

We struggled but lugged him to the gate area, albeit it took five more minutes that I wasn't sure we had. The gate I had seen was close to the split. It was getting dark already, and it was Sunday night, so hopefully, no one was outside. We had heard no hogs squealing or rooting, and, more importantly, had heard no dogs either, a commotion which I had been more worried about. The gate, a tubular pipe and mesh wire contraption, was actually a simple but perfectly engineered item. Hogs eat just about anything, but not steel pipes. They probably could, and would, eat the wire mesh, but they couldn't get through any of the openings, anyway. The mesh was actually to allow air movement in and keep coyotes and such out. Most farm gates can be opened from either side by just reaching through or around.

Tawon reached through the fencing and unhooked the gate. Damn! The gate opened outward, so we had to shut it and drag Zipper away from the arc of the opening. We finally heaved him through and the hogs had moved towards the barn. Our presence hadn't bothered them or caused a stir. As long as they stayed further up in the field and didn't begin to come to investigate, we could move him further into the corralled area. It was a little below grade from the house, but was in sight of the main barn. We drug him about twenty feet into the area. The hogs, depending on how many, would do the job quickly in the morning, or when they discovered their new meal.

Luck seemed on our side. We had retreated through the gate and had begun our trek to the car when we noticed the hogs had smelled us and had come out to investigate. Bon appetite.

Michelle explained to our passenger why we stopped at the hog farm. He understood immediately. He pissed his pants. She caressed his face and said, "Aw, you pee peed. Are you scared? Are you afraid? A big ole country boy like you. You shouldn't be scared. We just want to talk. Don't you think it would be wise to talk to us too?" He shook his head as violently in agreement as he could muster.

Tawon drove down the driveway, turned onto the frontage road and continued for about five minutes. He pulled over out of sight from lights in houses, farms, or the highway nearby. I had brought a tape recorder; I showed Tawon and motioned him not to talk.

I turned to Pedro's friend and said, "Okay, amigo. You're going to tell us your name and everything about the drugs and guns you're running for Muchido and anyone else."

By the expression in his eyes, he knew we knew about the organization, or at least enough to get his full attention ... if the hogs hadn't already.

Michelle cut away the wrap over his mouth. He took in a full breath and looked back and forth between all of us with yet wider eyes darting all around. It didn't take long to realize we were serious, and he knew we were still close to the hog farm.

I put the recorder down and motioned to him to start.

In broken English, he spoke, "Ah, ... my name is ... ah Tomas Engaflo. I used to work at Dos Amigos for Mr. Muchido. Ah, Pedro Lopez is my half-brother. He also worked at Dos Amigos. We were paid as employees, but we just sold drugs and guns." He looked at us with a gesture that's enough, right?

I turned off the recorder. "No, not enough, keep talking."

"Er ... Mr. Muchido worked closely with Mr. Tarant at a company called Rotten Tomatoes. We moved drugs and sometimes guns for him ... what? Oh, yeah, Mr. Tarant. I think he was Mr. Muchido's boss. He ...Tarant, is also in Mexico more than Texas. We worked for them for a couple of years. We only did deals in Texas and mainly in Dallas. I know they sold other places but I don't know where."

I kept the recorder on but swirled my hands like a basketball referee does when calling a traveling violation. Keep going.

Tomas continued, "Mr. Tarant has people in Mexico that control the town where our families live. He's ruthless. I saw him cut off a little girl's thumb because her father talked to the Federales."

He rambled on about various brutal actions of Tarant and others. I turned off the recorder. I spoke, "I want you to now tell us about when you and Pedro went to Indiana. I won't ask you questions about it. I want you to just tell us the complete story, and trust me, we know enough to recognize if you try to lie." I turned the recorder back on and motioned for him to begin. This time, he was even more nervous.

"Oh ... man. Okay, Mr. Tarant told us to go to Indiana and wait for a call. He said someone there was talking or stealing. I don't think he knew for sure. It was a couple months ago ... maybe four to five months. We were given a car."

"What kind of car?" I mouthed.

He looked at me with some recognition and stuttered, "Ah ...

yeah, a BMW ... kind of gray/silver. We got instructions on burner phones Mr. Tarant gave us before we left. We couldn't call anyone. He said they were programmed only to receive calls. We were in Indiana or Kentucky for about a month. We were told to follow two guys that worked at Baxter's Trucking. He wanted us to see if they were talking with the police. One guy was a manager named Sangweld, or something like that, and another guy named Woodford."

As he said my name, his eyes must have seen mine flicker recognition, and he now clearly recognized that I was the guy on the interstate highway. His eyes didn't lie, he knew.

He continued speaking while staring at me with visible fear the whole time. "Sangweld met with a truck driver several times around the area. The driver ... I don't know his name, but he was tall and skinny. He drove to Indianapolis a few times, and we were pretty sure he went to the FBI Building. Oh, the skinny guy ... to the FBI. We told Mr. Tarant. A couple of days later, he gave us an address and said to take care of everyone there at six o'clock one night."

When he said that, he again revealed fear, or maybe recognition, in his eyes. "We had to do it. Do you understand? We had to or our families in Mexico would be killed, or worse."

Worse? He began to sob a little. Tomas gave details of the murders, including riffling through the car in the driveway. The details made me sick to hear. I had to look away several times. Tomas saw my emotional responses and began to cry and plead forgiveness. I mouthed to him to continue.

"There were some papers in a car in the driveway we took and gave to Mr. Tarant later on. It was some pages with a bunch of numbers and letters. Looked like a drug balance sheet to me, but the numbers were too small. Pedro said they were guns. Anyway, Mr. Tarant said we did a good thing and told us to get rid of the car, so we burned it up outside of McAllen."

I had eventually stepped out of the car and walked around to the back passenger side and stood there with his door opened. He spoke a little longer, but no more pertinent information was forthcoming. I shut off the recorder, and in one motion, hit him harder than I think I had ever hit anyone in my life. I knew instantly that I had injured him ... severely. My fist and wrist were sore.

I was surprised at how I felt. It was as close as I had ever come to killing someone with my hands. It wouldn't be the last time. I was numb, but also could feel every part of my physical and mental being. My stomach was queasy and my legs rubbery. My mind had slowed down and replayed the punch repeatedly. In a weird out-of-body visual, I had reared back and had grabbed the doorjamb with my left hand and used it to catapult my weight and right arm into the side of his head just behind his right eye. It was close to the temple, and I heard an awful crack. I probably had fractured one of the four skull bones connected there. The perfect punch and a perfect sucker punch. He did not know it was coming, and neither had Tawon, who jumped a little. Michelle never flinched.

I stood there breathing heavily. Michelle got out and rubbed my shoulders and arm until I came back to earth. I heard her saying, "Honey, you're okay. Keep breathing. You're just coming off an adrenaline rush," and turning to Tawon, "Let's go back to the hog farm." Tawon looked startled, but regained his composure and did as asked.

We drove the five minutes back to the farm, and by then the world came to. The hogs had already begun their job on Zipper, and even though I hated that bastard so much, I couldn't even watch them tearing him apart. Michelle stood and gazed on with her fists clenched.

"Okay, now what?" Tawon wondered out loud.

Michelle said, "It's worth the risk. He's out cold. Let's drag him into the cage and let the hogs do their thing. I don't care if he is alive. The fucker killed Ashley and Terry."

Tawon said, "He'll wake up for sure if he's getting eaten alive

... don't you think?" With neither of us responding, he just shuddered, shook his arms, and grabbed a leg.

We drug him out of the backseat and onto the ground. One thing I had learned about using one's fists was there was seldom blood splatter. I truly had hit him hard. He was out and barely breathing. But there was the probability he would wake if being eaten. So, I grabbed one of the garbage bags, took my knife, and calmly but efficiently stuck him hard in the gut. Again in the heart. And again, until Michelle took the knife from me and coolly wiped it off on the shirt Tomas was wearing. Tawon found another gate around the left-hand drive and away from the hogs, tearing apart Pedro.

After again struggling with the dead weight of another of the murderers, we successfully got him far enough into the corral. We drove away without saying a word.

TWENTY-FOUR

We had discussed earlier to record any admissions in order to turn the info over to the FBI. Although we wanted to tear into Tarant ourselves, we figured that taking out the two who had killed Ashley and Terry was really what we had wanted to do. Tarant was a different story altogether. The FBI had more resources to take down someone like Tarant. Since Tomas admitted to being one killer, we would no longer be suspected of the murders.

During our drive, Tawon said, "Guys, what's in the backpack?"

I had completely forgotten about Pedro's backpack! I looked at Michelle and questioned, "What is in it?"

"I don't know. I assumed it was drugs. After all, that's what we were there for, right?"

I grabbed the pack and zipped it open. It was meth packaged in several one or two-pound bags, and a gun; a .45 Smith & Wesson. But what really wasn't expected was a small group of papers. The top row had locations, Dallas, Odessa, Shreveport, Memphis, Biloxi, and others. Under each column of locations, the column was split into two. Those two columns listed numbers and letters. The paper was green columnar pad paper that had once been used by accountants and in other business offices.

"What do you think?" I said to the crew.

"Well," Tawon ventured, "Those are initials for sure, bro. I've seen this kind of list before. But those numbers aren't weights, they're ... Michelle interrupted ... guns."

"Yeah, for sure," Tawon agreed.

"How can that be?" I said. "There are three pages of figures. That's, ah ... seven rows ... that's twenty-one."

"Damn." Michelle finally said. "How many locations?"

"Nine. Dallas has the most numbers noted in the maximum number of slots, but Biloxi has almost as many," I said.

Michelle questioned me, "Didn't you tell me you had a place there too?"

"What? Oh yeah, we did ... I do. Do you remember the papers I saw in Terry's car? HTF ... ah shit. It wasn't an H, it was an 'A' ... ATF: Alcohol, Tobacco, and Firearms."

"Makes sense," Michelle agreed. "But you know what? What if each number is a set or a group of weapons and not individual guns?"

"Oh, shit," uttered Tawon. "On the streets that could bring serious coin."

After a few minutes, I said to Michelle, "Why would we be involved in guns now? Terry himself recently told me that only a few drivers had ever been stopped, and the cops found nothing. Javier has been spooked. But he said nothing about guns. It makes little sense to change the entire organization."

The car went silent again. The type of eerily quiet that only happens when there isn't anything calming or reassuring that can be said. We all spent a few moments to ourselves pondering the possibilities.

Michelle then said, "They have changed the organization, or at least tried, Woody. If you had been at the house, the three most exposed members would have been eliminated."

"But guns? There would have to have been an organization in place for some time to be able to move them," I noted.

"Maybe Javier wasn't paranoid. Maybe he found out about the guns and realized what might happen next. You said it was he who set up the dinner. Maybe he was going to share with you and Terry what he had learned."

"And maybe he shared his feelings with … Tarant," I exclaimed.

Tawon broke the silence by kicking in the radio. It was a ghetto rap station he found, but the two whites in the car didn't care. We had tons of puzzle pieces to fit together without knowing how many puzzles to make or a picture on a box to use.

It was a clear, starlit night on the remaining drive to San Antonio. Finally, Michelle muttered, "Woody, we need to call Jimmy and ask him for his input. He'll have a much better view because he's not involved directly. I think he's who we need to look at this ATF thing."

"I agree. We won't be able to explain why we know, though."

"We'll have to just tell him what's happened."

"Who is Jim?" asked Tawon.

"He's a retired deputy sheriff who was a homicide detective."

"Wait, just a minute. We killed two people and you want to tell a cop?"

"He knows we didn't murder Ashley or Terry. He's our next-door neighbor in North Carolina. He's cool, Tawon."

"If you say so," Tawon said under his breath.

"I think you're right, Michelle. I think if we hand over the papers to him, he'll probably know how to disseminate them to the right agency."

As I punched in the phone number, I thought about what had happened to us. All because of greed. Damn!

"Hello Jim, hope we didn't wake you. How are you doing?"

"Good, Paul. No, I wasn't in bed yet. What's up?"

"Yeah, doing fine. We came across some papers and we think they might be some sort of guns or weapons lists for distribution or purchases in different cities. You can understand that we … ah … aren't really in a position to meet with the police. If I get these to you, would you forward them to someone you trust?"

"Sure, Paul. How'd did you happen onto these records?"

"Ah, well …"

"Yeah, that's what I thought. Are you all okay?"

"We're fine. I … we knew we could count on you."

"Hello. This is special agent Cottrell with the ATF. Is agent Burke in today?"

"He's on the phone, agent Cottrell. May I take a message?"

"Tell him three names he gave me are linked to a large gun-smuggling group out of Mexico. He can call me on my cell."

"Sir, he's motioning me to hold you from hanging up."

"Okay, of course, I'll hold."

"Hey, Seth. Thanks for holding," Kurt said.

"Sure thing. Three names you gave me jumped out of our computer."

"Awesome. Tell me what you found."

"Okay, Terrance Lincoln's name hit a few cross-agency investigations and all in the last several years. He was arrested five years ago in Texas for trafficking guns but agreed to a plea deal on a lesser charge and received twenty-four months by the state versus federal charges. Says here he was released after eight months served."

"Cindi Draper is connected through a name not on your list. She is considered being involved in moving guns into Alabama."

"Archie Wolfe is connected loosely with Lincoln and lives in the Memphis area. We know from interviews he has a connection with a trucking company in McAllen, Texas."

"Thanks, Seth, I owe you."

On the drive back to San Antonio, I decided we wouldn't drop off the tape of Tomas with the FBI. I wanted to give our local cops that information, hoping they could use it, especially since they're the ones we needed to exonerate us. We would FedEx a copy to our Sheriff's office. I gave Tawon the tape to FedEx via a flat rate box and told him to drive to Austin and drop it in a street canister. I also asked him to do some searching for anyone who knew anything about Tarant, Muchido, Schmidt, or anyone else in this organization. I gave him a check for $5,000 notated as consulting salary.

We found rooms for the night and then hit it fairly early in the morning. Michelle and I drove towards McAllen. Tawon went to Austin.

We had driven about fifty miles before Michelle finally asked, "Why are we going to McAllen."

I said, "We still have unfinished business with Tarant."

"I'm in," she said. "I was waiting for you to say it; what changed your mind?"

"We've got to stop whatever else he and his cronies have started with all the guns destined for who knows where. We have a chance to make a statement. Us. You, me, and Tawon! We were part of that world and I, for one, no longer want to be associated in any way … shape … or form, with that world."

"I've been thinking the same way ever since you told me you wanted to correct your wrongs. I feel the same because, Lord knows, I've made a slew of mistakes. But do you have any idea what, and how, we're going to do it?"

"Yep, we're going to call him and let him know he's going to die," I stoically claimed.

A few minutes later, I found and telephoned the main office. "Hello, Rotten Tomatoes. May I help you?"

"Yes ma'am, is Mr. Tarant in?"

"No sir, he's out. May I take a message?"

"Do you expect him to return soon?"

"He might be back. I never know. Who is this?"

"Tell him Woody called and that we need to talk."

"Okay, does he know you, sir?"

"Oh yeah. Tell him I'm in Kentucky now but I'm driving to Texas."

"Will do, honey. Does he have this number?"

"No, you can give it to him."

TWENTY-FIVE

We arrived in McAllen soon after my phone call to Tarant. We drove straight to Rotten Tomatoes and began scoping out the plant, including the trucking portion. It was a large complex. Bordered by three streets and an alley cutting through it, making an odd sort of triangle shape. The trucks entered from 3rd Avenue and generally departed onto Huertas Street. Lucinda Drive encompassed the main building and office space. The location sat within two blocks of both Interstates 69C and Rt. 2. The main office building was a two-story brick and mortar structure with windows only on the north and east sides of the structure.

We drove around the complex several times, making mental notes of what we saw and what we didn't see, noticeable security measures. We identified the parking lot for employees, which was on the corner of Lucinda and 3rd Avenue. Michelle pointed out a paint shop across the street from the parking lot. The paint shop was a good size non-national business. It used a medium-sized parking area; there were two shade trees near the sidewalk which offered some protection from the sun and helped our hope to remain part of the landscape.

Michelle said, "Do you know of a president or top brass that doesn't have an assigned parking spot?"

I thought a moment and realized what she was getting at. "Tarant had to have a prime parking space and most likely one nearest the building," I answered in agreement.

"Exactly." She took a stroll to see if a sign was presently marking the boss's spot. She gave the thumbs up slyly behind her back and kept walking around to the other side of the street and then returned to our car.

"Bingo! He has a sign marked as El Rey. My Spanish isn't very good, but that translates as The King. No car was parked there."

"Were there any other marked slots?"

"Just for visiting customers."

We could see his spot from several places, so we stayed put and discussed our next move and waited. A few minutes later, my phone rang.

"Hello," I said.

"I got a message you called Mr. Woodford. I was surprised to hear from you. You have some explaining to do."

"Really? Since I'm the only one alive now, I think you're the one who has some explaining to do."

A small grunt came through the other end of the receiver. "Listen here, you little shit. You've been stealing money, talking to the Feds, and being a royal pain in my ass."

"Well, that hurts," I said with a smirk. "I've never talked to any Feds."

"I don't care who you've been talking to. Stealing from us was plenty of a reason to send your balls up the flagpole. And for what? Didn't pay you enough, you little punk? You even set up the scheme for all of our retirements. We were all set, but you had to fuck it all up."

"We could talk about whose skills were more important to the organization until we're blue in the face, but that doesn't explain why you put hits on us."

"Me? That shit came from way up. You should know that."

Tarant paused for a second. "But it doesn't matter anymore. What's done is done. You and everyone else that knows about the hit has to go."

I tried to think clearly and turn the discussion in a way to get intel. "But you and I might be able to help each other."

"What are you saying?"

"Let's meet and talk about the finances and the problems with the numbers. I can explain to you where the money is and how you can pick off the other's share ... all for you. No one else needs to know."

A bit of indecision. Then more silence while he digested this offer and the possibilities. "How about at a local restaurant tomorrow?"

"I won't be able to get there until late morning," I lied.

"Meet me at Pueblos on Fourth Avenue at noon."

"Okay, and don't bring the cavalry."

I hung up. We waited for Tarant to return to his office, assuming he would want to gather copies of documents he had read reflecting the missing money. I still was wondering how he had figured it out, if, in fact, he had. In the end, it wouldn't matter if everything went the way I hoped.

We didn't have to wait too long. Tarant showed up in a black Cadillac. Black? In Texas. Really? He was in a hurry. He ducked into the office side door, quickly taking the steps two at a time. He looked to be about six feet and lean. He wore his black hair short. He moved with some sign of athleticism. He was probably forty-five. He was alone. We waited for another twenty minutes before he exited with a male Hispanic.

We followed them into town and straight to Pueblos. They drove around the restaurant noticeably scouting it out either noting a defensive position or an attack site. Tarant drove back to the office, but dropped the passenger off on Lucinda and kept driving. We followed as long as we could, but after a few red lights, we lost him. It was late afternoon, so we found another hotel room.

Michelle remarked, "Before we find a hotel, we need to switch out the car first. We have to assume he, or others, may have seen it, especially since yesterday's events." I agreed. We dropped off our car at the airport. We walked around to the taxi and bus pickup point and found the shuttle bus identified as connected to a La Quinta hotel. After checking in, we called and had a new rental car brought to us, a perk I had through the credit card company.

There was some time to kill, so we found Dos Amigos Trucking and conducted some surveillance there, too. It was a similar-looking structure to Rotten Tomatoes Distributorship. There were many eighteen-wheelers in and out of the facility. It was within a triangle of streets and avenues, much like the lumberyard. Each street gave an access point, but the main office building was accessed from Tenth Street. One other issue was that the perimeter was bordered by a six-foot-high-security chain-link fence, which limited visibility.

We found a suitable location to watch the main entrance. Michelle, again, took a walk. The entrance was wide enough for her to see parking slot markers.

"There is a slot for Javier and one for Hanson and no others except for visitors."

"You know this Hanson?"

"He may be the lawyer Javier used. It seems to me his name came up when a driver had been stopped some time ago."

"Okay, if Javier used him, we have to assume he was well aware of the actual business. We'll have to do some work to determine if he's a player too. Can you search the Internet for this Hanson and find out anything useful?"

"Of course. Let's drive to the nearest coffee shop. They all have Wi-Fi connections and sometimes a computer terminal too."

We drove away from Dos Amigos in an easterly direction for no other reason than to put the sun at our back. After six or seven blocks, we saw a prospective spot, Java Joe's. We parked at the rear of the store and walked in to find exactly what we needed. A counter of breadsticks, cookies, bisques, a coffee bar, and computers in cubicles along the opposite wall. Michelle sat down and searched. The search request linked Hanson to Muchido and Dos Amigos, but Michelle also noted: "He's a defense attorney, too. His practice specializes in all types of defense matters. He has a website." She continued on, "Let me open that up." ... "The clients that provided testimonials are all drug defendants. Imagine that."

In the morning, we drove to Rotten Tomatoes and parked again nearby to watch for Tarant. He arrived soon after nine o'clock. He was alone, and this time seemed more aware of his surroundings. He remained in the car, looking around, using his rearview and side-view mirrors. When he exited the car, he looked over his shoulder twice as he walked into the building. We had three hours before the proposed meeting.

Michelle said, "I'm going to ask for a job and get a feel for the office. I'll say I'm looking for anything."

We drove around the corner far enough away so that if any security cameras were working, no one would see us. I dropped Michelle off, drove away, and timed it so hopefully, my return would be close to Michelle's entrance, and as I turned the corner, I saw her walk in. About five minutes later, she exited and walked away towards the spot I had dropped her off. I left my location, traveling in the opposite direction, and then circled to pick her up.

Michelle told me, "There were only two employees I saw. The receptionist and an office worker in the back. I was told there weren't any jobs. Tarant's office is the second room on the left behind the front office where the receptionist area is. The receptionist took a call while I was asking about a job and told the woman in the back of the building she needed to leave and pick up someone around lunchtime. I didn't hear names or a location."

"Did you see Tarant?"

"No. I saw his nameplate on the doorway but his door was closed."

"There are only three cars in the parking lot. Hopefully, both of the women leave before Tarant does."

We sat in silence for the next few hours, several blocks away. We moved every fifteen minutes to avoid suspicion. At eleven forty, we traveled around the western path past Rotten Tomatoes when Michelle noted, "That woman walking to the light blue Oldsmobile was the employee I saw at the rear of the office." We saw her pull out and travel past us, never even looking up at our approaching vehicle. We continued in the original direction, which took us past Rotten Tomatoes on our right side. It took about five minutes to circle the blocks and eventually picked up Rotten Tomatoes back in our sights. A few minutes later, the receptionist left too, in a canary yellow VW. Michelle uttered, "Crap, Tarant's car is gone!"

We traveled straight away to the meeting at Pueblos. We circled the parking lot but did not see a black Cadillac. There were eight or nine cars in the parking lot and about the same number in the rear identified as employee parking only. We parked across the street for ten minutes and saw only two new vehicles arrive, but neither held any male occupants. During those ten minutes, we saw several groups of customers exit the restaurant, none of which led us to believe they were associated with Tarant. We continued waiting. Michelle said the obvious, "He will not show because he's got someone inside and probably outside doing surveillance to identify you for later."

"Yeah, I've been thinking that his agreement to meet seemed too easy."

"We should leave and check out from the hotel now," Michelle said.

"Right, and after that, we probably should reserve another hotel somewhere outside of town. Muchido and Tarant had, and have, many tentacles in this town, and we can't trust anyone. I don't want to leave yet because we at least have begun some communication with him."

Maybe forty-five minutes later, we had checked out of our hotel but hadn't figured out where to go next.

Michelle suggested, "How about Harlingen; it's probably less than an hour east of here."

I thought about her suggestion but countered, "I don't think so. That seems too close; he's got to be a powerful man in this part of Texas and Mexico. I saw a road sign for Laredo earlier. The sign read 161 miles. That's further than we both would like if there were a reason to respond quickly, but then again Tarant couldn't respond any quicker."

"I like that. Laredo it is. It's a larger city so we can get lost as tourists."

It took us two and a half hours before we found a decent hotel and one with a swimming pool. We had time to digest what had happened during the last seventy-two hours. Tarant had not called me to ask why we hadn't shown, probably because he knew we had figured out his plan. The bottom line: he knew I was alive, but he didn't know I knew what he looked like or what he drove. Also, as far as anyone knew, I was alone.

TWENTY-SIX

Michelle and I took advantage of the pool and relaxed as best we could. She was quite attractive in jeans and a real head-turner in the bikini she bought in a boutique down the street. I bought my swimsuit in the hotel's clothing shop. It was on a shelf between women's hats and gift cards ... classy.

We both envisioned specific goals. We had become more and more comfortable around each other. I guess it was inevitable. I would think it's much like the Stockholm Syndrome effect between kidnappers and hostages over a lengthy period. Each party ends up relying on the other for various needs. Michelle and I needed each other for day-to-day companionship and our collective safety.

In the morning, Michelle asked if we should try to contact Tarant or put him on the back burner and maybe try an angle for Hanson. She offered, "I have to believe Hanson is bigger than we thought, and with Muchido gone, wouldn't Hanson be trying to create a relationship with those above him to keep the organization together?"

"I'm tracking you, but wouldn't he be worried about

developing a relationship with the probable person who just had his boss murdered?" I countered.

"I guess so, but what if he was in on it? He's still alive, so the 'cleansing' was complete, except, of course, for you. He doesn't seem to be worried since he's still at work," Michelle accurately noted.

I mulled that over until Franklin Schmidt came to mind.

"What about Schmidt?" I asked.

Michelle remarked, "That's interesting. I was thinking about him too. I don't think Schmidt's main office is in McAllen anymore. Tarant seems to be the key man here. I think after Franklin took over, he moved to Nashville and set up there. My understanding has always been that Franklin kept his hands off as much as possible; moving to Nashville added another layer of insulation."

"I know I don't have any contacts close to Franklin," I said. "In fact, I don't think I ever met him more than a handful of times and always in a group setting. I'm not even sure what I said to him if I spoke at all."

Michelle said, "I met him a few times and also at dinner parties. I don't think I know anyone either that we could go to as a contact."

"We need to consider the possibility that Franklin is a bigger fish than we ever thought. If Tarant was the decision-maker, why didn't either of us know of his true role? Doesn't that seem weird?" I questioned.

"Okay, let's assume you're right. Why hadn't Terry ever said anything about Franklin having a larger role? I knew his direct line of power was through Javier because of the original partnership. I knew Tarant was an owner of Rotten Tomatoes and he had had a prior business relationship with Muchido at Dos Amigos. But the business relationship between Franklin and Tarant is still an unknown. Woody, it's too far to drive to Nashville and scope out Franklin. I vote for checking out Hanson."

"We could fly, but since we're closer, I agree with you. Let's drive back tomorrow to McAllen to see Hanson."

Tarant called Hanson. "Don? You sitting down? I've been called by Mr. Woodford."

Hanson squeaked, "That's the money man you told me about up in Indiana—right?"

Tarant growled, "Yes. He called to set up a meeting with me to discuss an arrangement for everyone. Can you believe it? He's brave or an idiot."

"Ha. Yeah. He's got balls," Hanson agreed. "What did you say to him?"

"I agreed to meet him. I was told he didn't show," Tarant again growled.

"You didn't go?" Hanson asked.

Tarant exclaimed, "Hell no! It was probably an ambush. I sent a couple of my guys instead. What I am telling you is, Woodford is being proactive. He's searching. If he doesn't already know about you, he'll figure it out soon. You've got to be on your toes. He's looking for revenge."

"Got it. What does he look like?" asked Hanson.

"I'm not sure. I don't know when we met. I relied on Muchido and Langfeld to handle the money side and only spoke with them regarding hiding the money. I know he's smart. We have to take care of this soon or Morelo will blow his top, and we don't want him to go off the deep end because then everyone becomes expendable."

"Okay, I'll be careful," Hanson answered nervously.

Burke took a call through his receptionist. "Yes, may I help you?"

"Yeah, Kurt. This is Mary in Forensics. We found two sets of prints at the Oliver residence that may be of help in the future."

"What do you mean, the future?"

"The prints aren't on file with us. So, until you get a second set of a known person, we have got nothing to compare these to."

"Okay, thanks, Mary."

Burke hung up and called another agent. "Skip, did you discover anything at the airport or car rental companies?"

"Nothing at Columbus Municipal Airport or here. I haven't yet contacted Muhammad Ali Airport in Louisville, but will. The rental companies are balking at such a wide-ranging subpoena."

"Narrow the subpoena time ranges to one month before the murders and two weeks after," Burke instructed. "Hey, get a subpoena out for Woodford's bank accounts. Maybe there will be something there we can use."

"Okay, will do."

Harris and Manna stood in the kitchen at the detachment, shooting the breeze. They were admiring the various food items in the refrigerator. Al asked, "Have we gotten through all the travel logs from Baxter's yet?"

"Yeah, they just completed it last night, and they created a spreadsheet of their findings, focusing on patterns. I took a quick look before you got in. What I've seen is that Baxter's return trips reflect that every twenty days, the same drivers traveled to various locations, including Oklahoma City and Atlanta. The comparison to the logbooks reflects its accuracy. There wasn't anything missing. The mileage is correct, and the drivers never exceeded the DOT restrictions on drive times. Basically, everything we've been told adds up."

"All right. Did you see anything that may have been suspicious?"

"Not really Al. Baxter's drivers followed DOT rules and guidelines to the letter."

In the morning, Michelle and I dressed for our return to McAllen, but we kept the hotel room open for two more days. We walked around the corner and breakfasted on what was billed as authentic Mexican food. It was good. We were happy with the authenticity advertisement. On the drive, I wondered out loud, "I think we need to do a two-car surveillance on Hanson and just see what happens. So, let's rent a second car nearer to McAllen, okay?"

Michelle agreed, "There's really no other way right now, anyway."

Michelle rented a Toyota Camry. We drove to Dos Amigos and used two new burner phones to talk. A Mercedes Benz was parked in Muchido's parking slot and Hanson's slot was empty. We had arrived at eleven-thirty. We took up positions within a block in either direction of the main entrance to Dos Amigos. Nothing other than trucks were using the entrance until twelve twenty, when two cars left and traveled past me. At twelve-thirty, Michelle called me and said she saw the Benz exit and come in her direction.

"Okay, Michelle. Just keep telling me the streets you're on and I'll follow hopefully on a parallel road."

Michelle shadowed the Benz to an office building with a small sign, Hanson & Associates, ESQ. "He's at his law office on fourteenth street. I remember the address on the website and this is it for sure."

I responded, "I'll stay back on the route to Dos Amigos, assuming he'll return for the afternoon. If he does, I'll track him so you don't get burned."

"Got it, Woody. I'll let you know when he leaves."

An hour and a half later Michelle called and reported, "Woody, a white male, brown hair, maybe six feet tall, just walked out and got in the driver's door of the Benz. He's driving back the same route so far."

"Okay, I've got him, but he's turning down a different street. I'm not sure why. This looks like a dead-end. Aw, shit! He's stopped! He's motioning me out of the car!"

I pulled up to his car, which was stopped across the roadway. I exited and yelled, "What the hell, man! What are you doing?"

Hanson got out and as sternly as he could, said, "I think you're tailing me, and I don't like it. Who are you and what do you want?"

My brain took off speeding at two hundred miles an hour. Was I being played, or maybe he didn't know who I was? The odds of him ever having seen a picture of me were slim and I had a grown-out five-day beard. My hair was a little longer too. I risked it. "Sir, I need a lawyer, and I understand you're a good one."

Hanson looked me up one side and down the other, trying to decide what to do. He finally answered, "I'm busy right now. Come back in an hour, and we'll see if I can help?"

"Yes sir, an hour."

He drove off. I called Michelle and asked her to meet me. She suggested the parking lot at a Walmart we had driven past earlier.

Michelle walked over to my parked car near the Yard and Garden of Walmart. "So, you sounded a little excited. What's up?"

"You need to sit down because this is crazy. I got burned by Hanson. Don't know how or when but he took me down a dead-end street, parked, and motioned me to stop."

"Holy shit, Woody!"

"Yeah, exactly. Anyway, there was no way to leave without drawing even more attention, so I stopped. He asked me who I was and why I was following him. I took the chance, and I said I needed a lawyer. He told me to come back in an hour."

"Oh, man! You're not truly going to meet him, are you?" Michelle exclaimed.

"Might as well. It won't hurt to gather some more intel ... can never have too much."

So, for the next thirty minutes, we discussed options, the pros and the cons. I said, "The reason I am considering telling him the truth is because of attorney-client privileges. If he became my attorney, I could hire him and he couldn't legally tell anyone. Now, if he is as involved as we think, the legality issue wouldn't bother him anyway, but being identified by me may be a problem for him. I could accuse him of being behind the murders, which might get me in long enough to learn some things. What do you think?"

"I think you're out of your fucking mind! You're going to walk into a building you've never been in, with no idea who else is there, all based on the assumption Hanson doesn't know who you are. Geez, Woody. Really?"

"I know it's crazy, but who would ever believe that I would get the chance to confront him?"

"I get that, probably no one, because he would never believe you're as crazy as you are," she barked.

"I think it's worth it. I'm going to try it and see what happens. The worst thing would be he can give Tarant a physical description."

"No, the worse thing would be he's waiting for you, Woody."

Michelle drove over to Hanson's office about twenty minutes before me. I saw her car, but only because I knew which car to look for. She was well concealed. She sent me a text, "I won't interrupt but you should know there are security cameras." I walked up the five steps to the entryway. I was barely greeted by a young woman in blue dress slacks and white short-sleeved blouse, who asked me as she skirted around behind her desk, "Your name, please, as she started to turn her computer on."

"Don't bother. I would rather speak to Mr. Hanson first."

She wasn't ready for my answer and with her back to me punched a button on the landline phone and through an intercom link announced the two o'clock appointment was here. She pointed me down the hall and to a conference room. She called after me that Mr. Hanson would be in a minute. She was still scurrying around her office, somewhat harried.

Hanson walked in, sporting a poor mood. "Okay, buddy. What the hell are you doing and why?"

I said, "I need an attorney. You're well known in the area, so I wanted to see how many clients you were seeing. Few that I can tell, so I figured I might have a chance."

"That's an interesting story, but most people just call and make an appointment. They rarely do surveillance. What exactly do you need me for?"

"How much do you need to officially hire you as my attorney?" I said, fumbling with my words. I could see the wheels turning. He was thinking: "Should I charge an exorbitant amount to just send him away, or simply name the normal fee."

"Carey, bring me a contract." Hanson finally announced.

I interrupted, "Here's six hundred cash. Is that enough?"

Hanson looked at the cash and said, "That's fine." Carey, still in the hallway, handed him a contract and Hanson requested she reschedule his two-thirty appointment.

Carey explained, "Okay, Don, but I have to pick up Angel at daycare. There's something going on at the daycare and they want the kids picked up as soon as possible. May I go after he fills this out?"

"Of course. No need to come back. Just go home and have a good night. I'll put the contract on your desk. You can file everything tomorrow morning. Hope everything is okay with Angel. See you in the morning."

Hanson walked out of the room, and I filled in my real name and "old" address.

When Hanson returned, he signed the contract without reading it, folded it over, and set it on Carey's desk. He then turned to me and eked out, "Okay, what do you need me for?"

I had visualized over and over what I might say in the event I would ever meet the boss. But even though I had, I felt nervous as all get out.

I stammered, "I am … ah … currently missing from … another state and may … ah … be considered a suspect in a murder. But I'm innocent."

"Well, tell me your story … ah, your name again?"

"It's Paul, sir," I interrupted.

"Okay, Paul. Your story please."

After the first exchange, I began to be more comfortable in the setting. I started with generalities of where and when. I was concentrating on Hanson's face and posture, looking for signs that he was aware of the murders. I kept talking with no names or places until he directed me to give him better details.

So, I said, "I was asked by two of my bosses to set up a meeting. I volunteered to have a dinner party at my girlfriend's and my house. I was ah … late getting home, and when I arrived at our house, I … I found they had all been … murdered. No reaction. No acknowledgment. Nothing at all. I couldn't go to the police because we all had been involved in some ah … things."

"I'm sorry to hear what's happened to you, but going to the police was/is the right thing to do, even if you're involved in some illegal activities. If not, the longer you're missing, the stronger their sense that you're the killer," he advised.

"Well, I thought I needed to protect others so, I didn't want to open pandora's box; if you know what I mean?"

I decided to push it a little more. "I left Indiana and just drove." Again, nothing.

"When did all this happen?" Hanson asked.

"Five months ago."

"Five months … and in Indiana. Why did you come here?"

"Well, I just started driving. I knew some of those involved were here in McAllen, so I figured maybe I should come here. I'm not thinking clearly. Maybe this was a bad idea."

"Who all were killed?" he asked with a faint look of a light bulb going on.

"Well, a guy named Muchido and," Hanson jumped. He was blinking a hundred miles an hour; his face had first turned reddish, and then paled.

"Excuse me. I need to make a call," he squeaked, as he began to rise.

I said, "No, I don't think so. You're my lawyer and you're going to sit down. You know Muchido, don't you?"

He wouldn't answer. He was trying to reach the phone when I grabbed him and threw him down on the table with an extra hard swing. He lost his breath. I took that opportunity to squeeze his shirt and tie at his throat. I leaned in and whispered, "You obviously know this Muchido. What I want to know is what else do you know and who else was involved?"

He jerked up as far as he could with me holding his neck, which wasn't a far distance. He was an average sized man. No sign he was a gym-rat.

"Listen to me," he said as strongly as he could, "you're not getting out of here alive. If you're lucky, you might live until midnight."

"That's a pretty fucking lame threat, asshole, and a stupid one at that. So, here is an actual threat. If you don't tell me who called the shots and carried them out, I'll just add you to the growing list of deceased. So, start," I said, angrily.

"No way, am I talking to you."

I brought my right hand and fist to my chest and swung my right elbow and struck the left side of his face. He saw it coming, but he had no real chance of avoiding a nearly perfect strike. I caught him more on the jaw than the cheekbone. Bone cracked loudly, and he went limp. Since he was still at the conference table, I was able to drag him into a chair. There was a long extension cord used to provide electricity to a multi-outlet used for computers. I grabbed it, unplugged it from the table, and quickly wrapped it around him. He was still pretty groggy. I ran around the conference table and drew the blinds, but as I did, I cut my leg on the corner. Some blood showed through my shorts. I couldn't stop. I took off his shoes and rolled down his socks. I took the socks and stuffed them into his mouth. I went to the front desk and found my contract and money. A glance at my leg proved some bleeding and dripping down my leg.

His office employee, Carey, must have been truly concerned about responding to her daughter's needs because she hadn't turned her computer off. When I checked, I could see my name, and any written documents hadn't been preserved anywhere. I deleted anything I found regarding a scheduled meeting from her computer, shredded the contract, and pocketed my money. I heard Hanson grunting and groaning. I stepped back into the room. "Well, Don. How's it feel to be on the other end of an attorney-client screwing?"

He was mad, but not yet significantly fearful of me. There was a glass pitcher used as a vase with some flowers. I put on my gloves and grabbed the vase handle. Hanson's eyes enlarged, and I wasn't sure if he feared the use of the gloves or the potential use of the glass vase. I swung it to the corner of the table, shearing off the glass, leaving the glass handle in my hand and a nice jagged edge. I snuggled the jagged edge to his throat and pushed hard enough to draw blood. His defenses were wilting.

"I asked politely. You've got another chance, but just one. I'd suggest you make the best of it."

"No, he'll kill me," he said.

I thrust the glass edge into his throat and down to the voice box. Along the way, I must have hit the jugular. The blood spurted ninety degrees to his left and more than I would have liked. His eyes rolled back into his head. I continued holding his necktie. He gurgled and struggled and tried to push me off him, but his strength was waning fast. He tried to speak or shout. I'm not sure which. I didn't care. I was lucky he spurted most of his blood away from my arm, and my legs were sheltered because of the table. He became limp with no more fight and huffed his last breath.

I stood back and called Michelle on my phone. I said, "I'm fine and the only one here. Come closer and watch the front door. Let me know if someone wants in."

I saw I had some blood on my shirt. Had to be his. My blood was lower and on the top of my shoes. Damn. I had avoided stepping in any of the blood. I went through the office looking for anything that might help us. There were several file folders of clients that meant nothing to me. There was a computer, but it was password protected.

Hanson used one of those large paper calendars on his desktop and had doodled while he was probably on a phone call. With each new month, he just folded prior months over. I rolled through them until I flipped to the month. "The date" was circled and marked with an asterisk. I saw a few other dates or other pages similarly marked, so I grabbed those months too. I took a flash drive that was in a desk drawer. I had seen nothing else that jumped out to me, but I kept milling around the office and, whoa, la. Clothes. Dress clothes, actually a man's suit he must have used when he had to go to court at the last minute. I checked for sizes. Legs might work, but the shirt and coat would certainly be tight. I changed. I was right about the fit, but I figured all I had to do was get to the car and worry about the rest later. I saw a garbage bag and put my bloodied clothes in it, along with other items.

Carey had an antiseptic container with those little ammonia-laden sheets or wipes. I used them to wipe anything and everything I could think of. I wasn't sure how much time I had, so I worked quickly, hoping I cleaned it all. No idea if it would contaminate my DNA or not.

Michelle called, "No one has driven up, but a police car drove by. I don't think they could see your car and license plate, but you need to get out soon."

"On my way. Keep a lookout." I started towards the front, but then it hit me, security cameras. I stepped into several offices towards the rear of the space. I finally found two computers. I didn't know what to do to erase files, but I grabbed the computer identified as security. The other computer I assumed was a network office server. I hoped one wasn't backed up to the other.

I walked out of the office through the front door, using the garbage bag on the door handle and cradling the computer laptop under my arm. I looked around from the front stoop and took in a long breath of air and felt better than I had when I had arrived. Getting closer.

I saw Michelle. She gestured to follow her, which I did, back to the Walmart lot.

"Well, you big ape. How'd did it go?"

I told her the details and said we needed to clear the hell out and get back to Laredo pronto. She didn't argue. She said we needed to drop off my car and go in hers now. Then she saw the blood. "Hey, I thought you said you were, okay?" Michelle said.

I could see Michelle had seen evidence of my cut on the leg. I answered, "I am okay. A slight cut only. A chink in my armor. Guess I'm not invisible."

Michelle said, "Don't get in the car yet. She took off the jacket I had removed from Hanson's closet and set it on the seat. She pointed for me to sit. I did. Michelle drove and occasionally looked over at me shaking her head."

I said, "What? It doesn't even hurt." She reached over and punched my leg. "Ow," I said, not-so-manly-like.

"Yeah, doesn't hurt. How bad is it really? Do we have to stop and get medical treatment?"

"It's almost stopped bleeding. Forget the emergency room. Just let's drop my car off like you suggested."

After dropping off my rental, I began leafing through the things I took while she drove her vehicle. But I still watched her right arm.

The desk top calendar papers revealed something interesting. "Look at this. The date of the murders is circled with an asterisk too. The date of Stewart's murder is also circled and with an asterisk. They're the only such indications in all the months. Most of the doodles and scribbles mean nothing to me. The flash drive will most likely be password protected, but who knows?"

"Have you forgotten about the security computer in the back seat?" Michelle asked.

"Oh, crap! You think? Let's try it."

The computer itself wasn't password-protected, probably because it didn't have any client data. I plugged in the flash drive, but it was encrypted. I threw the computer in the back seat and we kept driving.

TWENTY-SEVEN

During the several hours ride back to Laredo, Michelle asked me various times, "How are you, really?"

"I'm okay. I must admit, I wasn't ready for this," pointing to my leg, which had stopped bleeding. "When his secretary said she had to leave, he told her to file the contract in the morning. I felt I might be able to stay invisible. If he had talked, I was prepared to tie him up, but nothing else. I wanted Tarant, and whoever else, to know I was alive and proactive. But, well, he wouldn't talk, and so, you know."

"Okay, but you've got to confide in me if things get dark. You know, up there," as she pointed to my head.

I answered, "Sure. Thanks. What are you thinking? Hanson wasn't part of the group?"

"Well, I think Tarant, or Rotten Tomatoes, was running all or most of the organization through its subsidiary, Dos Amigos, and its relationship with Baxter's. No, I feel Hanson was involved as an attorney. But nothing yet explains Schmidt's role. I think he's farther up the ladder. Franklin might actually be the one pulling the strings. But that is hard to believe based on his personality," Michelle perfectly summarized.

"So, if we're wrong with the theory that Tarant is a key figure and we both agree that Franklin doesn't have the stomach to run this organization, then there's at least one other person neither of us is aware of."

Michelle said, "If we're going to dismantle this organization, then we need to know which one, Tarant or Schmidt, is next."

"I've got an idea. If I can call Miguel and act as though I know nothing much about Hanson's death and ask him to reach out to a friend about Hanson. It might be interesting how his death is felt through the businesses."

"I don't think we lose anything as long as Miguel doesn't get burned for asking about Hanson the same week as he is murdered."

I answered, "That's a good point. I don't want to put him on the spot. I'll just feel him out." I punched the favorite number for Miguel.

"Miguel, this is Woody. Can you talk?"

"Si. Give me a second to step down the hall. Okay, amigo. How are you?"

"We're fine, my friend. Do you know who Don Hanson is at Dos Amigos Trucking?"

"Si, he's their lawyer, and I think he also does defense work. I think he's known as a drug attorney. Why do you ask?"

"Ah, his name came up in a weird conversation I had with someone. Do you think he's involved with … you know, our stuff?"

"I think he was close with Muchido and probably Tarant, too. It always helps to have an attorney on board. But I don't know how, or what, he did for them. I can ask around if you want me to."

"Well, if you can. It's probably no big deal. If his name comes up when you're talking to your friend, well then, maybe you can ask. You've got to be careful first. The conversation I was in was squirrelly, you know?"

"Si. Did I tell you that Elizabeth is going to the University of Indiana in the spring?"

"No, that's great Miguel!"

"I know. She's really excited. Me too."

"You should be proud, my brother."

"I am. You take care, Woody."

I turned to Michelle. "I think that went well enough, don't you think?"

"Perfectly. We need to decide on our next move. My vote is to go to Nashville and figure out what Franklin is doing there."

"I'm with you. Things in McAllen will soon be too hot."

We'd been in a car for hours each of the last several days, and were pretty tired, so we dropped off the rental at the Laredo International Airport and hoped to get redeye tickets for Nashville. We ate at the airport and had drunk a few brews and slept on the flight. We hadn't any idea where to stay in Nashville, but I liked country music, so we found a room downtown at a ridiculously expensive rate; we booked it for a week. We did not know what we were to expect regarding Schmidt's.

Schmidt's plant in Nashville was in an industrial park at the intersection of I-65 and I-24. The main building seemed fairly easy to watch, except it wasn't safe from being crushed by all the trucks in the area. Michelle again claimed we needed two cars. We tried our luck at obtaining a home address for Franklin but weren't lucky. We took shifts at the plant. When not watching at the plant, we did whatever we could to determine where he lived. It isn't as easy as it used to be. Phone books are dinosaurs, and it's easier to stay out of the public eye if you want to, and Franklin did.

We tried it our way for two and a half days until I said, "I give up. Call Jimmy, please."

"Hello."

"Hi, Jimmy. This is Michelle. How are you?"

"Oh, Michelle, I'm fine, but the real question is, how are you two?"

"We're fine. As always, we have a favor to ask of you or at least some direction you think we could take."

"Sure thing, honey. What do you need?"

"The organization we ended up being part of, employed or, we think, is run by an individual by the name of Franklin Schmidt. He used to be in McAllen, but we just learned he's in the Nashville area, but we can't locate him. Oh, and only to talk to, honest."

"I'll try, Michelle. It shouldn't be too difficult, but maybe not today, okay?"

"Of course, Jimmy, whatever you can do for us."

We hadn't yet walked downtown to Broadway to absorb and enjoy the sights and the music. We stopped at several of the well-known places and a few I hadn't heard about. It was a pleasant escape for us both. We danced a few times and walked into a karaoke bar; we listened to a few really talented singers and more than a few drunks. They were entertaining nonetheless. By midnight, we had drunk enough and began the walk to the hotel. Michelle walked closer to me on the way back; she intertwined her arm under my arm and leaned onto my upper arm. She giggled, and I bellowed when we both almost fell on our faces when we stubbed our feet on a raised part of the sidewalk.

We made it to the hotel unharmed. Michelle had taken my shirt off before we left the elevator. We were kissing passionately, weaving down the hallway to the room. I had trouble opening the door because Michelle was nibbling on my now exposed stomach, inching her way south. We fell onto the bed and clothes sprang off at a rapid pace. I grabbed her from behind and cupped her breasts. I continued massaging her breasts while nibbling her neck and ear. She moaned a bit, turned, and with a velvet and silky hand held my throbbing penis and lowered onto me. I arched my back and let loose. We both fell on our backs, but pretty soon I was ready again. I returned the compliment, and when she grabbed me and pulled me up her body, I entered her and we exploded together.

We lay together for a long time without uttering a word, just some slow breathing and comfortable, easy sighs. We strolled together to the shower and made love once again. Afterward, we talked naked until the early morning hours about guilt, or not feeling guilty. About if this was a natural step for us while we began our lives over. We talked about how this might affect us going forward. We both felt we needed each other and loved each other in a manner no one else could know. We were okay. We relaxed. We breathed ... together.

Jimmy, good to his word, called later the next day. "Woody, this Schmidt fellow is a pretty big deal. He owns several companies. I suppose you knew that, but did you know he has friends in high places?"

"What do you mean 'high places?' I'm not sure I know much about him. He's the partner I had the least interaction with. His company, Schmidt's Distributors & Parson's Fruits and Vegetables, was the distributor in the U.S. using Rotten Tomatoes. But Rotten Tomatoes is owned or was a principal partner in Schmidt's."

"That's the part I found out that you need to know. He rubs shoulders with large international corporate officers and politicians too: Congressman Joseph Tyler in Texas for one and a Congressman Scott Landry in Tennessee for another. I'm not at all saying that the two congressmen are bad. I'm just wanting you to know that this Schmidt is well connected."

"We understand, sir. We appreciate your concern and everything you've done for us."

"I know you do. Just be careful."

With the address and a telephone number provided to us, we now had at least a chance to make headway.

Franklin lived in a gated subdivision, Harmony Acres. The perimeter of the entire community was a raised ground landscape with several types of shrubs and bushes. Inside, those visual impediments snaked a six-foot wrought-iron fence. The entire subdivision wreaked of privacy. We drove the perimeter twice, noting that there were two entrances, both of which were manned by a security guard. There wasn't a plaque or other signage reflecting a real estate company for vacant lots for sale. There appeared to be a golf course connected, or accessible, to the residents, but we couldn't see a clubhouse.

The main headquarters for Schmidt's wasn't any better for us. It was also gated, with one manned security booth. Over the top for a produce distributor, we thought, but we also assumed we knew why. We tried for a few more days to sneak a look at Franklin in any vehicle with no luck. For all we knew, he was overseas in the South Pacific.

We had spent a lot of resources with little to show for it. It had been at least a month since we had encountered Pedro and Tomas, and two weeks since Hanson. Michelle had searched the internet for news articles on them. Only Hanson and Muchido were mentioned in news reports having been killed. The news article stated the secretary reported she last saw him speaking to a new client. A white male in his 30s. The article did not mention a name, so she hadn't seen my name written anywhere. Reading further in the article revealed a quote from the Sheriff in which he identified a link with Javier Muchido. It further claimed the authorities were investigating both crimes as a possible business dispute and suggested others not yet known may be creating a sort of coup. Since the news was out of south Texas, it illustrated a distinct viewpoint that investors in Mexico were behind the coup. There was nothing written that showed any person or persons were suspects.

I shaved my head again to disguise myself further. We had

already rebooked the Nashville hotel for four more days, so I lay out at the pool and walked around downtown as much as possible to bring a normal-looking tan on the new head. Of course, I burned rather than tanned during our drive with a rented convertible on our travels back to McAllen to speak to Tarant. By the time we pulled into Hidalgo County, I had achieved a dark red tan color. Michelle had ridden with a halter top, and because of it, I drove painfully for the longest time.

We chose a different route this time, going through Harlingen about forty-minutes east of McAllen. We stayed at a different La Quinta Inn, and this time Michelle checked us in. We turned in the rental car and rented two new cars at two other rental companies. I used the hotel business office computer to connect online to insure the last several months of expenses charged on my credit card were paid.

We drove separately to McAllen. To bring our heads and thoughts together, she chose a small mall that had seen better times to park in while we decided on what we were going to do. Michelle had purchased two new burner phones outside San Antonio.

Michelle said, "I don't think I can approach the office again for another job without spooking him. You have any ideas?"

"Well, I was thinking we have to catch Tarant in his office alone, maybe we could set up an appointment for after hours."

"How are we going to do that? No job openings, he knows you, and I've been seen by his staff."

"I think Tawon could pull it off," I said and called Tawon with what we needed him to do. About an hour later, he called me back.

"Hey man, it went great. I told him I was traveling in from New Orleans and was representing an interested party that may want to buy part of the trucking company that Rotten Tomatoes owned. I wouldn't tell him the company's name and I insisted I would be in McAllen only this Saturday afternoon. He said I could come around 1:30 and began to tell me the address, but I interrupted him to say I knew everything I needed about the company and looked forward to meeting him."

Michelle said, "Tawon, that was excellent! You sound more and more like a true businessman. I'm impressed."

"Okay, Saturday it is. Thanks, Tawon."

TWENTY-EIGHT

For the next two days, Michelle and I managed more surveillance. We were fairly good at it, too. Michelle used her military training to explain how to conduct various types of surveillance, including urban settings. We learned Tarant always drove the black Cadillac and, except for one time, he drove alone. We put him into a residence and never saw any family type of activity. So, if the office angle didn't work, there was always his home for a visit.

On Saturday, Michelle sat on the residence and I drove to Rotten Tomatoes just to be sure there wouldn't be any others at the meeting.

No one drove by or walked up to the main office. At one twenty, Tarant pulled into the parking lot. He exited the caddy and didn't seem at all concerned by a Saturday meeting with someone he had not yet met. I couldn't tell if he had locked the front door or not. I had texted Michelle that he was here. She said she was on her way over. On the fly, I changed up our plan a bit. Michelle understood.

Michelle tried the front door while I stayed low around the corner of the small roofed porch. It was locked. She knocked on the door and Tarant opened the door a crack. "I'm expecting someone for a meeting soon. Come back Monday."

Michelle, to her credit, asserted, "What? I can't hear you."

Tarant dutifully opened the door to repeat his remarks.

Michelle said, "I used to work at Baxter's."

Tarant froze. I flew around the wall and barreled through the door, knocking Tarant's hand from the handle. I tackled him, driving him into, and almost through, the width of the lobby, landing on him with a thunderous crash. Michelle stepped in, shut and locked the front door, and suspended the closed sign. I placed him in a headlock and waited for him to recognize who I was. It didn't take long.

"Listen up, young man. You don't know what you're doing or who you're up against."

"Well, asshole, I know exactly what I'm doing, and I know what you've done. So now you're going to tell me who else is involved."

He thrashed and wiggled some, but my two hundred forty pounds and weightier anger were too much for him. He just ended up panting and wheezing.

"You won't get out of Texas if you do anything to me. You only hope to leave now. If you do, you both walk away, no questions asked."

I wasn't in the mood for negotiating. "Fuck you! You ordered me and Langfeld dead, but you killed my girlfriend instead, so no, I will not walk away without some answers. Who else knew of the hit?"

He was struggling to figure out how to escape his predicament. He would not talk without more incentive. I let him struggle to muscle me off him, but I wasn't budging, and it just made him waste energy. When he grew weary, I dragged him into his office. Michelle tied his hands and feet with an electrical extension cord she had cut, one used for two-floor lights. Michelle had grabbed a hand towel from the bathroom and I shoved it into his mouth. She also found packing tape; the real packing tape, with strings along its linear length, which we used to secure the towel.

"Here's the deal. I'm going to remove some of the tape and then ask you a few questions. If you're a good boy and don't yell or scream, I'll leave the tape off. Otherwise, the tape goes back on. Your choice. No one is going to be coming by today, so we have all the time in the world to help you cooperate." He nodded okay.

As soon as I started ripping the tape away from his mouth, he yelled and sprung up, struggling for the front desk. He was more explosive than I had imagined. I wasn't as ready for him as I would have liked, but I was able to grab him halfway to the desk. I then landed an uppercut to his stomach, rendering him without air. The tape went back on.

Michelle went to the desk that he had been valiantly trying to reach and discovered an alarm button. We pushed and lugged him more to the middle of the room. I pulled out my knife and said, "That was stupid. I could have killed you."

Michelle spoke up, "Listen, you son-of-a-bitch, I want to know who gave the orders?"

I added, "Who ordered the hit on Langfeld and me?" I removed part of the tape, but this time held onto it.

"I don't know what you're talking about."

"I should have been specific when I gave you instructions. I forgot to say that when you lie to me, you'll receive pain."

Before I followed up with my threat, Michelle leaned over him, put two fingers under his jaw, and with her other hand, grabbed his head on the opposite side. "Hey, asshole. This is called the hypoglossal nerve. With sufficient pressure, one can make a person stand up and bark like a dog." As she spoke, she applied pressure, and Tarant, inching to a standing position, looked as though he really might bark.

I said, "So now you have all the instructions and promises you need. Let's try this again. Who ordered the hit?"

Tarant tried to stay mum, but Michelle made him jump, and then we all jumped. My telephone rang. The ring sounded like an old-time Klaxon. It was Tawon. I let it go to a voice message. Michelle recognized the ringtone. I said, "We'll call him after we take care of this situation."

I had seen a movie where a person trained in anti-interrogation techniques can outlast untold types of torture, but almost always relents. I wasn't ready to use a knife yet. I used something else.

I grabbed his right hand and pinned it down with all my weight to the floor with my right knee. He started doing a pushup to earn leverage to throw me off. I hit him twice with a downward punch to his right elbow, and since I had the wrist locked, it broke. He screamed, but the sound was severely muffled by the towel and tape. My wrist lock now was unneeded, so I crab-walked over the top of him to his left-side and grabbed his left wrist, and kneeled on it with my knee as I had for the opposite wrist. Tarant continued to holler in pain, but even he began to wither and succumb, realizing he might lose the use of both hands.

Michelle had seen I was in control now, so she began scouting the office space for any information we might need. I leaned a little more on his uninjured arm and began our discussion once again.

"You, sir, must be having trouble understanding the situation. Let me help you … again. I know you were involved in the killing of Muchido, Langfeld, and my girlfriend. I also know you killed Mr. Stewart and his sister. You have shown no mercy. I'm inclined not to show you mercy either; especially if you refuse to tell me the truth. Why don't you try again and tell me why?"

Tarant was an evil being. He refused to talk. He didn't seem to care, so I grabbed his little finger on the good hand and began to bend it the wrong way. His eyes and his physical movements proved he was going to fight for his life by trying to outlast me. He was struggling, jerking his body as best he could, but I was pushing down hard and still had control of his good hand. I wasn't sure how long we truly had to get information, so I broke the finger with a quick snap. He screamed into the towel. Tears shot out of his eyes. His breathing and shaking lasted for at least thirty seconds. That doesn't sound very long, but I read somewhere that steady pain lasting longer than forty seconds can be debilitating.

He shook his head up and down aggressively, showing yes, he would talk.

"When I take the towel out of your mouth, you best be quiet or more fingers will go. Understand?" I took the towel out, and he immediately gasped and spit out, "Morelo is who you want."

"How do I find him?"

"Over there by my computer is an old Rolodex."

"You actually use a Rolodex rather than a computer or a cell phone to keep your contacts?" He didn't answer. He whimpered some and then cried when he looked at his finger pointing about sixty degrees backward.

"How does he contact you? And why did you kill Ms. Oliver up in Indiana?"

His eyes darted around, still dilated for fight or flight sympathetic response. He said, "Burner phones … never the same. Stewart's sister was … there. That was … Stewart's fault. A snitch."

"If you never call Morelo, what's on the card in the Rolodex?"

"There's a phone number for … an associate of his. I've never called … it. You know everything. Just leave. I … can't tell you anything … more." He said, struggling.

I was flabbergasted. "You didn't answer my question. Who ordered the murders?"

"It was Morelo."

"Why?" Michelle asked.

Tarant focused in on her for the first time. "Who are you?"

Michelle said, "I used to work for Langfeld and I want to know why Morelo wanted him dead."

"Morelo declared, Javier, Terry, and the moneyman were stealing and talking to the feds. They took all the money and were turning us in for a sweetheart deal with the FBI. He told me to take care of it. That's all. Now let me go, or else."

Tarant was totally in our control, yet he was threatening us. He wasn't worried at all about what could happen to him. How brazen could he be? Why?

I pulled out my knife. "Fuckoff, you're nothing more than a lowlife piece of scum." And I stuck him with the knife, ripping and tearing the muscle and tendons in his abdomen wall. I heard and felt the tearing of the gristle. His lungs leaked air. I held my hand over the towel on his face until he took his last breath, either through suffocation or the knife. I didn't care, and I hoped it was painful.

We had worn gloves and stayed away as best we could from the blood, but it had squirted more than I had planned. I would need to clean up. Michelle checked me for any defensive wounds and found none. She had found the security setup. It wasn't password-protected, so she downloaded the contents onto a CD she found in a desk drawer. She turned off the system, and we took the hard drive, hoping they didn't save the data to another device.

Michelle ran a sweep of the office we had been in and then trashed all the offices. She threw a couple of twenties in the hall and front lobby. We grabbed his stupid antique Rolodex and walked out.

Jesus, how many more levels in this association are there, anyway.

We drove away towards the McAllen International Airport. We saw a reservoir—Boeye Reservoir. Very few people lingered on or near the bank to take notice, so we walked separately to the rim and covertly threw the knife into the water along with parts of our disassembled guns. Before arriving at the airport, we stopped and Michelle went into a Walmart to buy me new clothes. I changed as she drove to the airport. We had left my rental at the hotel, so I called the rental agency; I gave them a song and dance that I had to leave for an emergency and had been picked up by a business partner. I said I would not argue about the pickup fee they would charge.

At the airport rental return, we spotted several trash containers where we deposited the rest of the gun, bullets, and my bloody clothes. Somehow Michelle had been spared any of Tarant's spurting blood. We purchased two tickets for Biloxi, departing in two hours. That gave us time to go through the Rolodex. Alonzo Morelo was in the file with only a phone number as Tarant had sworn. Don Hanson, Esq., also had a card identifying Dos Amigos. A few other names seemed to ring a bell to us, so we took those cards and threw away the remaining cards one by one in every trash can we saw.

We arrived in Biloxi at seven-fifteen. During the flight, I had racked my brain to recall the address of the townhouse Ashley and I had bought just three years ago. I finally remembered how to find the townhouses, but hadn't recalled the actual address. Michelle and I drove our latest rental car to the townhouse. The property was on the rental market. I would have to visit the office to see if the condo was currently rented and if I could get the key. Thankfully, an office employee was still on site. The townhouse wasn't rented. We didn't have any luggage. We called for a pizza to be delivered and asked for the driver to bring a six-pack of beer. She did, and I tipped her twenty bucks. We ate and drank like young kids who snuck away from their folks to see each other. The sensation we both shared having killed another human being cannot be described. Our actions were purely revenge. We hadn't meant to kill our way to the top. It had just happened that way. We both began rationalizing our actions more than before.

We ate, drank, and laughed. We let our hair down, so to speak, and gave into our mutual emotions that only we shared. No one else, just us. No one else could have the same emotional connections. We had just exonerated ourselves and had exacted revenge and I, ... we, liked how it felt. We were satisfied with what we had accomplished. We didn't care. We had killed those who had hurt us or our loved ones. We had become one. For the first time since Ashley and Terry were murdered, we comfortably slept.

In the morning, our exhilaration continued, albeit muted.

TWENTY-NINE

Jim was uneasy and pacing the floor. He hadn't heard from Paul and Michelle for some time. The last they spoke, he felt they were going to take out some type of revenge. He had warned them. One side of his brain was telling him to alert the authorities; the other side was saying to help them ... to save them. He paced around his living room just as he had for all those years as a detective. His gut told him something was ... off. He picked up the phone.

"Lenawee County Sheriff's Office, may I help you?"

"Yes, you can, Phyllis," he purred like a pervert. Phyllis had been his receptionist.

"Oh, Jimmy, you old fart! What's going on down there in the sunshine?"

"Well, the sun is shining, that's for sure. But it would look better if you were down here with me."

"You old flirt. You had your chance, honey," she seductively answered.

"Well, that's just my poor luck. Hey, is Pins around?"

"Sure is. You be good Jimmy, love you."

"Love you too Phyllis."

As Phyllis was making the connection, he was thinking back to when he and his wife had had typical family relationship issues caused by his being a cop. He had come on to Phyllis. She shot him down politely and was the reason he and his wife got back together. She had talked to him sternly or compassionately, depending on the particular circumstance surrounding his life at the time.

"Hey, Jimmy, what's happening?" Pinson said.

"Hey, Pins. I'm still curious about that triple murder. I don't suppose the detectives have reached out to ask about any leads you may have found, have they?"

"No, Jimmy, nothing, but there shouldn't have been a link—right?"

"No, I doubt it, but one never knows. Have you spoken with them at all?"

"No, not yet. I was waiting to hear from you. I'll call them now if you want me to."

"Yeah, if you wouldn't mind. I'd be interested if anything new has been uncovered. The people down here I mentioned asked me again."

"Okay, Jimmy. I'll make a call."

"Thanks, Pins. I appreciate it."

"Hello, may I help you?"

"Yes, I'm Detective Pinson here in Lenawee County, Michigan. I spoke with Detective Harris some time ago. May I speak with him?"

"Sure thing, sweetie. I'll put you right through."

"Detective Harris here. May I help you?"

"Yeah Al, this is Pins up in Michigan. I'm just calling back to tell you we've found nothing on your Lopez dude, and I'm sorry to say no one has made a link with your murders down there, either. Sorry. How have you guys done on this?"

"Hey, no problem. There have been several interesting twists to this mystery. For one, we received a tape recording of what appears to have been a confession."

"Appears to be a confession?"

"Yeah, it's obvious the confessor, a guy named Tomas Engaflo, was being coerced, or at least fearful, of the person or persons conducting the recording. The information provided was spot on; I mean, there was no way he and his half-brother Pedro Lopez didn't do it. He knew too many specific details."

"When you say it may have been an involuntarily given statement. What made you believe that?"

"At several points during the recording there seemed to be some coaching or prodding to explain an event or give more details."

"How did you get the recording?"

"It was delivered by FedEx. We tracked it back to San Antonio, but no way to identify who sent it. There weren't any fingerprints or notes, and no cameras in the area fixed on the sidewalk. We've had BOLOs out for Lopez and Engaflo, but no luck. We tracked them both to McAllen and to the Dos Amigos Trucking and Rotten Tomatoes businesses. I think I had told you about the Dos Amigos link to Baxter's, but Rotten Tomatoes was new to us. Anyway, there have been no sightings of either of them."

"That's weird. The recording can't be used as evidence unless this Tomas guy can verify it at trial, so I wonder why the interviewers sent it with no other information."

"Agreed, but that's not the half of it. A guy that worked at that stupid named business, Rotten Tomatoes, was killed during a burglary the other day. Tarant was his name. The boys down there said his company might have owned or had a financial interest in Dos Amigos."

"God Damn. I'm glad I'm not an employee at these trucking companies."

"Yeah, I agree, and there's more. A defense lawyer in McAllen was murdered a month or two ago which no one except his family would cry over, but he was also connected to Dos Amigos."

"What's his name?" asked Pinson.

"Don Hanson. Detective Manna and I had spoken with him when we called regarding the notification on Muchido."

"Wow, too many coincidences for me."

"Yeah, no shit. We're just sort of sitting on this right now. Unless we find the shooter to corroborate the recording, we have nothing … nada. The Feebs are handling the other two murders up here and the others are in Texas, so we're just sort of sitting on our collective asses."

"What other murders? Are they connected?"

"Yeah, they're connected. Another male employee at Baxter's was murdered, along with his sister east of here, but still in our county. The male ended up being an informant to the Feebs, so they're trying to work the case."

"Jesus Christ, Al, you've got a fucking tiger by the tail. Five linked murders in your county alone; a coerced confession; and two other killings in Texas. Jeez, what the hell is going on?"

"We're still missing the Woodford boy and the Freeman girl. They've not shown up anywhere, and no one who knows them has had any contact. We've just gone up on a wire on Thompson's daughter and a few others that may be close to them, but nothing yet."

"Well, my brother, I hate to say it, but I'm glad it's you and not me."

"I hear you. It's a cluster fuck for sure. You take care now," Harris said.

"Hello, Jimmy?"

"Yeah, Pins, that was quick. What did you hear?"

Pinson gave his old partner the scoop and all the details. He added some of his own speculations. He and Jimmy discussed the case like old times.

"Jimmy, this case seems to be more than just a curiosity story for you. What's really going on?"

Jim had pondered this question and when or how Pins would eventually ask it. He was quite torn about how to answer. "Nah, there's nothing going on. I spoke with someone down here who has family up in Indianapolis. The more we talked about it, the more it got me dreaming of the old days. They're aware of my being a cop, so they ask me a lot of questions. They knew one victim and were just upset. I guess I also was a sort of sticking my chest out and bragging some. I don't tell them any of the important evidence. I coddle their feelings sufficiently to appease their curiosity. Thanks for helping an old man relive some of those old war stories again. You take care now, Pins, and tell Alice hi from me."

"Okay, Jimmy. You take care of yourself; you know sunburns can be painful," Gary laughed and hung up.

We hadn't spoken with Tawon for some time. I had asked him to check on his sources to find out something, anything, about this Morelo guy. I telephoned him. It rang and rang, but no answer. Strange. I dialed again. Same thing again.

"Hey, Michelle, do we have a second number for Tawon?"

"I have this number. Is it different?"

"Yeah, try that one, okay?"

Michelle dialed with the speaker on. "Oh, hi, I must have the wrong number."

A female answered, "Who ya trying to call?"

"I was trying to contact my friend Tawon."

There was a swallow of air, an audible sigh, and another inhale, "Tawon's ... dead."

"Excuse me, what did you say?" Michelle and I gasped.

"Tawon's dead. This is his sister, Neesha. He was shot."

"Oh, no!" we gasped again.

I inhaled desperately to calm my nerves. It didn't work. Michelle couldn't breathe, she just stared … nowhere. What seemed like minutes passed by and I eked out, "This is Woody. What happened? When?"

We listened to Tawon's sister cry and tell us that Tawon died a week ago. He was murdered in Dallas. There weren't any witnesses, and no one had been arrested. He was shot and stabbed several times. The police gave a news release saying it appeared to have been a drug deal gone bad.

"That's bullshit, Michelle declared, her hand pressed over the receiver. He wouldn't have allowed someone to get the drop on him. He was murdered because of what we did and what we asked him to do for us."

I couldn't see straight. Every fucking person I loved was being killed. And all because of me! Tawon was like a brother, the brother I never had. He was loyal. He didn't ask questions and didn't judge. We did anything and everything for the other.

I told Neesha who I was again; she remembered me, and she cried, again.

I, again, as I did with Ashley's murder, saw Tawon and our lives together. He became excited when we had made an extra good deal. He gave his momma all the money he had made, so she didn't have to work three jobs to make the rent and feed his younger siblings. I remember him going without food so his sister could eat. He refused to buy himself shoes he desperately needed so his other sister could get a dress for a school dance. He would be street talking one second and the next second sound as if he was a banker. He cried when his boyhood friend was killed in a drive-by shooting by a gang that mistakenly thought he was a rival gang member. He should have lived a long and enjoyable life.

This was almost as devastating as losing Ashley. A million thoughts flew around my head. It couldn't have been our interaction with Lopez and Engaflo, could it? No one there knew him or us except the two that we killed. I could see Michelle was struggling with her emotions, too. She barely knew Tawon, yet they had become close.

After we all regained our composure, I asked Neesha if she by chance had access to his apartment and banking. She did for both. I told her I would deposit more money into the account for her and her family. She sobbed a thank you and I hung up. A long silence. Michelle and I held each other and touched every emotional button: anger, sadness, disgust; heartbreak, hopelessness, loss.

"What could he have found out in Dallas that spooked someone?" I finally asked.

Michelle sighed and answered, "No idea, but it had to be big."

"Yeah, that's what I was thinking, too. Had to have been major intel. He must have had important news that he hadn't the opportunity to tell us ..."

Michelle gasped and pointed at me. No, at my phone. "What is it, Michelle? I asked."

"Phone ... message," Michelle gulped.

Oh my God! We never listened to Tawon's voice message.

I jerked my phone to the table and selected the voice messages. Only one. It was from Tawon.

"Cracker," Tawon fought to say. "I fucked up, bro. I ... oh shit, ... it hurts so much."

I looked at Michelle desperately, hoping she could explain this was a ... dream.

Tawon continued, *"Oh damn, Cracker ... help me, ... please. I let them ... get too close,"* Tawon said, begging me. There was a pause. We could hear Tawon laboring for air. His breathing was getting shallower. I hugged Michelle. She placed her head on my arm and had her hand over her mouth. Finally, a break in his breathing.

"Thanks, bro, for ... you know ... helping me. I never saw ... it coming ... Dallas. Glad I met you Michelle ... take care ... of, oh damn ... hurts. Morelo ... he's the guy. My computer ...."

Silence ... forever.

I sat back again as if I just now heard Tawon had been

murdered. Michelle was equally stunned. We had heard Tawon's last words. Dallas, Morelo and computer. We held each other, trembling. A gut punch couldn't have hurt more.

"Call his sister again," Michelle suggested.

"No, let's just go to Dallas and see her. We need to get into Tawon's apartment. Let's call Jimmy to let him know about Tawon and that we're okay."

Before I called Jimmy, I recounted the events of the last year. The fall off the cliff couldn't have been any more sudden or steeper. There were only four close family and friends of mine still living. Everything pointed toward Muchido, Tarant, Schmidt, Hanson, and now Alonzo Morelo as the culprits. Of course, when I think of that cluster, I now conveniently ignore Langfeld and me in the group.

Muchido and Tarant and a few of their employees are now gone, and the others are untouchable. I had assumed that Schmidt would probably be the easiest one to approach, but that wasn't the case. In fact, he might be the hardest to communicate with. Morelo was an unknown quantity. Neither of us had any idea what his role and connection with Schmidt was or had been. For all we knew, he was above Franklin Schmidt. I had never heard of him and did not know where he would call home. Michelle hadn't heard the name either.

"Hey Jimmy, Paul here. Can we talk?"

"Of course, Paul. Before you start, I want to make sure you understand that I'm on your side. It's been tearing me up inside weighing this moral and ethical dilemma. But I've also never been closer to a set of victims than to you and Michelle. So, I'm here for both of you. I just wanted you to know that."

I was speechless again. I knew we had painted him into another corner. But here, he was essentially forgiving us for our transgressions—all of them.

"Jimmy, I don't know what to say. I'm speechless. Thank you just doesn't seem good enough to show our appreciation."

"Are you okay? You know, healthy?" Jimmy asked.

I wasn't sure how to answer. My head seemed on straight. Did he know about me cutting my leg? "Ah … yeah well, I cut my leg the other day. Why do you ask?"

"Just checking. I feel you two have been … active," Jimmy said.

"Thanks for your concerns, Jimmy. I really mean it," I answered.

"Okay, don't worry about it. Just be safe and start a new life with Michelle. You both deserve it."

"We will, again thanks for understanding. We just called to tell you we're taking a long drive to fully absorb the incidents of the last year and take care of some new business with Tawon."

"New business, huh? I know what has happened. I've kept track of Mr. Phelps ever since you had me find him for you. What happened to him is still being investigated, so you will get nothing there in Texas. So, do what you want to do but stay away from the police down there, okay?"

"Geez, Jimmy, is there anything you don't know?"

"Not too much, Paul. I was a cop for a long time. Be safe and come home soon."

I filled Michelle in on our conversation. She smiled and said, "I've never believed in angels, but if I ever start, Mr. Fleck would have wings."

"For sure," I countered. "We can still drive to Dallas and think about this thoroughly and more closely. But, as Jimmy said, we need to steer clear of the police investigation."

We took I-84 towards Quitman, Georgia, and then traveled Rt. 221 south into Florida and then I-10 west. I had driven Baxter's trucks enough that I had developed long-haul endurance. Michelle drove some just to prevent her from going crazy from the boredom of being the passenger.

The drive is a well-used trucking route and an easy east and west coast artery. In some ways, it looks the same as all other freeways, but if you take your time to assess the surroundings, you'll notice the southern charm and, of course, some questionable southern history. Sometimes, if you can view and touch everything on a finished slate, then a lot of charming aspects are grasped ... Southern belles and riverboats ... Sweet tea and fried chicken ... Rebels and healing ... Old oaks and Spanish moss. Down home hospitality along with some good old southern justice.

I had noticed during my long hauls in the south that a dry driving day was almost nonexistent. It always seemed to me that a charcoal-black storm front materialized, and a drenching followed soon after. Our trip was no exception. Although we were traveling west, it seemed though the storm front followed us for two hundred miles or more. I never really was a white-knuckle driver with Baxter's, but with Michelle in the car, I found myself almost terrified. The rain came in sheets, and the wind was unmerciful. A real toad strangler. We scanned every radio station for warning signs of tornados. None near us, so I released my grip just a tad.

We called Neesha. She had seen a computer but no signs of the other things we asked about, and of course, why would she. She said she took the checkbook and his other identity documents so no one else one could use them. She said all his clothes were still there, and as far as she knew, the apartment hadn't been taped off by the cops. She thought the rent had been paid up through the end of the month. She promised to meet us when we arrived to let us in. We figured it wouldn't be until late the next night, so we scheduled to call her the following morning.

We stopped in Biloxi. It was about halfway, anyway, so it was good to sleep in our bed. We picked up some clothes and a few other belongings, and left early the next morning. We couldn't forget why we were traveling to Dallas, but the time helped to calm nerves.

We pulled into Dallas in the early evening. I took Michelle around some of my old stomping grounds. I took her to the safer streets. We booked a room near where Tawon had rented his apartment.

The following morning, we called Neesha and set up a time to meet. At the apartment complex, we hugged and cried with her. Neesha was seven years younger than Tawon. She was a delightful young woman who was dealing with the loss of her older, adored brother.

She told me she had known for some time about me and him when I lived in Dallas. It wasn't a big deal. Everyone she grew up with was a dealer or a sports star. She reminded me that the stars were protected because the hood knew they got out and made it. She said she remembered Tawon saying he was so glad you had escaped before you took a hit. She said he was lucky until … her voice trailed off. I wrapped my arms around her slender shoulders and hugged until her trembling had ceased.

We entered our friend's apartment, and even though she had known him only a short while, it was clear Michelle had felt something for him as a friend. We walked slowly and whispered as if we might disturb him.

He had kept the apartment almost spotless. All the clothes were hung up properly. His queen-sized bed was made up with a gray and light blue striped bed cover. The kitchen was well maintained. There were no dishes in the sink or the dishwasher. I noticed a few photos of Neesha and several of Tawon with friends I didn't recognize. I must have been admiring the cleanliness more than I knew. Neesha said, "All of us in the projects aren't animals. When we get the chance to leave, we try to leave all the past behind, if possible. That includes living in a messy house."

Michelle spoke, "Woody, here is his computer."

"Turn it on, honey. See if we can get in."

She turned it on, but a password request came up. "Neesha, do you know if any of the stuff you moved out might have included paperwork with a password?"

"No. I didn't take any papers. I used to send him emails, so I know he used it."

"What the hell would he use as a password?" I said out loud.

Michelle looked at Neesha, "Any ideas?"

"Well, I use the name of my third-grade teacher because he was good-looking," she blushed.

I asked, "How many chances do we get before it locks up?"

"Normally, it's like three."

"Okay, Neesha, what were some things he used to talk about all the time or brag about? Maybe a sports team."

She thought a long while and said, "He talked about the Dallas Cowboys a lot."

"Anyone special player?"

"No. He was just ate-up with the Boys."

"All right, try, Cowboys."

Michelle typed in Cowboys, but it was rejected. "Anything else, Neesha?" I asked expectantly. Neesha, realizing her information was important, strained for a word or sentence.

"I know he used to say Crazy for you when he liked someone a lot."

"Okay, let's try that, Michelle." She typed it in just like it was spelled in a sentence. Another declined response.

"There's a shitload of combinations—Cr@z4U; Crazeefouryou, and on and on," Michelle said. "We only have one more chance. We can't try every combination. That's why it would be a good password."

"Think, Neesha. Anything else he talked a lot about?"

She gazed out the window and then turned to me. "Well, he talked about you when he was spaced out and remembering old times."

"How did you know he was talking about me?"

"He used to say, I wish Cracker was here; he'd know how to fix this. Stuff like that."

"You remember me as Cracker?"

"Shit, everyone on the Eighth knew you as Cracker."

"Michelle, let's go with Cracker. We've got nothing to lose at this point." She typed in Cracker and bingo! The computer opened up. Who knew?

Michelle was much savvier on a computer than I was unless it had to do with finances, so she navigated through the few files and applications Tawon stored on his computer. She clicked on a folder named Flour Power and laughed. I explained it was another street moniker for me and not a food recipe. I said I had earned that nickname from a group of older street men who thought I was crazy hanging with a poor black boy in their projects. I said the folder might mean something. She opened it up, and it listed one Word document titled Trigger Connections. Michelle opened up the file.

Tawon had created an Excel spreadsheet with 5-columns with state headings—Texas, Mississippi, Alabama, Oklahoma, and Tennessee. There were two other columns not titled. Along the vertical axis, several names were noted. Terrance Lincoln, Kevin Ungowan, Cindy Draper, Archie Wolfe, and Henry Tarr.

	TX	**MS**	**AL**	**OK**	**TN**
Terrance Lincoln	92				
Kevin Ungowan		49			
Cindi Draper			54		
Archie Wolfe				52	
Henry Tarr					72

"You know what? That looks a lot like the data that was in Terry's car," Michelle noted.

"Sure does, and remember the numbers and pages we've seen now at several locations? Some places, and now the names/initials, are the same. Can't be a coincidence."

Michelle motioned me over to the computer screen, "Woody, look at this."

In a sub-folder titled Read My Friend, Tawon had typed, Find A.M.

I took hold of Michelle and squeezed her tightly as we both looked over the computer screen as if it were Tawon's coffin.

"Tawon gave us a clue from the grave ... twice, Michelle. Find AM has to be Alonzo Morelo. Tawon said to find him. Well, brother, we're not going to only find him, we're going to kill him too!"

Follow Woody and Michelle on their quest to find Alonzo Morelo in ...

Deadly Reasons (The Search for Alonzo Morelo)

ACKNOWLEDGMENTS

To my principal editor, Kitty Frazier, who not only was a world of help as an editor but as a believer. Thank you just doesn't seem enough. A big thank you to Kathy O'Connor for her suggestions and her thumbs-up. To John Young, who first read my initial drafts of the series and believed in me throughout. To my son Doug, who walked me through the obstacles of writing and publishing, and lastly, to my wife Cindi, who understood my dreams and the time needed to tackle them.

Made in the USA
Middletown, DE
03 October 2022